IN PRAISE

The stresses of blue-collar family life, the formation of friendships in an ethnically diverse city, and other adolescent challenges are presented in colorful and humorous detail. The story is so expertly crafted and lively that the reader almost unavoidably becomes a football team member on this coming-of-age journey.

MICHAEL N. RYAN, PHD / PROFESSOR EMERITUS / STATE UNIVERSITY OF NEW YORK

Krull's novel allows readers beyond a certain age a humorous yet poignant opportunity to recapture what was lost years ago, their youth, and its many adventures. If your younger days involved sports, the opposite sex, crazy friends, and beer, you will enjoy reliving it all in these pages.

LEE OWEN / RETIRED INVESTMENT PROFESSIONAL

J.R. Krull captures what life was like for young people on the cusp of adulthood in 20th-century blue collar America. Krull has a voice. His narrator, Chris Simpson, speaks the language of friendship and football in this engaging debut novel.

CRAIG KLUGMAN / RETIRED NEWSPAPER EDITOR

There is something special about the quality time that we spend together as kids in our growing up years. This book is an adventuresome story and a portrayal of those happy, carefree days filled with trials, tribulations, laughter, fun, and good friends. Krull gives us an opportunity to reminisce about a time when life was less complicated.

JACK MAITLAND, FORMER NFL PLAYER WITH THE BALTIMORE COLTS AND NEW ENGLAND PATRIOTS, AND WINNER OF A SUPER BOWL RING

For information or permission, contact:

Mission Point Press
2554 Chandler Road
Traverse City, Michigan 49696
www.MissionPointPress.com

Cover and book design by Sarah Meiers

Printed in the United States of America

ISBN: 978-1-954786-92-9
Library of Congress Control Number: 2022906521

SINGLE WING

A STORY OF BOYHOOD, FRIENDSHIP, AND FOOTBALL

BY J.R. KRULL

MISSION POINT PRESS

DEDICATION

TO ALICE

1

THE AIR WAS ALWAYS HEAVY WITH THE SMELL OF ROTTEN EGGS, compliments of the two paper mills in town, located on the river. A very familiar smell. Somehow it was part of our identity, something unpleasant that you lived with, a reality that defined the place, a feature of our gritty town that you just dealt with. Maybe it even made you feel tough, and superior to the classy suburbs with their neat residential streets and strip malls, uncontaminated by smelly factories and slag heaps and power plants and coal yards.

The practice field was across the street from the high school. There were separate fields for the varsity, junior varsity, and freshman teams. There were two fields for the varsity team, and of course they were in the best shape, actually had a fair amount of grass. The varsity team would alternate practicing on their fields, one week on this one, next week on the other. Most of the grass in the center of the JV and freshman fields was completely gone, just mud with a fair amount of gravel mixed in.

When I first looked out over that practice field as a

member of the freshman football team, I remember feeling tremendously excited and scared to death. I always wanted to play football for Ganaway. It was a big deal in our town. One of my cousins played football, and when he made it to the varsity I got to see some of his games when my uncle took me with him uptown on a Friday night to the stadium behind the high school. It was a cool stadium, I think the largest one in the area, and it was always full to overflowing, even the visitors' side. Parents and relatives of the players and high school kids acting cool, some of them smoking under the bleacher sections at either end of the concrete grandstand. And lots of townspeople, who looked forward to the games as a welcome break from the tough, dirty, sometimes dangerous factories where they spent most of their waking hours.

Going uptown for a football game, or to the department store, or the movie theater, was a pretty rare event for me. The part of town where we lived, called Wittenberg, was an insulated, self-contained community, officially the Ninth Ward. It was settled by German Old Lutherans who came to the US in the 1840s to escape the doctrinal mandates of the Prussian king. They called their settlement Wittenberg because that was the town where Martin Luther nailed his ninety-five theses to the church door. They believed—no, they *knew*— that their Christian religion was true and correct, and anyone who believed differently was wrong and was headed for the everlasting flames of hell. Period. Theirs was "die einzig richtige,"—"the only correct"—religion, as my grandmother would sometimes remind us. She was an awfully nice person and I never really thought she would condemn anyone to eternal damnation, but this stuff was drilled into their heads and so

I guess sometimes it just slipped out. To their credit, most of my relatives really weren't too fanatical about splitting doctrinal hairs. But the founders of Wittenberg definitely were. After the initial wave of immigrants arrived and bought land and built fachwerk houses like they had in the old country, the first thing they did was build a church. And after the church was built it took less than ten years for a schism to develop, with two factions splitting hairs over fine points of doctrine. Because they couldn't agree and because they were stubborn krauts, a band of earnest, true believers left Redeemer Church and formed St. Peter's, not more than a quarter mile away, on the same street. Now there were two groups of Prussian neighbors who had braved the wide Atlantic to practice their einzig richtige religion in America. So whose religion was die richtige? Both groups knew theirs was.

My dad was a member of the Odd Fellows. I don't remember him actually doing much of anything with them or attending meetings regularly. I always suspected he joined as a rebellious act against the Lutheran church, which considered membership in lodges and organizations like the Odd Fellows and the Elks and the Masons to be a sacrilege. Just another one of their ridiculous fine points of doctrine that annoyed the old man and that I was also coming to wonder about. When you came right down to it, the Lutherans disapproved of these organizations, which they felt promoted a version of religion, simply because they were not Lutheran. Everybody was going to hell except the Lutherans—the Catholics (special place in hell for them), the Jews (same), the Baptists, the Methodists, the Presbyterians, the Seventh Day Adventists, lodge members. You name it, they were screwed.

My dad was an exception to the rule in his irreverent views. Most people in our neighborhood came across as pretty devout types who took their religion seriously. Dad went through the motions—made his offerings grudgingly, took his turn serving as an usher at church, went to communion when Mom nagged him. But he didn't have much use for the holier-than-thou attitude and the arguments about doctrine and interpretation of scripture. I don't know if he actually believed in any of it. He really didn't care for the minister, Pastor Reinhardt, who was a classic know-it-all, superior, often condescending "shepherd" of his parish. I couldn't stand the guy either.

Back in grammar school days, when it was time for our confirmation class to be "examined" after two years of attending twice-weekly indoctrination sessions—also known as religious instruction—all of us soon-to-be-real-Lutherans were pretty stressed out. According to tradition or some kind of rule, the class would get decked out in robes and sit in the front of the church on Confirmation Sunday, and each kid would be called upon by the pastor to stand up and answer some question about doctrine or faith or whatever. Some ministers would make it less stressful by asking practice questions in class leading up to the examination day. They would ask the same question of each kid for several weeks, so that you were pretty sure you were going to get that question on Confirmation Sunday, and you could be prepared with your answer. Not Reinhardt. That prick made a point of not giving you any clue as to the questions you'd be asked on the big day. So all the kids were stressed out, including me.

I remember that I was having trouble sleeping in the

weeks leading up to confirmation, and the old man could tell that something was bothering me. He asked me what was wrong and I told him about the examination question thing. I also told him about Margaret in our confirmation class, a girl who had trouble understanding things and who had a very bad stutter, and who almost broke down crying when Reinhardt would ask her a different question every week when we were preparing for the examination. The old man hit the roof. "That pompous asshole!" he yelled. "What the hell is wrong with that stupid idiot?" Mom heard this and she was aghast.

"Bill!" she said. "What kind of language is that? You never talk like that. And talk about the pastor like that? What is wrong with you?"

"What's wrong with me? What's wrong with me? What's wrong with that obnoxious, self-righteous jerk? What kind of 'love thy neighbor' is that? These are just kids for chrissake. They're not taking the goddamn bar exam."

So anyway, you can see why the old man didn't have any qualms about joining the Odd Fellows, even though it was verboten. Mom just shook her head.

———

GROWING UP IN WITTENBERG I walked or rode my bike to elementary school. I went to the public school, not to St. Peter's parochial school. I was really glad that my parents weren't into that. In fact my father often grumbled about the money—his money—the church was wasting running a "goddamn school" when there was a perfectly good public school a couple blocks away, and he was paying for that too, with his taxes. I hung out with friends and spent summer vacations playing pickup baseball and football at the community playground, or sitting around outside of Weber's store eating popsicles, or roaming the fields and backyards shooting tweetie birds with our Daisy BB guns.

Seventh grade gave me the first real glimpse of life outside of Wittenberg. We took the bus uptown to the old grammar school. That's what we called seventh and eighth grade—grammar school. But at the end of the school day the bus took us back to Wittenberg and dropped us off where we'd been picked up, in front of Weber's store. The kids who lived uptown, it seemed to me, were more sophisticated, worldly. They went to Central Pool in the summer, and got hot dogs at Barney's, and sat at the counter and drank milkshakes at The Sweet Shop. There were Catholics up there. Polish kids and Italian kids and Hungarian kids and Ukrainian kids. I felt like I was really sheltered and naïve compared to some of the kids I met in my grammar school classes. They seemed to live in a wider world than mine, and I wanted to find a way into that. I got to know some of the kids a little bit, but there wasn't time in the school day to get very well acquainted. Grammar school started to draw me out of my Wittenberg shell, but freshman football was what transformed me.

No more getting on the bus and heading back to Wittenberg. This was high school. Now after school I would head down to the locker room, suit up, and report for practice on that muddy, smelly practice field. And that was quite an eye opener. For one thing, I had never been with so many bare-assed guys before. I felt really self-conscious but tried hard not to show it. When one of the varsity guys snapped a wet towel on a freshman's rosy ass, and it made a loud, sickening crack, the kid let out a bloodcurdling yelp and I was scared shitless. Christ, take me back to Wittenberg, I thought to myself. What the hell have I gotten myself into?

The locker room was huge, with row after row of lockers with benches in between. The freshmen were relegated to the lockers farthest from the showers. Each player was assigned a locker and our practice gear was stowed there: cleats, socks, jock, pants, t-shirt, jersey, shoulder pads, helmet. The cleats were high-tops, considered old-fashioned and generally despised. The varsity backs were issued low-cuts, which were viewed as unutterably cool. The varsity linemen wore high-tops. All the JVs and freshmen got high-tops.

Our practice pants looked like something the Gipper would have worn. Tan-gray and stiff, and they felt like they were made of canvas. Maybe they were. They had pockets where thick thigh and knee pads were inserted. They also had hip pads that protruded above the waist, or maybe they were supposed to protect your kidneys. Like I said, very Knute Rockne. The pants got washed once a week. You would take the pads out of their pockets and put them in your locker before handing the pants over to the team manager, who would take them to the laundry. By the time they went to the laundry, those pants would be filthy and, depending on the weather, caked with mud. The only thing that got washed every day was your jock. That was done in an attempt to prevent crotch-rot, the plague that frequently turned players' groins into flaming, itching, raging fungal colonies.

And then there was the helmet. The freshman team actually had leather helmets, another relic that should have been long gone. For a school that was pretty fanatical about football, with a proud tradition of winning teams going back to the 1890s, to still be using leather helmets—even for the freshman team—now seems totally ridiculous.

But Ganaway was not a rich city. Money for schools and parks and playgrounds, for everything, was always tight. And we were supposed to be tough, and suck it up, and not complain, and do what we were told. We weren't pansies like the rich kids from Eastport or Parsons. Their equipment would certainly be the best and the latest. But equipment didn't win football games. To win you had to be in shape and you had to kick the shit out of your opponent. You had to have your offense and defense drilled into your head until what you did on the field was done by instinct, second nature, without thinking about it.

The football program had been shaped and led for thirty-five years by Coach Frank Helwig. His won-lost record leading up to our freshman year was the best in the state. He had won thirteen conference championships and had nine undefeated seasons. Still, some people were starting to think that Frank's approach needed an update, that it was outmoded, too old school. Lots of comparisons with Woody Hayes. Three yards and a cloud of dust. But Helwig, who was born at the end of the nineteenth century, was actually quite a bit older than Woody, and his system was even more archaic than Woody's. Ganaway was one of only a handful of schools—high schools and colleges—that still used the single wing offense. In the single wing formation, the tailback and fullback line up so that either one can receive a direct snap from the center. A flanker and a blocking back make up the rest of the backfield.

Mainly it was raw power that Helwig believed in and that his teams relied on to win. As freshmen we were taught that we didn't have to surprise our opponents. They might know what we're going to do but that doesn't matter because we're just going to run them over. We're tougher than they are and we have more guts and desire than they do. We know how to block, we know how to blow holes in their line. We have more passion, we have more fire. We want to win more than they do. Pain won't stop us. We will crush them, we will grind them down.

Our freshman practices started with stretches to loosen up, followed by jumping jacks, squat-thrusts, high-stepping in place, push-ups, shuffle steps side to side, all the typical calisthenics and exercises you'd expect. Then lots of time on blocking drills, pushing blocking sleds around with a coach standing on the sled yelling at the top of his lungs. Also one-on-one drills. Coach holding the blocking dummy yells, DOWN! You get down in your stance. Coach yells, HUT HUT! You charge into the blocking dummy grunting and groaning and sounding as mean and aggressive as you can. Coach yells, RELEASE! You stop pushing the dummy and sprint forward at top speed for ten yards, then circle back to the end of the line of players waiting their turn to block. Then do it all again when you get back to the front of the line.

Lots of time was spent on fundamentals, and not just for freshmen. You worked on alignment, blocking, tackling, agility, change of direction, pursuit. You used those skills to overpower your opponent, run him over, drive him into the dirt, pulverize him. On offense your playbook was simple. Snap the ball to the tailback, blow a hole in the defensive line with your blockers, run the tailback through the hole, gain a few yards, repeat. You would mix it up with the occasional reverse, or a pass by the tailback, and you'd go strong side and weak side, or up the middle. But the whole thing relied on power and execution, and not on finesse, or originality, or surprise. Same thing on defense. Just a few formations, very straightforward, rely on your fundamentals, nothing fancy. This formula had worked for Helwig for more than thirty-five years. An incredible run.

I had always wanted to be a quarterback. I watched Y. A. Tittle and Johnny Unitas on our black and white TV. I spent hours trying to perfect my spiral. I would make my younger brother play catch with me as much as I could, whether he wanted to or not. If I didn't have anybody to play catch with, I'd throw the ball and run to retrieve it, throw it again, go get it, throw it again. I could do that for an hour and think nothing of it. I didn't know then about the single wing offense. I didn't know that the QB in the single wing was basically a blocker. When I started practice freshman year I was surprised and disappointed to learn this. Why hadn't anybody told me about this when I was out in the backyard practicing my perfect spiral for hours on end? I guess because nobody was actually paying attention, or just never thought about it, or didn't give a shit.

There was one bright spot. In recent years Helwig had tempered his fanatical commitment to the single wing just a bit. There were some times, not many, when we would switch to a wing-T offense. In that formation, you had a Y.A. Tittle setup, where the QB would line up under the center, take the snap, and hand the ball off, or, wonder of wonders, every once in a while throw a pass. Helwig wouldn't admit it, but he was yielding just a little bit to pressure from his coaching staff to modernize Ganaway's game. So this trend worked in my favor. I decided to stick with my plan to try out for QB, but I had to work really hard on the grunt stuff, the blocking and hitting, because a lot of my playing time would be spent doing just that. I think my throwing ability got the attention of the freshman coach, Tim Parker, who was one of Helwig's chief critics, even though he couldn't be very vocal about it. Maybe he overlooked my blocking skills, which were mediocre at best, because he thought he could use me to make his point—to show that an updated offense could offer some real benefits. Parker was limited in what he could do; he had to stick pretty much to the Helwig playbook, which had only a few plays from the wing-T. But he did devote a fair amount of time in offensive practice to the handoffs, options, and passes he had to work with.

We only had a couple weeks of practice before our first freshman game, so the coaches had to decide pretty quickly who was going to start and at which positions. We didn't have August practice sessions like the JV and varsity teams; we started practice when school started. The day the teams were going to be announced I was really nervous. I thought and worried about it all day in school and when we went down to the locker room everybody crowded around the bulletin board where the roster was posted. I got as close as I could but I still couldn't read the typewritten list at first. Guys up closest to the board started moving away after they'd had a chance to find their name. Some were obviously happy while others looked dejected as they went to their lockers. Finally I got close enough to read the type— First Team—QB—Chris Simpson. Holy shit! I made it! I couldn't believe it. I really thought I wasn't going to make it. There was at least one guy who could throw pretty well and was really built. He was bigger than me and when he did the blocking drills and ran the offensive plays from the single wing he looked like an animal. His name was Peter Gorlukovich; he was known as the Gorilla. Honestly, he kind of looked like one and definitely acted like one on the field. I couldn't believe I had beat out Gorlukovich for the starting spot at QB. I knew if I was going to be able to keep my starting position I would have to work like hell at blocking. Because even though Coach Parker was trying to mix things up on offense and introduce some finesse, there was only so much he could get away with working under Helwig. We would still be running mostly single wing and I would basically be a blocking back.

I ran down the roster to see who else would be in the starting backfield. Tailback was Joe Palmisano, a kid with great speed and great moves. No surprise there. He looked like a natural for the position because not only was he really fast, he could also throw, and sometimes the tailback would be called on to do that. For starting fullback Parker had picked Stan Hanuszewicz. A good pick, I thought. From what I'd seen of him he looked like a mean ass-kicker, the kind of kid who would run at you and run over you and love it. He was big, at least six feet, weighed maybe 190, and pretty agile for a big guy, with good speed. Starting at wingback would be Tyler Barrett, not a big kid but pretty well-rounded. I didn't know then, staring at the team roster on the wall of the locker room, that these guys and I would become inseparable friends.

2

THE FRESHMEN ONLY PLAYED FIVE GAMES, not the full eight-game schedule the JV and varsity teams had. I don't remember how it was decided which schools the freshman team played, but it really doesn't matter. Of course, we wanted to win every game, but the focus was always Bell Island vs. Ganaway, the BI-G game. And it was the big game, acknowledged throughout the region as the greatest rivalry, without even a close second. Even if you had a pretty lousy season, if you won that game it kind of redeemed the whole year. This rivalry had been going on for a very long time; in fact, it was the oldest rivalry in the state and Ganaway led in the won-lost record, but not by much. The school was a bit bigger than Bell Island High and so had more boys to draw on. Somehow the size of school advantage wasn't as important as you might think.

Our won-lost record freshman year was 2-3. As QB I was the play caller in the huddle, but I was told by Coach Parker going into our first game that we would be running mostly single wing. That meant that my job was mainly to block for the runner, usually the tailback. As I said before, the plays were pretty straightforward with few surprises. As I recall, the ball kept changing hands with neither team scoring and by halftime we were tied at 0-0. In the locker room Coach Parker gave us a typical rah-rah pep talk about desire and focus and toughness and "you gotta take it to 'em!" and Ganaway pride and all the usual stuff, which actually sounded very rousing and motivating and really made you want to go back out there and kick some ass! Unfortunately, most of the ass kicking that took place in the second half was being done by the other side. Their defensive line was big and pretty damn mean and I was doing a piss-poor job of smashing into them and opening up holes for our runners. It wasn't for lack of trying; I just wasn't that good at it, and it was disturbing to admit this.

In the fourth quarter we were behind, hadn't scored at all, and I guess Coach Parker was feeling desperate, so he called for a pass from the wing-T formation. This was my big chance. All my backyard perfect spiral drills would be tested here, on the field of battle. One big difference, of course: on the field of battle you had aggressive big guys coming at you wanting to pound your face into the dirt. Which they did, quite effectively, on the first pass play we tried. We went back to the running game, turned the ball over, and our defense went back out on the field and promptly gave up another TD. It was getting ugly. The only good thing I remember about that first game was that just as the clock was winding down, and we were more desperate than ever, Coach called another pass and this time our line gave me some protection and I saw Tyler Barrett, our wing-back, way the hell downfield, wide open, and I uncorked a perfect spiral that dropped right into his hands on the twenty-yard line, and he ran with it untouched into the end zone. Damn, that felt good! We missed the extra point, which would become another problem, and lost. Not even close.

After the game the coach gave us a little review of the game, laid out what we did wrong and tried to find something we did right, told us to look ahead to the next game and work on the stuff we needed to work on, and rah rah. Our second game, as I recall, was pretty much like the first: couldn't move the ball, couldn't stop the opposition, we lost. This was not looking good. This was not what you expected from Ganaway. At practice the following Monday the coach took me aside and informed me that Gorlukovich was going to start at QB next game. Nothing against me, I had looked really good throwing those passes (he kindly didn't specify the small number of passes) but we needed to shake things up and try some new combinations and it was early in the season and this was not unusual and we all need to pull together and hey, we may start you again so keep working on your fundamentals, and-and-and. So Gorilla was QB now and I was relegated to second string. After practice he came up to me and said, "Hey man, I'm sorry about that." I said, "What do you have to be sorry about? I wasn't sorry when the roster was posted. I was happy as hell! You go for it. Maybe one of these days I'll get the starting job back."

The best thing about freshman football was the friendships I was making with guys from uptown. All the guys in the group except for me lived close enough to school to walk home from practice. I had to get picked up, usually by my mom. Freshman games were played after school during the week, usually on Thursdays, and everybody went to the varsity home games on Friday night. I was usually able to talk my mom into taking me to the game and coming back later to pick me up. The other guys, like I said, could walk. At the games we would hang out, trying to act cool and look like ball players out of uniform, trying to impress... who? Who were we trying to impress? Doesn't really matter because nobody was the least bit impressed. After the game there really wasn't anything for us to do but go back home, and then we wouldn't see each other again until school on Monday.

Even though we didn't have much time to social-ize outside of practice and school, we began to develop a pretty tight-knit group of friends. We thought we were quite the creative and inventive young geniuses, and we came up with nicknames for everybody. Gorlukovich was already the Gorilla, like I said. Stan Hanuszewicz we started calling Ham Sandwich, but that didn't really stick, so we decided his initials, S. H., stood for Shit Head, or as we finally decided it should be—and I don't know who exactly came up with this—ShiThead. That was pro-nounced Shith-eed. That way you could call him shithead without anybody outside the group knowing you were calling him shithead. As time went on other kids figured out what we were doing, but it didn't matter. Stan was ShiThead, and no going back.

For my initials, C. S., we thought up a bunch of pos-sibilities. Cock Sucker, Chicken Shit, Cork Screw, Crock o' Shit, to name just a few. We were always dreaming up impolite alternatives for people's initials. Once you start doing this it drives you crazy because you can't stop. For me, we eventually settled on Crock, because everybody thought most of the stuff I said was a crock of shit. Then Crock became Croc, just because I liked it better.

The Backfield, as we started calling ourselves, ate lunch together at school every day if we could. Most of us brought lunch from home because the food the cafeteria put out was practically inedible, and the amount you got for your thirty-five cents wasn't nearly enough to fill the gullets of the growing boys who made up the Backfield. We had five guys in the group, including both me and the Gorilla at QB. The short freshman season had been enough to create a pretty strong bond, and we found that we shared a weird sense of humor and enjoyed trying to one-up each other with highly creative but totally absurd shit. The business of inventing things for initials to stand for was an example of that. And the name ShiThead for Stan, the Ham Sandwich. And the name we came up with for Joey, who was always talking about eating, and his grandmother's cooking, and the big dinners his family would have. Mama Palmisano would love to watch Joey enjoying her food, and she'd egg him on, saying, "Mangia! mangia!" Which in Italian means "eat! eat!" So one of us came up with the name Joe DiMangio for him—obviously a take on Joe DiMaggio. We later started calling him J.D., which made no sense to anyone except us, and that was exactly what we wanted.

We needed a name for Tyler Barrett, the aristocrat of the group. His father was a lawyer, and they lived in the Forest Park neighborhood, which was the oldest residential section of town and had some cool old houses, some of them built by the early industrialists of the Gilded Age, and even before that. It took a while, but we came up with a good one. Tyler Barrett. TB. Tuberculosis. What was tuberculosis? A scourge. So Tyler henceforth was known as Scourge. But what was his middle name? Lewis. TLB. The Little Bastard. Or, when we discovered that this kid from what we considered a wealthy family was actually quite a little tightwad— Tight Little Bastard. And once we learned what a cheap little shit he was, we could, if the situation warranted, turn Scourge into Scrooge. There was no end to our cleverness. We had fun with his father's law firm too. Barrett, Logan, Stewart, Harris & Taft. BLSHT. Bullshit! Too bad lawyers and doctors weren't allowed to advertise in those days. We would have had a ball coming up with ads for the Bullshit Law Firm.

3

IN HIGH SCHOOL WE DIDN'T KNOW THAT FOR MOST PEOPLE, the twin cities were Minneapolis and St. Paul. We thought everybody knew that the twin cities were Ganaway and Bell Island. Ganaway was an adaptation of Cayuga and Onondaga words meaning "sun." Kind of an ironic name because the sun was not a regular feature in our sky, which tended to be gray more often than not, either because of heavy clouds, or thick smog from the factories, or both. Bell Island got its name from a foundry that was located there in the early 1800s and produced bells for churches and schoolhouses and clock towers and village greens. A bridge over a narrow section of the river connected the downtown sections of the two cities, and there was another bridge farther down the island where the foundry, long since closed, used to be. Ganaway and Bell Island were part of a sprawling metropolitan area, at the center of which was a large municipality that we always just called the City. The City had a population maybe ten times that of Ganaway and Bell Island combined.

Ganaway and Bell Island both had lots of factories, many of them along the river, where they could dump their waste, and residue, and runoff, or whatever you wanted to call the pollution that they disgorged night and day. Most of the kids we knew had fathers who worked in the chemical plants, and paper mills, and steel mills, and auto plants, and just about any kind of factory you can think of. A lot of the plants were unionized, and guys who worked there made good money, enough to have a house, and a car, maybe even a boat to run around in on the river.

A lot of the men, including my father, had gone off to fight in the war. Many knew guys who had not come back. The ones who had come back were proud that they had kicked the shit out of the krauts and the japs, and had not forgiven them for the wreckage they'd caused in the world. On the positive side, the US was now the dominant power in the world. Europe and Japan were on their knees. America was the leader in manufacturing just about everything, and the guys working in all these factories were enjoying that position of dominance. Their unions could negotiate good pay and job security. There really wasn't any competition. Sure, GM competed with Chrysler and Ford, but they really didn't have much leverage over the unions.

Most of the plants ran three shifts: 8:00 to 4:00, 4:00 to midnight, midnight to 8:00. Some guys worked the same shift all the time but some plants ran swing shifts, where you would work a different shift every other week or so. I guess swing shifts were supposed to allow guys the flexibility to go to a doctor, or go to a store, but from what I could tell, guys who worked swing shifts never could get into a groove, or develop a sleep pattern, or whatever. When they got off shift a lot of guys would go to the corner tavern before going home. To an outsider it might look weird to see a bar full of customers at 8:30 in the morning but that was normal in our town. There was a bar on every corner, or it seemed like it, because they were everywhere. In fact, Samuels Street was reputed to have more bars per mile than any other street in the country. We actually believed this and bragged about it. I guess we'd never heard of Bourbon Street.

Another "fact" that you also heard was that it only took a relatively small number of regular customers to keep one of these gin mills in business, because the customers came there so often and probably spent way too much of their paychecks when they should have been home getting some sleep and paying attention to the wife and kids.

Since there were so many Catholics in town, a lot of these places offered fish fries on Friday nights. For some of the bars, the Friday fish fry was the only food they served, other than the ever-present pickled eggs in a huge glass jar that sat at the end of the bar, or maybe some crappy packaged sandwich that they heated up in a kind of small oven. But I'd say most of the bars did have a "restaurant" of sorts, even if the menu was very limited. And some of them had damn good food.

When you went to one of the neighborhood bars for the Friday fish fry, you'd typically have a choice of yellow pike or blue pike. The blue pike was always a little more expensive. I had no idea what kind of fish these were, or why blue pike cost more. Years later when I got interested in cooking, I did some research on this. Yellow pike is another term for walleye, a fish that's found in a lot of northern lakes. Blue pike was another variety of walleye, but just a local thing, not widespread. Both of these fish came out of the big lake, which was getting extremely polluted back then, to the point where not too many years later the fish started disappearing. Pollution killed off the blue pike completely, while the yellow pike managed to make a comeback when the lake was cleaned up, thanks to environmental regulations and the decline of industry in later years. None of that really matters because on Friday nights people weren't thinking about the genetic makeup of their fish dinners, they just wanted a big plate of deep-fried fish, french fries, maybe German potato salad, and coleslaw, washed down by some cold beers.

These gin mills were mostly nondescript, totally unremarkable buildings, with the bar/restaurant area on the first floor and an apartment upstairs. Usually the family that owned and ran the bar lived upstairs. We had two of these places in Wittenberg, Volcker's and Hoffmann's. Volcker's was just a couple blocks from St. Peter's and that was my old man's hangout. Every night after supper he would sit down with his coffee and a cigarette and read the paper for about an hour, then he'd head down the street to Volcker's, where he'd spend the evening drinking beer and knocking back a few shots of Smooth as Silk Kessler's. To get to Volcker's he'd walk past St. Peter's parsonage and the church, looking pretty happy and sometimes whistling a little tune. He never stayed too late; he'd head home around 10:00, walking straight as a stick, weaving a bit, probably pretty damn plastered, but actually I never really knew how drunk he was. He didn't get mean, like some of the guys did when they were shit-faced. He usually watched the eleven o'clock news and then went to bed. Got up, had breakfast, and went to his job at Rollins Boat Co. He was a skilled cabinetmaker, never missed work because of drinking. However, he must have spent a pretty hefty sum of money on his nightly trips to Volcker's. In fact, the only arguments my folks really had were about the cost of Dad's "hobby." Every once in a while, Mom would bring it up and it would always go the same way.

"Why do you need to go down there every night? Every night! You're just wasting our money down there. Buy your beer at Weber's and drink it at home! You could still get drunk every night for a lot less money. I just don't understand you!"

"Goddamn it, Doris, how many times do I have to tell you I need to get out of the house and have some time for myself?"

"You were never like this before the war, Bill, when we were first married. You know that. You never drank so much and you actually seemed to enjoy my company."

"I do enjoy your company! Don't tell me I don't enjoy your company. We have supper every night. All weekend I'm hanging around here. I cut the grass, I shovel the snow, we go to your mother's for picnics, I do all kinds of stuff around here and with you. Why do you begrudge me a little time for myself?"

"Well, it's more than a little time and it's a lot of money. So, you'll do what you want."

Knowing what I know now about how traumatic stress can affect people, I'm almost certain that the old man had seen some really horrendous stuff in the army in Europe and was struggling to cope. They talked about guys being shell-shocked but that never really meant much to me; I couldn't quite picture what that would mean. But I look back on what my mother always said: "You were never like this before the war, Bill." And that puts some of the stuff I observed about the old man's behavior in a little clearer light. I've asked my sister Donna about it, but even though she was born before the war, she was still too little when he went away to have any recollection of what he was like, and how he might have changed.

You never saw a Black person in the Twin Cities. There was an unwritten rule that everybody knew and even bragged about, that no Black person better be in Ganaway after dark or…or what? Nobody ever said exactly, but they just better not be there. Looking back now, I can't imagine why any Black person would have wanted to be in Ganaway, at any time of day. It was as segregated as any place down south. I literally never saw a Black person in person until our freshman football game against Roosevelt High School. They had a lot of Black players, actually most were Black, and they were a tough team. This was our third game, and Gorilla had replaced me as starting QB/blocking back. We were behind and the coach called a pass from the wing-T formation. Scourge ran a down and out pattern and he was wide open but Gorilla didn't see him, and Scourge was screaming at the top of his lungs, "Gorilla! Gorilla!" but the offensive line had done its usual lousy job of protecting the passer and Gorilla got his ass canned before he could throw the ball to anybody. One of the Roosevelt players who heard Scourge yelling came running at him like a maniac and cold-cocked him and screamed, "Who you callin' a Gorilla? I'm gonna pound the shit outta you!" The ref ran over and pulled the Black guy off Scourge and called a penalty against Roosevelt, and Scourge tried to explain that he wasn't calling the Black guy a gorilla, and that was the end of it. But it was an eye-opener for the naïve and clueless white boys from Ganaway. This incident got us thinking that maybe that nickname was not too cool. Also, we knew that Gorilla himself hated being called that. Actually, to our perverse way of thinking, the fact that he didn't like it was a great reason to keep using it. But it wasn't too long until we started calling him G-man, or just G. And actually, everybody liked that better, so that's what we stuck with.

As high school kids we thought Ganaway was a pretty great place, even though looking around you couldn't miss seeing that it was dirty and smelly and in some sections pretty run-down, with factories belching smoke and spewing fumes. I suppose it wasn't much different from many industrial cities. It had some tree-lined streets with stately old houses, and a nice park with big trees. Most of the residential sections had two-story houses, really close together in the older neighborhoods, where some streets had alleys behind the houses and garages facing the alley, and so no driveways. Some of these had been converted into two-family houses, with apartments up and down, and I suppose some had been built as apartments originally. In some neighborhoods the houses were on bigger lots and had driveways leading to separate one-car garages. As you got a little farther from the older parts of town, you would start to see streets with newer one- or one-and-a-half-story houses. The one-stories were called cigar-boxes and the story-and-a-halfs were Cape Cods. Most of the older houses were heated with coal or oil, and some of the newer ones had natural gas. Bell Island was the same. Both cities had a small central shopping area. Bell Island had a department store,

Ganaway had a Woolworth's. Both had a movie theater. It seemed like Ganaway had more bars, probably because of Samuels Street.

The year we played freshman football, the varsity lost to Bell Island for the first time in five years. The town was really shaken by this and people were not happy. Bell Island's young coach led their team to a 7-1 season, and they were getting lots of attention throughout the whole region. There was more grumbling about Helwig. He was a main topic of conversation in all the gin mills where workers would gather for a shot and a beer, or two, or three, or… after their shifts. Something to talk about other than bitching about work or bitching about the wife.

With G at QB our freshman team won two of our remaining three games. We finished with a 2-3 record, but we lost to Bell Island. I did get to play a little. Coach put me in a few times to run both single wing and wing-T, and I did OK. My blocking was respectable but not as good as G's. I got to throw a few passes, or try to throw a few passes. Our line somehow was better at pulling and blocking on power plays than it was at protecting the passer. I did actually throw another nice bomb like the one in the first game, although it didn't go for a touchdown this time. I felt like maybe next year, on the JV team, I'd have a chance at winning back the starting job.

4

AFTER FOOTBALL, BASKETBALL WAS THE BIGGEST SPORT and we tried to get to the varsity home games so we could hang out. I was the only one of the group who had to get a ride to the high school, and my mom was pretty good about dragging out of the house on a cold winter night to drop me off, and then come back later to pick me up. The old man couldn't be bothered because of course he was at Volcker's. Sometimes I could talk my sister into doing it, but not very often. She was still living at home but she was twenty-two and had a serious boyfriend and had pretty much checked out of the family, or at least was trying to. She had a job as a secretary at Cooper Chemical and was trying to earn enough money to get an apartment of her own uptown.

A lot of the varsity b-ball games were on Friday night, and we started trying to convince our parents to let us go somewhere after the games. There was a pizza place called Gino's that was really popular. It wasn't a bar, but it was in another one of the two-story houses with the apartment upstairs, business downstairs. I think some of these places were built that way and some were converted from regular one- or two-family houses. They were all over the place and Gino's was on one of the main business streets in Ganaway—Samuels Street, the one with the most bars per mile of any street in the country. Samuels Street was pretty rough. Not dangerous, just worn and gritty looking. The exteriors of a lot of the houses were what I would call fake brick—asphalt shingles made to look like bricks. As a kid I probably didn't even think about how tacky and cheesy they looked, because they were everywhere and that's just the way everything looked.

After a lot of pleading and whining I got Mom to agree to let me go out for a little while after the games. The best I could do was to get permission to stay out until 10:30, which was the latest that Mom would agree to drive uptown and pick me up. The games started at 7:00 and were usually over by 9:00. We'd leave the game and start walking to Gino's, freezing our asses off in the frigid weather that we had all winter back then. So we only had about an hour to order a pizza and sit around trying to be cool, while actually looking like the freshman dorks that we were, and being ignored and privately mocked by the older crowd. We would all leave at the same time, and all the guys who lived close enough to walk, everybody but me, would head for home. I had Ma pick me up a couple blocks down the street so I wouldn't be seen at Gino's getting picked up by my mother.

Our occasional post-game outings were brief, but they made us feel more grown up, independent. We heard some things and learned some things. For example, some of the older kids would talk about going to Angelo's, where apparently you might get served without having to show ID. We were always trying to figure out ways that we could hang out together. Gino's was great but you could only afford so much pizza and there were only so many home b-ball games.

One Friday night, instead of going to Gino's we walked to G's house. G's father worked second shift at Cooper Chemical and his mother was a waitress at the Ukrainian Social Club, so there were lots of nights when neither of them was home. We started going over to his house more often, not just after ball games, but still usually on Friday or Saturday nights. We'd go down in the basement, which wasn't fixed up or anything, but it had a beat-up couch and a couple of chairs so we could sit around and shoot the shit and listen to records. There was also a cheap pool table down there. G had an older brother who wasn't usually around and even when he was, he didn't pay much attention to us. We were really into Dylan. This was in Dylan's early years, and we played his albums so much that we had a lot of the lyrics memorized. We thought that some of Dylan's stuff was really good, and the lyrics were true poetry and had a lot of meaning. Other songs we thought were just pretty brilliant bullshit; crazy, absurd words that basically meant nothing but just rhymed. We loved that kind of stuff most of all.

Probably the most bizarre thing we got into was Mitch Miller. There was a TV show called *Sing Along with Mitch*, featuring Mitch Miller, a goofy-looking guy with a stupid little goatee and his all-guy chorus or whatever it was called. They sang all these corny old songs that G's folks apparently really liked, because they had several of their albums. Don't ask me why a group of high school guys got into this cornball stuff, but we loved it. We memorized a few of our favorites and sometimes we would actually sing along with Mitch. Here's one that was a classic. The song was called "There Is a Tavern in the Town" and the tune was the same as the kids' song that goes, "Head, shoulders, knees and toes. Knees and toes." The first few lines went like this:

> There is a tavern in the town. In the town.
> And there my true love sits him down. Sits him
>   down.
> And drinks his wine as merry as can be,
> And never, never thinks of me.

We were all taking German, and mostly we just memorized conversations. The recording in language lab would say "Hören Sie zu, und wiederhören Sie," which means "listen and repeat." Sometimes we would try to throw a few German expressions into our conversations. Like "Links um die Ecke, bitte" ("Left around the corner, please"). One night, somebody came up with the idea of substituting some German words for the "Tavern in the Town" lyrics. Why? Who knows? Made absolutely no sense. So, obviously, we loved it. Instead of "There is a tavern in the town. In the town," we sang, "Wie ist das Wetter heute, boys? Heute, boys." You pronounce that like "vee ist dahs Vetter hoyta, boys. Hoyta, boys." It means, "how is the weather today, boys? Today, boys." Yeah, you had to be there.

G's old man had lots of beer down in the basement. It was just a matter of time before somebody asked if we could sneak a couple. It was a little tricky because the beer was in returnable bottles in cardboard cases of twenty-four, and we were afraid that if we weren't careful, his old man would notice that there were more empties in the case than there should be. So the first time we just took two bottles and passed them around, taking swigs. I don't think any of us actually liked the taste of beer very much then, but we definitely liked the idea of drinking beer. Most or all of us had nipped some beers at our own houses at some time or other. Every time we got together in G's basement, we checked out the beer situation. If there were only a few beers in a case, and a lot of empties, we would have to forego our libations. If there was a case with mostly full bottles, we felt fairly safe in snagging two or three, sometimes four. Naturally the beer was always warm, but we couldn't do anything about that. We couldn't raid the fridge, because it was up in the kitchen and we didn't want to take any chances. It was safer to stay in the basement and drink our beer warm.

One day when the beer situation didn't look too good, somebody thought of dipping into the hard stuff. Most families would have a bottle or two of whiskey in the house, maybe a Smooth as Silk Kessler's for everyday and a Seagram's Seven Crown or a Canadian Club for special occasions. The booze was upstairs too, but we decided that if we were careful and made sure that nobody was around, we could sneak a couple of quick nips and then head back down to the basement. We knew that G's old man would be drinking the Kessler's most of the time, and he might notice if the level was mysteriously going down, so we had to be careful not to drink enough to make it noticeable. On the other hand, the Seagram's would be used less often and since it was more expensive, the old man would be likely to be paying more attention. We thought about taking a few nips and then just adding water to bring it back to the level where we started. But we rejected that idea because we figured we'd forget how many nips we took and how much water we added and before we knew it, the booze would be watered down so that it was obvious what was going on. We only did this a couple of times because we didn't think it was worth the risk of getting caught. We didn't drink enough beer or booze to get really ripped, although we could all feel some effect, and it was a good feeling. I had to be careful not to smell like beer when Mom picked me up. She definitely knew what beer breath smelled like since she smelled it every night on the old man. So I always made sure I had some Wrigley's spearmint gum with me.

The other guys had an easier time slipping into their houses and not having to worry about booze breath since they could walk and didn't have to get picked up by dear old Mom. ShiThead lived in the Third Ward, not too far from G's house. In that area you had a lot of Polish, Ukrainian, and Hungarian families. We called the Third Ward the Turd Ward, because that's how most of the older people there pronounced it. Families there were more recent immigrants than the Germans in Wittenberg. Same for the Italian families, most of which were in their own little enclave between Fourth and Crozier Streets. The ethnic identities were fading somewhat as the years passed but we still had the Italian-American Club, the Ukrainian Social Club, and the Polish Eagle Club. These places were used for weddings and birthday parties and baptism parties and whatever, and they were basically open to everybody. Each one had a bar where anybody was welcome, but I will say that most of the older guys who hung out at these places tended to belong to the identified ethnic group. You still heard people talking about polacks, and dagos, and wops, and guineas, and hunkies, and krauts, and heinies, but it was more and more getting to be seen as rude and disrespectful. We called each other those things sometimes, though, just to be pricks. Maybe only Scourge could have been considered beyond the ethnic identity thing. Actually I don't think we really knew what the hell he was, only that his old man was not a polack or a kraut or a dago, but he was a member of the Commercial Club.

ShiThead's dad was a foreman at International Bolt Co., which put him in somewhat of an awkward position, since he was considered management and most of his neighbors, regardless of where they worked, were union members. He came up through the ranks and a lot of the guys resented him, and after he became foreman he didn't really feel comfortable hanging out at the Polish Eagle, where everybody knew him. He would still go there sometimes to drink, and for the Friday fish fry, and obviously for weddings and such, but he also frequented some of the other gin mills in the neighborhood. It was pretty shitty that the guys resented him for being a foreman because he had definitely paid his dues. He worked for years as a catcher, a dangerous job where you have to grab red hot steel, like a steel bar, as it comes out of the furnace and guide it to a set of rollers that lead to where it will slowly cool down. The International Bolt plant was really old, and too small to let the red-hot bars just shoot down one set of rollers to the cooling area. Instead, the catcher had to grab the bar, which was shooting at him red hot, and turn it onto another set of rollers going in the other direction. A really dangerous setup, and one that resulted in lots of injuries. It was so hot that you had to wear two sets of long underwear to provide enough insulation so that you wouldn't burn your skin just from the heat of the furnace. ShiThead told us about all this. He had heard lots of stories from his old man, who would then say, "So make sure you study hard so you can go to college and get a job where you won't always be worried that you're going to get your balls burned off."

Joey Palmisano, a.k.a. Joe DiMangio, aka J.D., had a large family who owned Palmisano's Market on Lombard Street, right in the heart of the Italian neighborhood. His married sister lived above the store, and J.D., two older brothers, and two younger sisters lived right next door in a big clapboard house. The building that housed the market and the apartment was one of those fake brick asphalt shingle deals. The upstairs sister was married to an Italian guy named Danny Rizzo, whose family was said to have some shady connections to the mob. That was just a rumor but most people seemed to believe it, although you never really heard anything specific. J.D. worked in the store sometimes, and so did his older brothers. The store had some regular customers and had pretty much whatever you needed in the way of groceries, although it was starting to lose some business to the new supermarket over in Bell Island, called The Union. It didn't sell much meat other than cold cuts—mortadella, salami, capocollo, prosciutto, baloney, some ham, that kind of stuff. For serious meat you went to DiSimone's meat market, right down the street. Palmisano's sold beer, and it would become a source for us in the future.

5

EVERYBODY IN THE BACKFIELD PLAYED THREE SPORTS. J.D., ShiThead, and I played basketball, G wrestled, and Scourge was on the swim team. In the spring Scourge and I played tennis, J.D. and ShiThead played baseball, and G ran track and was a broad jumper. I learned to play tennis from my sister, who was a counselor at the playground near our house. We took all of our sports seriously and worked hard, but football was by far the biggest deal, the most important.

Sophomore year we were on the JV team and again we had our freshman coach, Tim Parker, who had been promoted to coach JV. We really liked Coach Parker, although he did have some kind of cornball quirks and we found many opportunities to imitate him behind his back. One of his favorite utterances was, "Ooooeeee boys, ooooeeee. Down ready to go! Down ready to go!" And then he'd give us some command and make us do some drills, like running in place, and he'd yell, "Short choppy steps! Short choppy steps! Ooooeeee boys, ooooeeee!" And then we'd do pushups and he'd change it to "Gettin' up! Gettin' up!

Ooooeeee! Ooooeeee boys!" Needless to say, we imitated coach's trademark calls until we had them down pat. One of his favorite phrases that year was that when we kicked off or punted, we were supposed to run down the field with "reckless abandon" to demolish our opponents and lay waste to the kick returner. Really? Reckless abandon? Wasn't that a bit too literary for the football field? I think it was J.D. who said at practice one day, "Who's this kid, Freckles Kramden? We're supposed to run down the field with Freckles Kramden? What the hell?" After that, Freckles Kramden was always a member of our special team and we ran down the field with him to demolish our opponents.

In spite of his pep talk style, Parker was a pretty good coach—more than pretty good. But the reason he got promoted from freshman coach was because the JV coach quit. This was quite a shock because it was very rare for a young coach to quit unless he was leaving the school and taking another teaching—and probably coaching—job at another school. We didn't have any coaches who weren't also teachers at the school. That was pretty much the rule everywhere. Everybody in town was talking about it, and everybody figured Ray Timmins quit as JV coach because of his disagreements with Helwig about modernizing the offense, and to some extent the defense. Timmins was a young guy, and I'm sure he was frustrated trying to introduce some new ideas, plays, and formations, to keep the program up to date with how the game was changing. But Helwig was a stubborn Dutchman and just wouldn't be swayed. Just like the Lutherans—and he was one—"die einzig richtige." He was right, everybody else was wrong. If you don't like it, you can lump it. Unfortunately, stubbornness will only get you so far, it seems. The varsity did even worse our sophomore year than they did our freshman year. And they lost to Bell Island again, the second year in a row. Not good.

As for the JV team, we went 4 and 4. Better than our freshman record, but still pretty pathetic, plus we lost to BI again. G was the starting QB, and I settled into my status as second stringer, the only member of the Backfield who wasn't a starter. I did get to play some, and not always in the last thirty seconds when the game was either safely won or irreversibly lost. Coach Parker put me in mostly to run plays from the wing-T, where I might have had a little more finesse than G, and I did complete a few passes and felt pretty good about that.

As the season went on, another guy on the team started to hang out with us sometimes, like at lunch and at varsity home games on Friday nights. He was the starting center and his name was Dave Frank, huge guy, one of the biggest players on the team. He really fit in with the Backfield. Had the same stupid sense of humor, was able to come up with ridiculous shit just like the rest of us. It didn't take us long to decide what his initials stood for: D. F. Dumb Fuck. But could we really call a guy Dumb Fuck in front of everybody? One of us said something like, "Hey he's got two first names. David and Frank. They could go in either order. Frank David. F. D. How about Fumb Duck?" And Fumb Duck stuck, shortened to just Fumb. He would never get rid of that name for his entire life, at least as far as the Backfield was concerned.

At the end of the season we decided that Fumb ought to be formally initiated into the Ancient and Honorable Order of the Backfield. After some careful plotting we came up with a plan for a formal induction ceremony. Since Scourge's old man was a lawyer, we assigned him the job of drafting a suitably legal-sounding document to certify Fumb's acceptance into the group. Scourge didn't let us down and he came up with a great document. I still have it. I've got a file folder with some of the crazy shit we came up with.

Know all men by these presents, that
David Carl Frank,
Affectionately known to his few friends as "Fumb Duck,"
Is hereby admitted into membership in the
Ancient and Honorable Order of the Backfield
With all the rights, honours, and privileges appertaining thereto.
In witness whereof, this Certificate of Membership is presented to the said
David Carl "Fumb Duck" Frank
This Thirteenth day of December
In the Year of Our Lord Nineteen Hundred and Sixty-Three

We met in G's basement for the induction ceremony. Scourge gave a reading of the certificate of election and admission into membership, appropriately decked out in a black robe of some kind that he had spirited out of his old man's closet. Who knows why his old man had a robe; he wasn't a judge. What made the whole thing perfect was that this ceremony took place on Friday the thirteenth, which in our twisted world we considered a symbol of good fortune. We had been stockpiling beers for a few weeks, so we had enough for everybody to have two and get a little buzz on. We had also managed to set aside a couple shots of Kessler, which we administered to Fumb as his rite of initiation, so he probably wound up getting a bit shit-faced, although he didn't really show it. Probably because he was such a big guy.

After we had completed the initiation ceremony, Fumb thanked us for welcoming him officially into the group. "But," he said, "there's just one thing. As far as I am aware, the position of center—the position that I play—is not a part of 'the Backfield.' Does that pose any kind of problem?"

"Of course not," said ShiThead. "Have you ever seen this group give a shit about what is accurate or correct? No."

"And if it will make you feel better," said Scourge, "we can always change our organization's name to the Backfield Plus One, BPO for short. But I doubt we'll ever get around to doing that, so just revel in your initiation and don't get bogged down in the details."

"Yes, I will do that," said Fumb. "And again, I am truly honored."

We were starting to get more interested in girls, but nobody had anything even close to a girlfriend. Occasionally there would be a sock hop in the gym, usually after a varsity basketball game on a Friday night. This was really a '50s term and it was starting to sound corny, but it was still used sometimes. The Backfield almost always attended these dances, where you actually did have to take your shoes off so you wouldn't scratch or scrape the hardwood floor of the gym. The cheerleaders would have their uniforms on from the basketball game, and one time they did this thing where they recognized all the players, including the JV guys, during the dance. The disk jockey announced that the Ganaway basketball team was going to be recognized by the cheerleaders. They had this standard cheer they did that went: "Joe Blow, he's our man. If he can't do it, Smith can. John Smith, he's our man. If he can't do it, Miller can. Tom Miller, he's our man..." Like that.

So, after the varsity team got showered and dressed, the varsity and JV players lined up outside the entrance to the gym, and we were supposed to stroll in our stocking feet out onto the floor one by one and be cheered by the cheerleaders. The JVs went first, setting the stage and building suspense for the varsity. I was right behind J.D. and ShiThead. The cheerleaders were waving and jumping and yelling "Joe Palmisano, he's our man. If he can't do it, Hanuszewicz can! Stan Hanuszewicz, he's our man. If he can't do it..." and then came the embarrassing part. The cheerleaders didn't know who I was, or they weren't sure, and they had to do a quick consultation, and apparently somebody knew my name and they managed to get back on track: "Simpson can! Chris Simpson, he's our man..." Needless to say, I was pretty mortified to be cheered on as an unknown nonentity. Somehow my ego managed to weather that little hammering. I never really did any dancing at these things anyway. J.D. was probably the most suave and debonair and he would actually dance with girls occasionally. Same with ShiThead. Scourge, G, and Fumb were more klutzy like me. But even though these dances were pretty weird and awkward, they did provide an opportunity to scope out some wenches, as we were fond of saying, and fuel our hormonal fires.

When we admitted Fumb into the Backfield, we didn't realize that we would be gaining a very valuable extra resource. It turned out that Fumb was a year older than the rest of us. His family had moved to town at just about the time that he would have been starting kindergarten.

Because of the disruption and confusion of moving and because Fumb was a bit immature for his age, or so his parents thought, they decided to hold him out of school for a year. This probably was not the greatest decision because Fumb was not only quite intelligent and no doubt as mature as most kids, but he was also a really big kid physically. Anyway, the advantage for us was that he could get his driver's license a year before everyone else in the group.

You could get a driver's license at age sixteen but you weren't allowed to drive at night. During daylight hours you could have one passenger, I think. Or maybe back then you could have more than one passenger. Anyway, we definitely had more than one passenger riding in Fumb's '58 Chevy on numerous occasions. Fumb's dad was in the auto parts business, manager of one of the local stores of a national chain. Fumb knew more about cars than all the rest of us put together. It was great that he could drive because he lived beyond easy walking distance of the school, and G's house, and Gino's. His house was in a new area called Chestnut Glen. This was the newest housing that had been built in Ganaway in quite a few years—a subdivision, which was a term we hadn't heard much before. The houses were mostly split levels or two-stories with good sized lots and two-car garages. A few even had swimming pools, which could really only be used for a couple of months in the summer. We used to say that we had two seasons—winter and the Fourth of July. Quite a few of the people who lived there had moved from out of town, like management people and their families, managers who worked in the plants all over town. But there were also local people who saw Chestnut Glen as a step up and moved there if they could afford it.

Fumb had to toe the line pretty closely on the driving at night thing. If he'd gotten stopped by the cops his old man would have yanked his car keys for sure. So he was careful to follow the rules on that. That was probably a really good thing because if he had been driving at night, there would certainly have been times when he was at least slightly drunk. But just having someone with a car who we could ride around with during the daytime, especially on weekends, was a great thing. We didn't really use much gas but all of us would chip in once in a while and help pay to fill up the tank.

All of us had some kind of job. I worked a few hours a week at Weber's store in Wittenberg and in the summer mowed lawns for a few people. J.D. worked at his family's market, stocking shelves and sometimes waiting on customers. ShiThead washed dishes sometimes at fish fries and other events at the Polish Eagle. G worked as an usher at the Tate Theatre in Bell Island. Scourge worked at the marina where his old man had their boat serviced. Fumb worked at an auto repair shop. None of us earned much working fairly limited hours, but it did give us some spending cash and made us feel somewhat self-sufficient. But it was Fumb's car that really gave us our freedom, and we were happy to help him keep it gassed up and purring like a kitten. He took us down to Grothmann's, the repair shop where he worked, a few times and showed us around. We were impressed. The mechanics treated him more like an adult than a kid, and he obviously knew his way around everything that had to do with cars, from body shop stuff to engine tune-ups.

Fumb was the only one of the guys who had his own car, or even had access to a car. I call it Fumb's car, but

I'm sure officially it belonged to his mother or father, but because he had worked to earn enough money to pay for it, or at least a good portion of it, he was allowed to say it was his. None of the rest of us were old enough to get a driver's license. But we were definitely looking forward to the day when we would. We all planned to sign up for driver's ed as soon as we were eligible.

6

GANAWAY HIGH SCHOOL WAS AN IMPOSING, formal-looking red brick building, built in the 1920s and expanded in the 1930s. When we were there it was overcrowded and definitely showing its age. It had a swimming pool, and every student was required to pass a swimming test freshman year. The girls were issued frumpy swim suits that looked like they were made when the school was built. The guys? We swam buck naked. We'd go to the locker room, get undressed, and go out and line up at the edge of the pool. The first time I did this, I was glad that I'd had the experience of being with lots of naked guys in the football locker room. We got used to it, and it became some kind of weird rite of passage thing. After the formal class time, when we learned different strokes and practiced by swimming laps, we had about ten minutes just to goof around. What a bizarre scene that was, with guys jumping off the diving boards, balls and peckers flapping in the air on the way down into the water.

Academically, the school was probably mediocre at best, but we had nothing to compare it with, so I guess we just didn't really think about it. There was an "accelerated" program for kids who were somewhat ahead of the crowd in math and science. If you were in this group, you took algebra a year before everybody else, and you were allowed to do the same thing with some science classes. I took algebra and earth science in eighth grade, and I think the other guys in our group were in accelerated too. We all thought we wanted to go to college, which probably put us in the minority. There was an extensive shop program, including auto shop, and home economics and secretarial programs. Some snobby types looked down their noses at kids who took these courses, but at that time there were a lot of jobs for people who had practical skills. It made a lot of sense. My mom had taken the secretarial course, and I'm pretty sure my dad had gone through one of the shop programs. A lot of the guys on the football team took the shop route. Even if you took the college prep route, everyone was required to take two shop classes somewhere along the line. Boys took wood shop and metal shop in grammar school. Girls took home economics. Still a big boy-girl divide in those days. The old grammar school even had a boys' entrance and a girls' entrance.

We had some good teachers, a couple great ones, and some real dopes. A prime example of the latter was Mr. Morris, who taught freshman social studies. Every day, you would go into his class and he would have written on the blackboard, word for word, complete pages from our textbook. There would be some missing words, blank spaces with an underline. Then we were supposed to sit there and copy off the blackboard, word for word, everything he'd written, and fill in the blanks. So you would get out your textbook, find the sections that he'd copied onto the black-board, and sit there and copy the whole section into your notebook, filling in the blanks. At the end of class you would hand in your notebook so he could check to see if you'd copied it all. I know that sounds totally absurd, because it was, but that's what we did in that class. All year. By the end of the year, we had copied pretty much the whole textbook into our notebooks. Then we'd turn in our textbooks and throw away our notebooks. I still can't believe the school district let that idiot do that, year after year, until he finally retired some years after we graduated.

At one point or another, I think all the guys took chemistry, so we had the memorable experience of studying under the penetrating glare of Mrs. Margaret Baxter, known to her adoring students as Batshit Baxter. The Bat for short. She was a short, dumpy lady, maybe in her fifties. When you're in high school you don't really have a very good idea of how old adults are, especially your teachers. The Bat spoke with a kind of southern accent, and we got very good at imitating her. Certain things would set her off, and these things were well known and got passed along from one class to the next. One of the things that caused her great consternation, annoyance, and frustration involved the way you describe a liquid or a gas. If you were called on to discuss your chemistry experiment during lab, and if you said something like, "It produced a clear liquid," that would get her going. She would step back from her counter, place her hands palms down on the surface, and kind of rotate her head in a slow, deliberate circle, like she was stretching her neck muscles, prepping to unleash a verbal blast, and then she would lean forward and almost shout in her southernish accent, "Cleah

is not a cullah!" (Translation: Clear is not a color!) Most
likely the student who described the liquid as "clear" knew
that the proper scientific description was "colorless." The
Bat's "Cleah is not a cullah!" was a legendary exclamation
that often rang out in the halls of Ganaway High School.
If you had a chance to make her say it, you would not pass
up the opportunity. Even if some innocent student didn't
do it on purpose, and just said "clear liquid" because that's
just what naturally comes to mind, the effect was the same.
The Bat was furious, and the class would love it when she
blew her top. Then she would look down, shake her head,
and look up to the ceiling and say, "I tell them and I tell
them, but they don't listen," sharing her frustration with the
almighty, imploring him to deliver her from this pit of snig-
gering, ignorant adolescent tormentors.

I think it was in The Bat's class that we were introduced
to British Thermal Units, or BTUs. Maybe it was physics
class. Somewhere along the line we decided that BTU stood
for Batshit Technological University—our alma mater.
It may have been J.D. who came up with that, but maybe
not. Who knows? We decided that we all played football
at BTU for our beloved coach, Cyril Throckmorton. Again,
who came up with that? I don't know. Nobody remembers
and it has never mattered. BTU became a part of our private world, our parallel universe that was constantly under
construction.

In math we learned that QED meant "quod erat demon-
strandum"—"that which was to be demonstrated." You
would put that at the end of a math proof to indicate that the
proof was complete. QED became the name of our fraternity at BTU—Quelta Epsilon Delta. Quelta? Not exactly a

Greek letter but it sounded like one, so close enough. When we got started with shit like this, one thing would lead to another. Certainly BTU would have an archrival, so we needed another university. Around that time you were hearing a lot about LSD. Somebody came up with the brilliant idea that LSD stood for Louie's School of Dentistry. So now BTU had its archrival, and we had the beginning of a saga that we added to and built on year after year. I guess it's one of those you-had-to-be-there things, but believe me, we had a hell of a lot of fun making things up and inventing stories about our days at the Quelt House, which is what we called our fraternity house at BTU. As we often said, "It doesn't take much to amuse us."

One of the English teachers, Mrs. Fetters, would make us take turns reading aloud in class. Usually it was poetry, but sometimes it was a passage from a novel or some famous historical document. I was in her class with ShiThead and one day he was called on to do the reading. I have no idea now what he was reading but it had the word "epitome," which he pronounced "ep-i-toam." The whole class snickered and ShiThead looked up, puzzled about what was so funny. Mrs. Fetters said, "Stanley, that word is pronounced "e-pit-o-mee." ShiThead was obviously embarrassed but tried to act nonchalant and unfazed. He said something like, "Right, I know, I was just going too fast." Most of the kids in the class I'm sure never gave it another thought after the initial laugh. But I made sure that the entire Backfield heard about it. ShiThead's mispronunciation started another tradition. When we planned to get together, we said we were having a rendezvous, which we pronounced "ren-dez-vouse."

A big, raucous meeting was a "horrendezvous." Truly, it didn't take much to amuse us.

From time to time we would issue a "writ." Sometimes this was done to recognize a member for some achievement, but usually it was to condemn a member for some act, or statement, or perceived shortcoming or offense. Scourge was often called upon to draft these, using his advanced skills in legalese, but other members were known to come up with their own versions, on occasion. All this ridiculous stuff—BTU, and LSD, and QED, and writs, and horrendezvouses, and more stupid things we were constantly inventing—gave us endless laughs and made us feel like a band of brothers, set apart from the crowd, and joined in a bond of friendship unlike any other in Ganaway High School. We never got tired of retelling the old stories.

1

THE SUMMER BEFORE OUR JUNIOR YEAR was when we started spending a lot of time on the water. Scourge had a really cool boat that was kept in a boathouse that his family owned on the river. It was a Rollins wood boat, made by the company where my dad worked. I don't know the model or much about the exact features and specifications, but it had a small cabin where I guess you could actually sleep a couple of people, the steering wheel was under the covered part, a couple of other seats were to the rear of the cabin and a bench seat was in the stern. I know it had a 100-horse Mercury, because we all thought that was incredibly powerful.

The first time we went out on the boat it was just Scourge, J.D., ShiThead, and me. We had set up a plan where we would meet at the Ambassador Theatre in Ganaway, go to a movie, then have Scourge take us for a boat ride. Mom agreed to let me hang out with the guys and said she would pick me up at Gino's at around 8:00 p.m. I remember being really impressed by Scourge's nautical skills and knowledge. He checked all kinds of stuff, looked at dials, pressed some buttons, started the engine, and while it warmed up he opened the boathouse doors and then got back on the boat in the captain's chair. Slowly he backed the boat out of the boathouse and into the river, which looked wider and more imposing from the inside of the boat than it had ever looked to me before, more like a lake than a river.

My own nautical knowledge at that time was very limited. I had a canoe that I kept behind a neighbor's house on Eel Creek, and I'd been in fishing boats with small outboard motors on family vacations, but I'd never been in what I thought of as a serious boat with a serious engine. Once we got past the buoys, Scourge jammed down the throttle and we all jerked back in our seats as the boat accelerated and we took off across the water at what seemed like a hundred miles an hour. It felt incredible! The wind blowing in our faces and our shirts blowing and flapping around our bodies and the boat bouncing and crashing through the waves, with water splashing on us as we crashed along. Of course Scourge had to show off, and he started swerving left and right and we were jostled back and forth in our seats, loving every minute of it.

"Whoa!" yelled J.D. "You tryin' to kill all of us?"

"Does this asshole know what he's doing?" screamed ShiThead.

"What's the matter?" returned Scourge. "You pussies can't handle a little speed? Grow some balls, girls!"

Girls were supposed to grow balls? At the time it didn't sound quite so stupid. The main thing was, we were totally eating up the boating experience, which I believe was a first for all of us, except of course for Scourge, the aristocrat.

I don't know how long we stayed out on the first boat

ride. I was surprised that there weren't more boats out that day, but there was a lot of water, so maybe it just didn't get very crowded, I thought. All of us could swim, and there were life jackets and rescue floats as required, but obviously we weren't wearing life jackets. That would definitely not have been cool. After we got back to the boathouse it took a while for Scourge to get everything secured and tied up and locked down, or whatever you do to a boat in a boat-house. He knew what he was doing and he had us pitch in and help where we could. Once everything was ship shape, Scourge gave us a tour of the boathouse, which had a kind of apartment upstairs with a refrigerator, sink, small stove, kitchen table and chairs, a couch, and a couple of comfort-able chairs. There was a small bedroom and a nice living area. It also had a bathroom with a shower. We were all totally impressed by this, and we tried and failed to hide how impressed we were.

"Jesus," said ShiThead, "you own this place?"

"Yeah. Well, you know, I mean my old man owns it," said Scourge.

"Business must be pretty good at the Bullshit Law Firm," I said.

J.D. said, "Hey we should hang out here instead of G's basement. This is so cool. How come you been holdin' out on us, man?"

"Well, maybe we can come here sometimes," said Scourge, "but my old man can be a real prick, so I don't want to start anything that will screw things up for us with the boat. I think for now we should just use the boat and not sneak in here at night because the old man might be pissed if he found out we were hanging out here at night. Let's just see how it goes."

This sounded reasonable to us because we still had G's basement where we could scarf a few beers and play some pool. And we definitely didn't want to do anything that might jeopardize our newfound love of boating. So we closed up the boathouse and headed for Gino's. It wasn't too busy because it wasn't after a game, and there wasn't much going on in Bell Island or Ganaway on a Saturday night, or really anytime, for that matter. We ordered a couple of pizzas, which were always great, and really different. Not that we had a huge range of pizza experience in those days, but just compared to the pizzas we'd had at different places, Gino's was one of a kind. The crust was almost like a pastry, a pie crust, but not exactly. It had a kind of flaky texture, but still was pizza, with the feeling of bread, but very light and airy. It's really hard to describe it.

"So, when can we go out on the boat again?" J.D. asked.

"Yeah," said ShiThead, "that was seriously cool. Do you have any water skis?"

"What are you gonna do with water skis?' said J.D.

"What do you think you do with water skis, asshole?" said ShiThead.

"I know what certain skilled people do with water skis," J.D. said, "but what are you, a stupid polack who just went out on a boat for the first time in his life, going to do with water skis?"

"Shove 'em up your sorry guinea ass, that's what!"

"Boys, boys," I said, "enough of this acrimony and name-calling. Be kind to each other. For remember what Mitch Miller and the Gang have said: 'Be kind to your web-footed friends, for a duck may be somebody's mother. Be kind to your friends in the swamp, where the weather is very very damp. Now you may think that this is the end. Well, it is!' So let there be an end to this senseless conflict! I'm sure if Scourge has water skis, he will endeavor to instruct us in their use."

"I don't see how that is appropriate to this situation," said ShiThead. "The only duck we know is Fumb Duck and he's not even here."

"OK, very funny," said Scourge. "Yes, we have water skis, and yes, next time we go out on the boat I'll let you assholes make fools of yourselves trying to use them. Now, eat your pizza."

8

ONE DAY THAT SAME SUMMER, Fumb picked up all of us in his car and we went to Palmisano's Market, where we knew J.D. was working. We parked across the street and all of us went into the market and looked around. It wasn't very big, and it had a nice appetizing smell to it, like sandwich meat and fresh produce, if fresh produce actually has a smell. Anyway, it smelled like you thought a market and deli should smell. A guy who was stocking shelves saw us wandering around and said, "Can I help you?"

"Is J.D. here?" said G.

"Who the hell is J.D.?" asked the guy who, we noticed, closely resembled J.D.

"Joe Palmisano," G said.

"Who wants to know?" said the guy who was probably J.D.'s brother.

"We're just some friends from school," said Scourge. "We just wanted to say hi."

"Joey!" the guy yelled. "There's five assholes out here want to see you."

We heard some scuffling in the back room, and pretty soon J.D. came out with an apron on. He said, "Hey, what the hell are you guys doing here?"

"That's what I wanted to know," said the probable brother of J.D.

"We were just out driving around and we decided to come by and check out your market," said Scourge.

"Well, this is it," said J.D. "Not much to see, I'm afraid. Oh, by the way, speaking of assholes, meet my brother Rocco."

"Bafongool, you little shit!" said Rocco.

"Hey, you guys want a sub?" J.D. asked. "What kind do you want? I'll make one for everybody."

"Yeah, and everybody will pay for them, too," said Rocco.

"Don't pay any attention to him," said J.D. "So who wants what?"

We all ordered subs; I got the Italian assorted, and J.D. went behind the deli counter and made them all really fast. My god, they were good. I found out that they got their bread from Amato's Bakery, fresh every day. Amazing. J.D. let us come into the back room where there was a table and chairs, and we ate our subs and talked about the usual stuff. And we didn't pay for the subs.

While we were there a few customers came in and Rocco waited on them. I asked J.D. what he did in the store, what kind of work. He said he did whatever needed to be done, stocking shelves, waiting on customers, taking out the trash, sweeping the floors, wiping down the shelves and counters, whatever. He said he worked wherever he was needed, depending on his school schedule, sports practices, and so forth. Rocco was the oldest brother in the family and he worked there full-time as second in command to their father, Tomasso.

While we were there eating our subs, J.D.'s other brother, Tony, came in the back door of the market. "What's this?" he said. "Are we turning into a restaurant now?"

"These are friends of mine from school," said J.D. "We're all on the football team together." He introduced all of us to Tony.

"Hey, Tony," Rocco said, "can you work tonight? I got somethin' I gotta do."

"Jesus Christ!" said Tony. "I just got off shift at Cooper. I'm wiped out. Plus I need to spend a few hours on the oxygen tank after working at that fucking place. There's so much dust blowing around in there sometimes that you can't see your hand in front of your face. Look at this." He pounded with his hands on his chest and shook his shirt sleeves and dust just flew out everywhere. "First thing I gotta do is take a shower."

"Yeah, well after you take a shower and spend some time on the respirator, can you work tonight, paisan?" asked Rocco. "You're gettin' sent to college, you privileged little shit. You should be thankful for your good fortune and help out your older brother, who is helping to pay for your bright future."

"Oh, give me a break," said Tony. "I'm working at Cooper to pay for college and taking my life in my hands while I'm at it. You should see what goes on at that place."

"I know what Cooper's like," said Rocco. "I know lots of guys who work there. They get paid good money, and so do you. For a summer job you're getting paid a lot more than you're worth. So stop bitchin' about it."

"Well, if you think Cooper's so great," said Tony, "why don't you get a job there?"

"Oh, right. And who's gonna keep this fuckin' place goin'?" said Rocco. "You know the old man's gotta have somebody to pull some serious weight to keep this place running. Because I'm the oldest one, I got stuck with it. I'll be stocking shelves and sweeping floors till I'm old and gray while you and Joey here, the college boys, sip your cocktails at the country club."

"Ah, bullshit," said Tony. He didn't really have much to say to counter what Rocco said. He probably had a point, although who knew what would happen in the future? For sure Tony didn't want to wind up working in Palmisano's Market or Cooper Chemical for the rest of his life. None of us did. So he probably felt bad that Rocco might have gotten stuck in the family business, but hey, if he really didn't want to do that, he should talk to the old man and work something out.

"Joey," Rocco called, "customer." So J.D. got up from the table and went out to the desk to ring up a customer and the rest of us were there with Tony. Just for something to say, I asked Tony what he did at Cooper Chemical. We really got an earful.

"I usually work in the resin room," he said. "That's where they mix up this compound in huge kettles, like maybe seven feet tall and seven feet wide. Whatever they put in there gets heated and cooked and stirred by a big blade inside the kettle that rotates around and mixes the stuff until it looks kind of like thick, shiny red goop.

"When a batch of this stuff is done cooking, they call a few guys over to the kettle. Each guy gets a short shovel. There's a ramp that runs from the big concrete floor right up under the bottom of the kettle. You go up the ramp with your shovel and put it under the kettle. The guy in charge turns a lever and the hatch cover flops open and the red stuff starts coming out. You swirl the stuff onto your shovel and it looks like a soft-serve ice cream cone. Once you get a shovel full of the stuff, you run back and let another guy in. He sticks his shovel under the hatch and gets a load just like you did. You run down the ramp out onto the concrete floor, slide the goop off your shovel onto the floor, and then start stomping on it. If you don't stomp it out like that, it will swell up and explode.

"You keep doing this until the kettle is empty and all the red stuff has been stomped out and flattened. When it cools it gets hard and solid and you take a sledgehammer and smash the stuff into chunks. You shovel the chunks into large cardboard drums and a forklift picks them up. Where the stuff goes from there, I have no idea.

"While you're doing all this, the kettle is slowly cooling down. Once it cools down just enough so that it won't fry your skin if you touch it, some lucky bastard gets to climb down inside the damn thing through the hatch in the cover. Why do you have to get into the kettle? Because you have to chisel off all the resin that's dried on the inside, and then you shove that down through the bottom hatch hole. Nothing goes to waste.

"So, you squeeze your ass down through the hatch with your chisel and start chipping and scraping the resin off the walls of the kettle. And the damn agitator is still hotter than hell. You have to balance yourself with one foot on the curved wall of the kettle and one foot on the agitator, and you're sweating your ass off, and who knows what kind of poisonous shit you're breathing in there."

"God," I said, "that is just nuts. I can't believe they make people do that."

"Yeah," said Tony, "and some guys do that for years and years. I wonder how many years it takes off your life to work in that dump."

Then I said to G, "Your dad works at Cooper. Does he work in those kettles?"

"He really doesn't talk about it much," said G, "plus I don't see him very much because he works night shift. I'll have to ask him sometime if I get a chance."

"Sounds like Cooper is a real shithole," said ShiThead. "Kind of like the Bolt." The Bolt was what everyone called Iroquois Bolt Co.

"Well, I'll tell you one thing," said Tony, "everybody who works at these places will always tell you, 'Stay in school, kid, go to college. You don't want to spend the rest of your life in a dump like this.' Of course they also like the money, and the fact that they have a house, and a decent car, and that the wife can stay home and cook and clean and raise the kids. And they can buy shots and beers at the local gin mill. But I'm not gonna wind up working in one of those plants, or running this place, either."

We finished our subs and thanked J.D., who was still out in the store, and headed across the street and got in the car.

"Wanna go to the boathouse?" said ShiThead.

"Yeah, how about it, Scourge?" said G.

"Yeah, OK. I guess so. What the hell," said Scourge.

So we drove down to the river and pulled into the parking area behind the boathouse. Scourge unlocked the door and we all went in. It was pretty dark in there, with light coming in under the bottom of the walls. It smelled nautical, with the smell of stagnant, dirty water, and wet wooden pilings, and gasoline. There was a wooden deck or walkway around three sides of the boat. The stairway up to the second floor ran across the back wall, the wall that faced the street. We went up the stairs and Scourge unlocked that door, and we all went in and sprawled out on the couch and chairs. Fumb went over and opened the refrigerator door and said, "Now that is a sight to behold!" The fridge was full of bottles of Schlitz—"the beer that made Milwaukee famous."

"Leave the beer alone," said Scourge. "I'm sure the old man has an exact count maintained by his secretary or something."

"Close the door, Fumb," I said. "Lead us not into temptation."

"You assholes want to make fools of yourselves?" said Scourge. "Want to try the skis?"

"Hell, yeah, man," said ShiThead. "Let's do it!"

We went down and raised the overhead garage-type door while Scourge tended to the various details of revving the engine and casting off. He backed us out and soon we had left the no-wake zone and were in open water, under a clear blue sky with the sunlight dancing off the waves. There was a steady breeze and a pretty good chop on the water.

Scourge announced that it would be three strikes and you're out. If you didn't get up on the skis in three tries, the next guy would take his turn. I got to go first, and I found out that it was a lot harder than it looked. Floating back there with my life jacket on I had a hell of a time just getting the skis on my feet. Everybody was getting frustrated and impatient with me.

"Hurry up, asshole," ShiThead yelled. "It's going to get dark before you get the goddamn skis on."

"Up yours," I yelled back. "Wait till you try it."

When I finally got the skis on my feet, I had trouble keeping them pointed up in the air with the tow rope between them. Scourge moved the boat slowly forward and the rope tightened up and I was being pulled through the water just a little bit. The skis were wobbling back and forth as they moved slowly through the water.

"Wave your hand when you're ready," Scourge yelled.

I took a deep breath. Here goes. I waved my hand. Scourge slammed down the throttle and the 100-horse Merc let out a scary growl and the rope snapped taut, but the skis didn't seem to move, and I was yanked headfirst over the skis and dragged face-first into the water. I let go of the rope and came up with a nose full. The boat roared away and Scourge circled it around and came back and brought it up next to me.

"Very graceful," said ShiThead, looking down at me from the boat.

"OK, try it again," said Scourge. He moved the boat forward slowly and swung around so the tow rope came around and I grabbed it. He slowly pulled me along to where the skis were floating in the water and I was able to get hold of them. I had a little less trouble getting my feet into them this time, and Scourge slowly brought the boat around until the rope was straight between me and the boat. I stuck the skis up out of the water and the rope tightened up. I steadied the skis. OK, here we go. I raised my hand. The Merc growled. For a split second I felt myself rising up out of the water and almost felt myself standing on the skis, which were wobbling and wiggling underneath me. Then it was all over. The skis went under and I went headfirst over, just like the first time.

"Shit!" I yelled when I resurfaced.

Scourge came around again. "Last try," he said. And we did it all again. Another failure. I was feeling pissed and very frustrated and discouraged, but on the third try I felt like I was getting somewhere, and I thought, "Goddamn it, I know I can do this."

G was next. He got up on his third try. He had the same problems I had, but on the third try he wobbled to a her-ky-jerky standing position and Scourge towed him around for a few minutes and even swerved the boat around a bit so that G had to ski over the wake. I have to admit that I was jealous and did not have charitable feelings for my friend. Shame on me.

Fumb struck out like I did. That made me pretty happy. More shame. Then it was ShiThead's turn. Of course I was hoping that he would fail miserably. Shame, shame, shame. But that son of a bitch, I mean dear, beloved friend, got up on his first try and looked completely natural and comfort-able. Goddamn it! We would never hear the end of it. But actually, he surprised us. When he got back in the boat, he said, "Fuckin'-A, man. I think I got really lucky out there. When Scourge hit the engine, the water seemed really smooth and not as rough as when you guys were out there."

Fumb looked at him and said, "Please, spare us your good grace and sensitivity. We all know you're an obnoxious, egotistical piece of shit, so don't offend us with your phony modesty."

"So that's what I get for trying to build up and encourage my so-called friends? You assholes don't deserve to be treated with any kind of courtesy and respect."

"Ah, now there's the ShiThead we know and love," said G.

By that time it was getting dark, so we headed back to the boathouse. It was a great day. By the end of that summer all of us, including J.D., who learned as quickly as ShiThead, knew how to water ski. Some better than others, but we could all get up with confidence, and zig-zag across the wake, and feel like we belonged out there on the water like old pros.

9

A NEW DANCE PLACE OPENED THAT SUMMER in the rundown former Rollerdome skating rink. This place was a little way out of town and was quite a dump but it quickly became a popular spot. Something different in our town where there wasn't a hell of a lot to do. They hadn't really renovated the place, so it still looked like a roller rink. The counter area where they used to rent the skates they turned into a kind of snack bar where you could buy pop, and chips, and pizza, and burgers, and hot dogs, and candy. This place was open to younger kids and was supposed to be kind of a wholesome, safe place to go. It was only open Friday and Saturday nights. No alcohol was sold but some of the older kids would bring their own beer and drink it out on the edges of the parking lot, which was adjacent to a field with trees and undergrowth. We might have gone out there to check things out but typically we didn't have any beer. We didn't smoke but lots of people did and the air was literally a blue haze in there. Of course, the houses where we all lived were full of smoke too, so it wasn't anything new to us. Most of the kids couldn't drive so there was a lot of dropping off and picking up by parents and older brothers and sisters. Fumb could drive at night now, so whenever possible, we got him to drive us. The people who started this thing called it the Rockin' Rollerdome, which most people thought was pretty weak. Everybody started calling it The Rock.

The real draw was live music, plus it was a good place just to hang out and meet people. They had mostly local bands and every once in a while they'd have a band that had a bit of a wider following, trying to make a name for themselves. One time—and I have no idea why he would have come to The Rock—Jerry Lee Lewis was the featured attraction. He pounded on the piano like a wild man and when he finished with "goodness, gracious, great balls of fire!" the place went nuts. I actually got to talk to him that night. I don't remember what he said but I'll never forget seeing him there on his piano bench, just shooting the shit with the kids who were crowding around him.

Unlike at the sock hops, most people at The Rock tended to get out on the dance floor. Those were the days when dances had names: the Freddie, the Frug, the Loco-motion, the Mashed Potato, the Shimmy, the Swim, the Twist, the Watusi, the Bristol Stomp, the Chicken, the Jerk, the Monkey. Don't ask me how to do any of them, except the Twist. You would see some kids who were obviously more into it, very definitely making certain planned moves that belonged to one of the dances with a name. But most of the time you could get away with just bopping around in time to the music. I always stayed away from girls who obviously knew what they were doing and were good dancers. Unfortunately, a lot of girls seemed to know what they were doing, so that limited my potential partners. Some of the guys were good too, not as many guys as girls, and some just didn't give a shit and went out there and bounced and jerked around and looked ridiculous. I was self-conscious and immature enough that I couldn't just cut loose like that. So I kept a low profile and watched the people who were pretty good and eventually I mastered a few moves that I could use in most situations.

J.D. was the best dancer in the Backfield and he wasn't shy about asking girls to dance. The cheerleaders often hung out as a group and they were quite full of themselves. One night he asked one of them, a girl named Peggy Harrison, to dance and they were pretty good. Peggy was really good looking and had a great body—built like a brick shithouse, as we would say. They spent quite a bit of time out on the dance floor together that night. On the way home in Fumb's car we started giving J.D. some shit about his new love.

"So, tell us about your little Pubic Hair," said ShiThead.

"What are you talking about?" said J.D.

"You know, Peggy Harrison, P. H., Pubic Hair," said ShiThead.

"Very funny, asshole," said J.D. "I saw you out there with Pam Frazier, your little Pussy Fart. Tell us all about her."

"OK, enough," said Scourge. "We need to move on to a higher level of humor. By the way, did you know that Peggy Harrison's dad is the general manager of Cooper Chemical? He's a member of the Commercial Club and he has a boat at the marina. Damn nice boat. It's a Rollins cabin cruiser, big-ass son of a bitch. I don't know if he ever takes it out. I've never seen it leave the dock. But sometimes he has little parties on it, probably other business execs and their wives.

I've seen Peggy sunbathing on the deck a couple times. I think you've got yourself a tasty wench, there, J.D. Play your cards right and maybe you can get in her pants."

Maybe, but certainly not a given. We weren't yet into the free love days and the girls tended to limit the game to second base, or maybe third. We always said, years later, that we were born just a few years too soon. But we definitely were meeting some girls, and we had the Rock to thank for that. J.D. and Peggy became "a thing" and so did ShiThead and Sally Summers, whose brother, we found out, played football for Bell Island. G wound up getting pretty serious with Linda Gregg. She worked at the Tate in the ticket booth, and he was an usher there. Fumb, Scourge, and I didn't hook up with anybody in particular at that point. I was kind of sweet on a girl I had in one of my classes sophomore year, but she never came to the Rock. When school started up in the fall I tried to find opportunities to talk to her, but I didn't have any classes with her, so nothing ever came of it.

We spent a lot of nights at the rock that summer. One night a guy showed up in his snazzy Marine uniform. Some people thought it was cool and acted impressed, some thought it was kind of pathetic—showing off, strutting around like some kind of worldly soldier boy to impress the hometown civilians. Why would you wear a military uniform to a dance place? I'd say we were in the second group, except for G, who had a cousin in the Marines and took offense when somebody made a negative comment about Mr. Semper Fi. Vietnam was not a big issue yet, at least in our minds. If it came up, you could be pretty sure that almost everybody was onboard with the domino theory and thought we should do whatever was necessary to oppose the commies. There were people who were more tuned in to the issues and knew more about what was going on, even some who actively opposed what was happening over there. But they were definitely in the minority.

For most of us, I think only the really big news stories and events made much of an impression. The Buddhist monk who set himself on fire the previous summer was a big story and brought some focus on what was going on in Vietnam. Must have been something serious to cause a person to do that. And of course President Kennedy's assassination and the Lee Harvey Oswald and Jack Ruby stuff. But like I said, we didn't think or talk much about the news or about political issues. We had more important stuff to deal with. Like making up obscene nicknames for people and learning to dance the Watusi.

10

THE VARSITY FOOTBALL TEAM HAD TWO WEEKS of preseason practice sessions at the end of August, sometimes into September, depending on the school calendar. Even in our area, you'd get some pretty hot days in August. The workouts were tough and intense and after a couple of hours of calisthenics, and wind sprints, and blocking and tackling drills, you'd work up a hell of a sweat. Your gray t-shirts would be totally soaked and you'd be thirsty as hell. Gimme a drink of water! Oh, but no, not on your life. No drinks of water for the Ganaway Rivermen. Back in those days the theory was that if you drank water when you were out there sweating and working out, it would give you cramps. So you were allowed to have a slug of water that you were supposed to slosh around in your mouth and then spit it out. Seemed pretty stupid to me at the time and sounds really stupid all these years later. But that was the common wisdom back then.

Moving up to varsity from JV you could sense something different, more intense; somehow the pace was faster, crisper. The hitting was harder. It's hard to explain. You could also sense the pressure that was on the team, pressure because the last two seasons had been disastrous. Losing records both years, losing to Bell Island both years. Even my old man, who didn't take much interest in football, had asked me if I thought Ganaway was going to be able to turn things around. I'm sure he heard all kinds of talk about the state of Ganaway football at his nightly visits to Volcker's. He even asked me if I thought Helwig was over the hill, which was being said a lot around town. Of course I knew about Helwig's firm belief in the power of his single wing offense, but I really had no context to put that in. Were we really way out of touch with modern trends in the game? We'd heard Helwig's philosophy from the first day we set foot on the practice field as freshmen. We were thoroughly indoctrinated with his way of thinking and doing things. We were just kids and of course we wanted to respect and revere our coach and have him lead us onward to victory! So I really didn't know what to say when the old man asked me if I thought our coach was over the hill. I certainly didn't want to think so.

On the varsity now, we had a new rallying cry. We were no longer running down the field with Freckles Kramden as we had under Coach Parker. Now we were to be at all times Agile! Mobile! and Hostile! And these were not pronounced "ag'l, mob'l, and host'l." No. We were to be A-gile, MO-bile, and HOS-tile. This was drummed into us at every practice session and repeated in every pep talk.

It really was beastly hot that August and the practices were rough. It seemed to me that if we could get through that we must be pretty damn tough. Of course all the other teams were having preseason practice too, but Helwig just made you feel like you were capable of running over everybody. Like he always said, we don't care if they know what we're going to do. We're Ganaway and we're tougher than they are and we're going to have our way with them. This had worked for Ganaway for decades under Helwig's leadership, and this team would make it work too.

Most of the starters were seniors, but not all. As we got near the end of preseason practice and close to the first game in September, it was looking like J.D. and ShiThead both had a good shot at starting. They were both natural athletes, plus they worked like hell and were really competitive. That's not to say the rest of us were slackers. We worked hard and did our best and were totally committed to the team. But there was just something about their instincts, and really good coordination, and agility (A-gile!) that seemed to give them an edge. Fumb, because of his size, and because he was quite well coordinated and quick for a big guy, was a good fit for center. G had good speed and athletic ability, and was tough and very aggressive, which made him well suited for blocking back. He was an OK passer, and that's where I had a bit of an edge, in the wing-T. But with our offensive approach, G was a better fit than me. Scourge was quick but a little on the small side. He had good hands and could also throw, which came into play on rare occasions when we might run some kind of reverse.

One of our biggest weak spots was our kicking game. We had a mediocre punter, Eddie Lewandowski, and a pretty bad placekicker, Adam Dudek. Back then you basically never saw a high school team attempt a field goal. The kickoff was from the kicking team's forty-yard line and the point after touchdown was kicked from about the ten-yard line. Dudek was a pretty small guy. On the kickoff he would make a straight run at the ball, and sometimes he'd hit it pretty solid and it would go maybe thirty-five or forty yards. That would be a good kick for him. Sometimes he'd top it or hit it off center and it would bounce along the ground at the opposing line or squirt over their heads and maybe go out of bounds. If it went out of bounds, the receiving team could make him kick again from five yards farther back or they could take the ball on their own thirty-five-yard line. On extra points you never knew what you might get. He might kick it right through the goal post or he might kick it into the center's ass. He was a junior but apparently the best we had. I don't recall anyone challenging him for kicker.

Our first game was a home game against Eastport. Friday night as always. A good crowd, the stands were full. J.D. had made starter at tailback and ShiThead was starting fullback. G wasn't able to beat out senior Kevin Wiley at QB/blocking back. Fumb, Scourge, and I were also warming the bench, pretty much as we had expected. Eastport was usually an easy team to beat. It was a well-to-do suburb, so the team was well supported, but we always thought they were a bunch of pussies. I don't think there was a single big, dirty factory in the town and we just assumed that the kids were all rich and spoiled and had no balls. It had been a very long time since Ganaway had lost a football game to Eastport.

We carried on the winning tradition that year with a 34-7 win. Helwig's single wing power offense definitely did the job as we ran over them pretty much at will. Dudek had a typical game, for him. He kicked the extra point on the first two touchdowns, missed on the third and fourth, and Helwig called for a two-point conversion on the fifth touchdown, which was good. The reason I remember this much detail is that I was really tuned in to this first varsity game of my career. It seemed like a very important game to me. A traditionally weak team. The fact that Ganaway's two previous seasons had been really bad. Talk around town about Helwig being over the hill. This win felt good. Maybe the last two years were just some kind of fluke. Ganaway was back, and we were part of the comeback.

After the game, Helwig gave a post-game pep talk in the locker room. It was the same stuff we had heard since the start of practice, but I think we all felt pumped up. He really did have an inspirational style. As kids, deep down, do you really know it's all a bunch of bullshit? I think sometimes we did. But then sometimes you couldn't help but get charged up by it. It made you feel like you were a warrior, going out to do battle, to defend your school, your town. Us against the enemy! We will bury you! Wait a minute, that was Khrushchev.

We may have been psyched and inspired and all that, but the second game, against Summit, didn't go as well. They weren't as easy to run over. Helwig's classic principle, that we didn't care if they knew what we were going to do, that we would just overpower them with our fundamentals, and strength, and determination, seemed to be called into question by their defense. We ran our power plays to the strong side, but they wouldn't just let our blockers blow them out. Yeah, they knew what we were going to do, and they prepared for it and adjusted their defense, and lots of times that day, they stopped us. The only thing that saved us was that they didn't have much of an offense. Of course they ran from the T formation. Our running game was better than theirs, even though they weren't pushovers and we didn't plow through them the way we were supposed to. Their quarterback had a good arm, and they scored both of their touchdowns on passes. We won 19-14. Dudek made one of his extra points, missed two. Their guy made both of his extra points. Helwig was not pleased, and he made this known in the locker room after the game.

"Boys," he said, as he paced back and forth in the middle of the room, "we've got a lot of work to do. The way we played out there tonight is not going to win us a conference championship. That was not Ganaway football. We were weak, not strong. We did not take it to 'em. What are we supposed to be?" Silence.

"A-gile! MO-bile! HOS-tile!" he yelled so loud that some of us actually jumped.

"What are we gonna be?" he screamed.

"A-gile! MO-bile! HOS-tile!" we all yelled.

"I can't hear you!"

"A-gile! MO-bile! HOS-tile!" we yelled again, literally screaming at the top of our lungs.

"OK, boys," he said, "we're going to put this game behind us, but we're going to learn from it. Get some rest this weekend because you're going to work your tails off next week. OK, now hit the showers. Go!"

———

TUESDAY NIGHT WAS FILM NIGHT. The varsity team would come back to school at 7:30 and crowd into Helwig's history classroom to watch the 16 mm film of the previous week's game. The coaches would analyze each play and point out missed blocks, missed holes, incorrect lineups, penalties, poor pass coverage, weak line penetration, sloppy tackles, and missed cues. Both offense and defense would be dissected in detail. The backfield coach might say, "Hanuszewicz, what was that? What did you miss there?" Everybody dreaded getting called on like that. You had to think fast and try to pick up on what the coach thought you had done wrong.

"Uh," ShiThead might hesitate, "uh."

"You should have cut left! Timmins had the defensive tackle rolled up and shoving toward the sidelines. You just kept following the block and the defensive tackle got loose from Timmins and shut you down. You've got to be more aware of holes when they open up. It happens in a split second and you have to react. A-gile! MO-bile!"

'OK, Coach, yeah," ShiThead would say.

One night after the film session we went to Gino's to shoot the shit and order a pizza. Somebody said, "Did you notice that Helwig goes out in the hallway several times during the films? Like when one of the other coaches is talking about something or other or asking questions."

"I think he's taking nips," said J.D.

"What do you mean?" asked G.

"I've heard Wiley say that you can smell booze on Helwig on the sidelines at games," said J.D. "And I think he's right. I've noticed it when he grabs you by the shirt and gets up in your face to give you instructions about something or to chew you out."

"So you really think he's out in the hall takin' a snort?" G asked.

"It wouldn't surprise me," J.D. said. "I mean, the guy is a legend. But you know, maybe he is actually slipping. Look at how many passes we throw compared to pretty much everybody else. Yeah, the single wing is a solid, plow-ahead offense, but how many other teams use it? I can't think of any around here. I've heard there are maybe a few colleges that still use it. But none of the pro teams. It's all T formation. We don't have any innovation at all, offense or defense. Even my old man, who's not much of a football fan, said something at dinner the other night about it. He said, 'Is it true that Ganaway is old fashioned in football? Somebody was in the store talking about how Ganaway needs to get up to date or we're not going to keep up our reputation.' I didn't want to get into it with him because he doesn't really know anything about football, but I think if my old man is talking about it, it's got to be a pretty big issue."

"Yeah, but how about the drinking?" I asked.

J.D. shrugged his shoulders and put his hands palms-up on the table. "Well, like I said, Wiley talked about it, and I've noticed it too. We'll have to pay closer attention and see what we think."

I said, "I'll try to get close to him on the sidelines at a game sometime and see if I can smell it on him. I should be pretty good at it since my old man comes home smelling like booze every night. Problem is, when you're a scrub you don't get much chance to get up close and personal with the coach."

11

ONE FRIDAY THE GUYS DECIDED TO GO FOR A FISH FRY at the Polish Eagle. This was located on Samuels Street up in the Turd Ward—Little Warsaw. It had been there a long time, since the early 1900s, and was the social center of the Polish immigrant community for many years. It was still really popular, and on Friday nights you often had to wait for a table. Out behind the club were three soccer fields. All of the ethnic clubs and even a few volunteer fire companies had club soccer teams. They had youth soccer for little kids and young teenagers, a team for high school-age kids, and a team for adults. Since there was also a soccer program at the high school, some kids chose one or the other—club soccer or high school team. Some did both. A lot of us thought of soccer as a sissy sport compared to the big masculine sport of football. Soccer was BORE-ing. Up and down the field, back and forth, hardly any scoring. You get penalized for hitting somebody. What the hell? Pardon me for bumping into you. Oh my, may I just run around you kicking this bouncy white ball? Thank you. ShiThead was working his job in the kitchen but he was able to take a break and join us for a while. The food at the Eagle was great. On Fridays, you would normally order the fish fry, which was the classic yellow pike or blue pike, deep-fried with a light, crispy batter—not a thick beer batter—along with perfect french fries and coleslaw. Some places served the vinegar-based coleslaw but we all liked the creamy kind, and the Eagle had the best. You could also order some of the other Eagle specialties, like pierogi, golabke (stuffed cabbage rolls), kapusta (sauerkraut), kielbasa, and my all-time favorite, a kind of breaded pork chop called kotlet schabowy. Delicious. If you were really adventuresome you could try kieczka (sausage made with fresh pig's blood) or czernina (duck's blood soup). Yeah, sounds kind of disgusting, but if you can get past the images in your head and try it, really good.

We got our table and pretty soon ShiThead came out of the kitchen and joined us. I made some comment about the soccer fields and why would anybody want to play such a pussy game. I was surprised when ShiThead jumped all over me.

"What do you know about soccer, asshole?"

"Well," I said, "I know it looks like a game for pussies."

"Well, that just shows how ignorant you are," he said. "Hey, I love football, but there's no comparing football and soccer. One's not better than the other, they're just different, very different. Everybody on a soccer team has to have skill and dexterity. Everybody. In football you can play some positions based on size and strength. Offensive tackle, for example. You've got one job—blocking. Sure, speed and agility are important, but your skills and assignment are pretty specialized. In soccer, everybody needs to know how to dribble the ball and kick with accuracy and power. Totally different. You should open your mind and learn some stuff about soccer so you won't sound so ignorant, dipshit. Or offensive."

"OK, sorry," I said. "I didn't know you felt so strongly about soccer. So, did you ever play soccer, or what?"

"Yes, I played ever since I was a little kid," said ShiThead.

"I never knew that," I said.

"But when I got to high school," ShiThead went on, "I wanted to play football. Soccer is a great sport, but in Ganaway nothing compares to football. Everybody knows that. My dad was kind of disappointed, but he didn't stand in my way. He knows about football and Ganaway."

Our fish came and it was delicious. We talked about how the season was going. We were 2-0 at that point and feeling pretty confident about our chances for a winning season, maybe an undefeated season. God, wouldn't that be great? We'd be part of the team that turned things around, turned things back to Ganaway being on top. So we had Eastport and Summit behind us, with Ironton, St. Ignatius, Roosevelt, Parsons, Norfolk, and Bell Island left. J.D. was doing a great job at running back. He had great speed and an uncanny instinct for finding his running room and he could cut and turn on a dime. You could count on ShiThead to plow ahead for three yards up the middle. Fumb had gotten his chance at center when Roger Nelson, the senior starter, twisted his ankle and looked like he'd be out for several games. Fumb's blocking was strong, but he needed work on his snaps. He could get a good tight spiral on the ball but he didn't always lead the runner, usually J.D., the tailback, properly, and that would mess up the flow and timing of the play. He really needed to work on that.

G shared the news that his older brother, Tom, who had started college but dropped out, had been drafted. That was kind of a shocker, because like I said, we weren't too terribly focused on the Vietnam War and the whole draft business, and now this made it seem more real and serious. This was before the draft lottery, and nobody really knew how people's names got picked to be drafted.

Fumb asked him, "Why did he drop out of college? If you're in college you won't be drafted."

"Who knows?" said G. "I guess he didn't really know what he was shooting for, didn't know what he wanted to do."

"Well, it seems to me that wandering aimlessly through college is still better than being in the army and probably getting shipped off to Vietnam," said Fumb.

Things in Vietnam were heating up since the Gulf of Tonkin Resolution at the end of the summer. We didn't know much about the details of that, but we knew that it had something to do with giving the president authority to use armed forces to stop the commies.

"What's wrong with the army?" G asked. "Somebody's got to protect our country."

"Yeah, and how many senators' and congressmen's kids do you think are fighting to protect our country? How many of them are getting drafted?"

"I don't know," said G. "What do you mean anyway? There's some system and some guys get called up and you just have to go do your duty."

"Bullshit!" said Fumb. "The people who get drafted are

suckers like us, who don't have any connections or anybody to pull strings for them to keep them out. We're supposed to do our duty but the people who have some pull just get out of it. There's a system, all right, and it's totally bogus. How about it, Scourge, how many of your old man's country club friends have kids in the army?"

"I really don't know," said Scourge. "I never really asked."

"Yeah, well you can bet your sweet ass that their kids manage to get out of it somehow, some kind of deferment or whatever. Or maybe they join the navy and get to be a legal officer and sit around pushing paper while G's brother gets his ass blown off in some rice paddy."

G was really upset by this. "Why would you say that, asshole?" he said. "Why would you talk about my brother getting killed? That's a really stupid thing to say."

"Sorry," said Fumb. "I shouldn't have said that. That was stupid. I just think the whole draft thing is totally unfair and I have no idea what anybody can do about it. But yeah, I'm sorry I said that. I take it back."

"Getting back to soccer," I said.

"Why do we want to get back to soccer?" J.D. wanted to know.

"I was just thinking about Dudek," I said. "He's a pretty mediocre kicker at best, and there doesn't seem to be any-body else who can replace him. At least nobody has come forward to try out. I was just wondering if maybe some good soccer player could be a placekicker in football."

"No," said ShiThead, "believe me, it's a totally differ-ent thing kicking a soccer ball and kicking a football. And even if you could do it, I don't know any really good soccer player who would give up soccer just to be a placekicker on the football team. Some people—like you, dick brain," he was referring to me when he said this, "look down on soccer. Well, I've got news for you. There are some people who think football is a totally stupid sport. No, you're not going to see anybody doing what you're talking about."

"Not to change the subject," said G.

"You are changing the subject," said Scourge.

"OK, well then, if I may change the subject," said G, "I'd like to talk about beer."

"Good topic," said ShiThead.

"OK, well, I was just wondering," said G, "if J.D. could sell us beer from his store. I mean, could we give him money and then he can sneak it out when he's working and Rocco or Frank or his dad aren't around?"

J.D. thought about this for a minute. "We could, I guess, but I'm not sure I'd want to take the chance of getting caught. If somehow we got caught selling to someone under eighteen, the store could lose its liquor license. I'm not sure how we would ever get reported, if we're just doing it when nobody's around, but I'd have to think about it."

"I thought you guys had some kind of protection. Because of being Italian, or something," said G.

"What are you talking about?" said J.D. "Protection from getting reported to the cops or the state liquor authority? You mean some kind of mob thing? No, I'm afraid not."

"Well, I've just heard about some kind of protection that you get from certain, shall we say, shady organizations," said G.

"God, you're totally messed up, man," said J.D. "Protection was money you paid to the mob to keep bad things from happening to you. Like the store owner would have to pay a hundred bucks a week or whatever to keep from getting beat up, or having some kind of 'accident' or something. And these bad things would be done by the mob, so protection was just extortion. I don't think there's too much of that going on anymore. I don't know. I've heard that Amato's bakery once was burned because old Grandpa Amato said he was done paying protection. But that was like in the 1920s or something. But, back to your question, no, we don't have any kind of Italian protection from getting charged with selling to minors."

"Well, it was just an idea," said G.

Fumb said, "Maybe we just have somebody over eighteen buy it for us. We could ask Nelson, I'm pretty sure he'd do it. And he wouldn't even have to buy it at J.D.'s place. He could get it anywhere."

After thinking it over, J.D. decided that he could sneak beer out if he was careful. We would give him cash and he'd ring it up when he was alone in the store and no customers were around. He'd hide it in the garage on the alley, which was full of all kinds of shit, and nobody would notice a couple six packs or a tap-a-keg. It wasn't unusual then for sixteen- and seventeen-year-old kids, maybe even fifteen-year-olds, to be drinking some beer. The drinking age was eighteen in New York, and in most households, especially the ethnic ones, drinking was no big deal and even little kids would be offered a little sip. The grown-ups would laugh when the kid screwed up his face and gagged on the bitter taste, thinking or saying, "You want beer? Well, there you go, how do you like it?" That's not to say that J.D.'s father would be happy if he found out what we were doing. We still had to be careful. He could lose his liquor license and there would be hell to pay for that.

12

THE FIRST GAME AGAINST EASTPORT HAD BEEN GREAT, but we only squeaked out a win against Summit. Coming off that game we got our asses chewed out pretty good, and the coaches really worked us in practice the week before the Ironton game. Usually Ironton was a pretty strong team, made up of hard-nosed kids from blue collar families whose fathers worked in the auto plants, or the big steel mill, or one of the many other factories in the town. Pretty much like Ganaway, but they had some Black players, not many, where we had absolutely none. Nelson was still out with his ankle injury, and Fumb was starting at center. He was doing a good job and it looked like there might be some chance that he'd take over as center. So we had three start-ers from the Backfield on the field as we squared off against Ironton. It was a close game, low scoring. From our side, it was a perfect example of the Helwig style. Mostly running plays and almost everything out of the single wing. The few passes that were thrown were thrown by J.D. at tailback. We ran a few plays from the wing-T, but just handoffs or maybe a pitch. Nothing very imaginative or exciting. But we won, and that's what counts.

Our fourth game was against St. Ignatius, which was one of the two private schools we played. The other was Norfolk Academy. They were both all-boys schools, and we thought that all the kids who went there were rich stuck-up assholes who saw themselves as superior beings and better than everybody else. Therefore we always wanted to beat the shit out of them. Of course you didn't need to be rich to send your kid to St. Ignatius, a Catholic school, you just had to think the public schools were no good, or you had to want your kid to be surrounded by priests and nuns and holy water and incense and rosaries and all the other Catholic stuff, whatever that was. But if the parents thought their little darlings were being sheltered from the crude, profane, and sinful ways of the world, they must never have sat near the student section at one of their football games. The team name for St. Ignatius was the Saints. Very original. There was always a group of guys who, at some point during every game, would break out with the school cheer. This was a totally disgusting chant. Hilarious, but kind of shocking for a Catholic school. It made reference to rat and bat excrement and human bodily fluids and ended with a shout: "Saints, give 'em hell!" St. Ignatius, the namesake, would be proud. I'm sure this was frowned upon by Father Montrose, the principal, and maybe some of the guys got in trouble for raising the cheer, but it happened at every game, so either Father wasn't much of a disciplinarian, or the guys in the cheering section had ways of keeping their identities confidential.

St. Iggie, as the school was known around town, always

had good sports teams. This was because they didn't just draw from the good Catholic families around the diocese for their players. They actively recruited from the whole area, using scholarships to attract good athletes, some of them Black kids from neighborhoods where you wouldn't find a Catholic church, or a Catholic for that matter. They also had a coach who wasn't a teacher, something you never saw in a public school back then. That gave them something of an advantage because they could recruit former football players, maybe really good ones who had excelled in college ball, who loved the game but didn't go into education, who still wanted to be involved with the game. St. Iggie's coach worked for some company, doing what I don't know, that gave him enough free time that he could devote the hours required during the season to run the football program.

The St. Iggie game was close. They were ahead in the fourth quarter, but they didn't have the game sewed up. Ahead by less than a touchdown, they couldn't afford to coast; they needed to score again to get a more comfortable lead. With about five minutes to go, they were on about their own twenty-five-yard line, third down and four or five. They called a pitch-out. Our defensive end was right there and as soon as the halfback took the pitch, our guy nailed him. The ball came loose and for a split second it hung there in the air, then our guy grabbed it and sprinted untouched down the sideline and into the end zone. Dudek made the extra point and had one of his better kicks on the kickoff, and St. Iggie wasn't able to move the ball. We didn't score again either, but we didn't have to. We chalked up our fourth win out of four games. We beat the Saints, which was always especially sweet.

So we were pretty pumped up going into the Roosevelt game, which was always a tough one. Roosevelt was a pre-dominantly Black school. There were some white players on the team, but most of the starters were Black, "tutsoons," as J.D. and the Italians called them. I assumed that it was a derogatory term, but I didn't think much about it. We were totally oblivious to the fact that our whole attitude and way of thinking was racist and bigoted. We had heard about the time that some Black people had tried to sit at the lunch counter somewhere down south and were arrested by the cops. Yeah, those southerners were racists. But there was nothing wrong with us talking about tutsoons, and our coaches talking about "those sun-tanned boys" we'd be fac-ing off against on Friday. Since those days the language has changed, and lots of minds have been changed, but unfor-tunately there are still a lot of people whose attitudes and opinions haven't changed a bit.

The "sun-tanned boys" comment came up at our meet-ing to watch films of the St. Iggie game and get ready for the Roosevelt game. Assistant Coach Rudnik got up and started analyzing the Roosevelt team, talking about specific players we needed to focus on, what their strengths and weaknesses were. At one point he said something like, "We're going to be playing against a lot of those sun-tanned boys, if you know what I mean. They're tough and more than anything, they want to beat the white boys and mess up our season. They know we're 4 and 0. They're 4 and 0 too. They sure don't want to lose to the white boys. This is a crucial game for us. We've got to keep our momentum going. We've got to win this one. OK, so here's what we're going to do." And from there he launched into the Helwig spiel we'd heard so many times before, about how they might know what we're going to do, but that doesn't matter because we're gonna take it to 'em and they can't stop us because we know how to execute and we're tougher than they are, and on and on. A-gile! MO-bile! HOS-tile! Looking back now, I can't really say for sure if we believed it, or maybe wanted to believe it but were starting to have doubts. Maybe the latter because we were seeing other teams playing a more inventive, imaginative game, the kind of football you saw on TV with the pros and college teams. And we were hearing talk around town about that stuff.

The Roosevelt game was a disaster. They knew what we were going to do, and they had prepared for it, and they stopped us. Instead of three yards and a cloud of dust, it was one yard, or zero yards, and a cloud of dust. Their defensive line wasn't going to be overpowered. They were big and strong, and the fact that they could readily anticipate what we were going to run at them made them hard to move. J.D. called some pass plays, and completed a few, but it wasn't enough to keep us in the game. We tried a few plays from the wing-T, but this was not something we worked on a lot, and we weren't very good at it. Wiley, the QB, was a better blocker than a passer, which made sense when you're running the single wing. And that's why J.D., as tailback, threw most of the passes.

We lost that game, 35-13. Dudek made one extra point and missed the other. Roosevelt bottled up our running game, which was really all we had. Our defense, which was pretty good, was just no match for their speed and for the varied stuff their offense threw at us. They were a lot more agile, mobile, and hostile than we were. It was an away game for us and on the bus ride back to school nobody said anything. What was there to say? We knew the coaches would work us hard the next week, and we weren't afraid of that because we wanted very badly to win and were willing to do whatever it took to make that happen. We had three games left—Parsons, Norfolk, and then the big one, the Bell Island game, the BI-G game. A 4-1 record was definitely not bad, and we could still pull off a good season, so we had to put Roosevelt behind us and concentrate on the games we had left.

13

I WAS GETTING MORE AND MORE SKEPTICAL of the dogma and doctrine we heard every week at St. Peter's. The old man would go off on it sometimes. Reinhardt's sermons always started with "Grace be unto you, and peace from God our Father and our Lord and Savior, Jesus Christ." And then, after twenty minutes or so of the usual, he'd wrap it up with: "May the peace that passeth all understanding keep your hearts and minds in Christ Jesus. Amen." I remember one Sunday we got home from church and changed our clothes and sat down to lunch and the old man said, "Reinhardt is always talking about this peace that passeth all understanding. He's right, it does pass all understanding. Do you understand where this peace is in the world? Did we have a peaceful time fighting the goddamn krauts and japs? It was so peaceful in Korea, wasn't it? Now it looks like we're having some of that peace that passeth all understanding in Vietnam. If that's peace, I sure as hell don't understand it. It really passes my understanding. Seriously, I'm getting sick of hearing about it. It sounds like a complete crock of shit to me."

Mom didn't want to hear this. "What's wrong with you, Bill? That kind of talk is sinful and shameful. Coming from a Christian who should know better and certainly shouldn't be talking that way in front of your kids. You should listen to pastor's sermons and take to heart what he says. He's our shepherd and we should hear him and follow him."

"Oh, he's a shepherd, is he?" said Dad. "Yeah, I guess that's right. You didn't see him joining the army and fighting in Europe, did you? I sure as hell never saw him over there. Ha. No, he was out in the peaceful field tending his flock. He was probably even…" I thought I knew where he was going with that. Mom probably didn't. Luckily, he didn't continue. But he did go on to say that he was sick of hearing Reinhardt's sermons and his talk about God's peace. If war and killing millions of Jews was God's idea of peace, then it must be a pretty sick God running the show.

I thought Mom was going to pass out listening to this. The old man had never really cut loose like that before. Well, I take that back, he did go off on the confirmation class thing. Anyway, I had heard him make comments that showed he had doubts about many things. I agreed with what he was saying. A lot about the whole Christian religion didn't make sense to me, and the more I thought about it, the more it all seemed like a silly fairy tale that only little kids or total idiots could believe. And yet you had highly educated people who somehow put reason and logic aside and embraced these beliefs and made them a central part of their lives. Somehow they could have faith, even if it defied logic and reason. At least that's the way it seemed to me.

I think what grated on the old man and made the religion thing even more annoying to him was the fact that he was not a native Wittenberger. His family had moved to Ganaway from Pennsylvania when he was in elementary school. His father had come to work in one of the steel mills and they lived in a neighborhood near the factories. I never knew my grandmother on my father's side. She died from a heart condition when Dad was in grammar school. We saw my grandfather Simpson occasionally, but it was the Lindke family, my mother's family, that was always getting together for holidays, and picnics in the summer, and the annual one-week vacation to Canada to fish, play euchre, and drink beer. My mom and dad met in high school. When they graduated, they both had jobs; he worked in the mill where his father worked, and she was a secretary in a printing plant.

When they got engaged it was apparently a minor scandal because Bill was not a Wittenberger. In fact, not a Lutheran. He didn't see why this should be such a big deal, but he had a lot to learn. I guess he was a Presbyterian, or maybe nothing, but not being a Lutheran was a problem. Before Mom's family would approve of the marriage, Dad had to take religious instructions and officially become a practicing Lutheran. He did that, but I always sensed that he never got over being forced to adopt this religion in order to marry his true love. And I'm not sure if he resented just the family, Grandpa Lindke, the patriarch, in particular, or if he also held a nagging grudge against Mom, for not having the guts to tell the family to go to hell and then just marry the guy she supposedly was in love with. They got married in 1938 and my sister was born in 1940. He was drafted after the deferment for men with children was eliminated in 1943. He would never talk much about his service in the war, like a lot of guys who fought and came back, but Mom often made comments to the effect that he was very different when he got home. He got a job at Rollins Boat Co. I guess he started going to Volcker's back then, but as time went on his visits started to be more frequent. By the time I'm talking about here, it was getting to be more of a problem.

Volcker's, like all the gin mills that stayed in business, had a crew of regular customers. They didn't all come every day, but a lot of them certainly were there two or three times a week. It had a typical setup, with a long bar facing a main room with some tables, a kitchen toward the back, and an apartment upstairs where the proprietors lived. Volcker's didn't have a pool table like some of the places did. It was more of a euchre place, and some guys would play poker sometimes. Dad liked to play euchre. That was one thing he liked about Mom's family—whenever they got together you could be sure that it wouldn't be too long until the foursomes teamed up and you'd have a game or two going on. So we just assumed that he'd be playing euchre down at Volcker's.

One night it was getting late and he wasn't home yet. Mom didn't want to call down there, so she asked me to go see if everything was all right. I couldn't think of what might not be all right but I headed down there like she asked me to do, not sure exactly what I was going to say when I got there. When I went in the front door the place was a blue haze as usual, with practically every person in there smoking. I looked around and there were three or four groups of guys playing cards. I saw Dad at a table back in the corner and at first nobody paid any attention to me, but then Elmer Schmidt, who was playing euchre at a table near the bar saw me and waved. He looked over at Dad's table and said, "Hey, Bill, your boy's here."

Dad looked up and saw me and said, "Chris! What are you doing here?"

I told him that Mom had asked me to come down because she was getting worried that he wasn't home yet and it was later than usual. He acted kind of annoyed and said he was fine and I should tell Mom not to be silly and worry about him, like what did she think could happen at Volcker's? He said to tell her that he'd be home pretty soon. I said OK and turned around and headed for the door and a few guys looked at me, but nobody said anything and I left and started walking home. I did notice that he had been playing poker, not euchre, and that was unusual. I wondered if that was the reason that he was staying later than normal. Maybe he was behind and was trying to win back some money. I never thought of him as a gambler. In fact, I don't think I ever heard him even talk about poker, wasn't sure if he actually knew how to play, although when I thought about it I realized that anybody who's been in the army probably knows how to play poker. I knew he played the numbers, but everybody did that, and it wasn't any high stakes thing. You could just bet pocket change and that's what most people did. Somehow the runners made money off it and just about any bar you'd go into would have somebody coming around every day taking bets.

It turned out that this night of staying late at Volcker's set off quite a crisis in my parents' relationship. When I got home, Mom of course wanted to know what was going on at Volcker's. I told her what Dad had told me to say, but she wanted more details. Who was he with? Was he drinking liquor? Was he at the bar? Was he playing cards? I was in a tough spot. I didn't want to lie to Mom, but I didn't want to rat on Dad. I tried to be as vague as I could and walk some kind of line. When Dad got home, Mom laid into him about how much time he'd been spending there. And how much money. She was literally having trouble paying all the bills. He was definitely spending more money down there. What was he doing? How much was he drinking? Was he gambling? Oooh, this last question hit a nerve.

He cut loose with a tirade that I knew he was going to regret, but I guess he'd had just enough to drink that his usual control just snapped and he couldn't hold in his anger, or resentment, or whatever it was. He said that he'd gone off to fight the damn krauts, the same damn krauts that Mom's family was descended from, and when he got home it was as if everybody was sick of the war and just wanted to get back to normal. Just forget about it. Well, he could assure you, it wasn't that easy to forget about it if you'd been there and if you'd seen what those bastards were like and what they'd done. And that's why he was so sick and tired of listening to that asshole Reinhardt every Sunday spewing his bullshit about the peace that passes all understanding. And yeah, maybe he needed Volcker's to take his mind off of all that shit, so Mom should just get off his back and leave him alone. She had her card club, and her Altar Guild, and her Sunday School, and could do anything she wanted to do, while he had to go bust his ass every day building boats that only rich bastards could afford, and earning enough money to have a nice house, and a nice car, and go on vacation and…on and on he went. He was yelling so loud that my brother and sister, who'd been in bed, came downstairs to see what was going on. Mom was speechless. She just stood there staring at him, then she turned around and went upstairs. Nobody knew what to say. It was pretty awkward, to say the least. Dad went out in the backyard to have a cigarette, and we went to bed. We didn't know what else to do.

The atmosphere around the house was strained for quite a while after that night. Maybe there was conversation between Mom and Dad, but if so, we didn't hear it. My sister was busy with her job, my brother was in grammar school uptown, and I was into the second half of the season with the team, and things had taken a turn for the worse. We spent as little time as possible with "the family," and were happy to be absorbed in our own individual worlds. So it came as somewhat of a shock when one day, just a couple of weeks after the late-night-at-Volcker's incident, Mom announced that she would be going to work for Ernest Stenzel, owner of Stenzel Insurance Agency, as the office secretary. The Stenzel Agency was affiliated with Lutheran Mutual Insurance Co., and, obviously, catered to Lutherans. Not only Lutherans, of course. They would sell insurance to anybody. But probably most of the people in Wittenberg had their homeowner's, and auto, and life insurance policies with the Stenzel agency, and that would have been a big piece of their business. After his tirade about working his ass off every day, the old man apparently didn't feel like he could object to this move by Mom. And anyway, she was a prime example of a stubborn kraut, and once she had made up her mind to do this, nothing her husband could say would make her change her mind.

Even though Ernest Stenzel lived in Wittenberg, the Stenzel agency was located uptown. There were quite a few Lutheran churches in the Twin Cities so the customer pool was pretty good. When I told the guys about my mother getting a job, Scourge said that Mr. Stenzel was a member of the Commercial Club and that he had a very nice Rollins boat that he docked at the marina. I thought, Oh boy, the old man's gonna love the idea of building boats for the likes of Mom's new employer. A fringe benefit of Mom's new job, in my opinion, was that she needed a car to get to and from work. Dad was really pissed about this, but there wasn't anything he could do about it, so he helped her pick out a decent used Chevy. So now we had three cars, which was quite unusual to see in Wittenberg.

One positive thing about church was the minister's daughter. Karen Reinhardt had gone to St. Peter's through eighth grade, naturally, so I'd had little contact with her except in Sunday school and confirmation class, when we would have been thirteen or fourteen. That's when I started to take notice of her. She looked like she could be a cheerleader but she wasn't one, and I don't know if she wasn't interested, or went out for the team and didn't make it, or if her old man didn't approve of such things. But she did belong to the pep club and was pretty sociable, and she was in a couple of my classes, so I saw her on a regular basis. By the time we were juniors she had developed into a pretty hot chick, as we would have said back then.

14

J.D. WAS ALWAYS TALKING ABOUT THE GREAT FOOD his family had, and the big Sunday dinners when Mama Palmisano pulled out all the stops and everybody sat down at the table together. So we were always giving J.D. shit about his big Eye-talian family and if the food was so great, how about inviting your friends over to try it? So finally we got an invitation for a Sunday dinner. J.D. said they always had the big dinner at two o'clock, "after Mass," although it seemed to me that two o'clock would be quite a bit after Mass. I had never been inside a Catholic church and I was kind of curious about what went on there. Once one of my older cousins took his girlfriend, a Catholic, to church at St. Peter's, and she told him that the Lutheran order of service was very recognizable to her because it had many features like the Mass. When my cousin told his mom—my aunt—what his girlfriend had said, she almost lost it. The Wittenberg Lutherans, at least our family's version, were highly suspicious of Catholics. Martin Luther broke away from them because they had lost the true faith and were corrupt, selling indulgences and making up all kinds of elaborate rituals. The Lutherans believed you were saved by grace alone, none of this doing good works and penance and saying Hail Marys and all that other mumbo jumbo. "For by grace are ye saved through faith; and that not of yourselves: it is the gift of God: Not of works, lest any man should boast." How many times had we heard that, in Sunday School, in confirmation class, in church? Any suggestion that their Lutheran church service resembled, in any way, the Catholic nonsense, was repugnant to the Wittenbergers.

We all arrived promptly at two o'clock. The house next door to the market was very large. At one point Grandma and Grandpa Palmisano had lived in the apartment above the store and J.D. lived with his parents and all his brothers and sisters in the big house. That would have been Mr. and Mrs. Palmisano; Rocco, the oldest; Marie, the next oldest; Tony next; J.D. next; then Rose and Jenny. Eight people. Now Grandpa was dead and Marie was married and lived above the store with Danny Rizzo. Grandma had moved over to the big house with the family. Rocco was not happy to be the oldest and still living at home, the reluctant heir apparent to the Palmisano market empire, stuck running the store with his father.

The house almost seemed like it could have been a rooming house at some point, although I don't think it actually was. We all came in at the front door, and J.D. greeted us and showed us through the house. There was an entry vestibule, I guess you'd call it, a comfortable-looking living room or sitting room or parlor, a big dining room, and the heart of the house, a very large kitchen with lots and lots of white cupboards and a linoleum floor. Off the kitchen was a pantry and a room that looked like a sewing room with fabric and clothes on hangers and a sewing machine against one wall. The whole house had a warm and welcoming feel, with wide woodwork and hardwood floors, the kind with narrow boards like you find in houses of that age. Some of the family were already sitting at the dining room table. J.D. took us into the kitchen and introduced us to his mother, Carmella, and grandmother, known as Mama. The food smelled wonderful and my stomach was growling. There was the traditional spaghetti sauce simmering in a big pot, and the aroma of garlic, onions, and who knows what all. The Germans in Wittenberg did have some old family recipes that were brought out sometimes, but basically they'd had enough time to get pretty Americanized, so I was used to getting a lot of tuna noodle casserole, and scalloped potatoes and ham, and meatloaf and mashed potatoes, and broiled hamburgers, or hamburgs, as we called them.

Mama could speak enough English to get by and J.D.'s mother and father would talk to her in both English and Italian, depending on the situation, I guess. Rocco knew some Italian but didn't like to use it. J.D. was young enough that he really couldn't converse much in Italian, but he liked to try to impress us with some Italian words and expressions whenever he could. The whole family was there, so there was a huge group to feed. J.D.'s mom, two younger sisters, and Mama ate in the kitchen. But actually I don't think Mama and Carmella had time to eat anything because they were constantly running back and forth from the kitchen to the dining room, bringing more food to the table. I have to say that J.D. had not been exaggerating about the food that his mom and Mama cooked. But before we even sat down,

J.D. had us all come into the kitchen and tear off a piece of crusty bread and dip it in the big pot of sauce. His mom wasn't too thrilled with this, but Mama seemed to approve. It was a tradition, and J.D. was really proud of it and just wanted to show off and give us an insider experience of Mama's kitchen—what it's like when everything smells so good and you're hungry and it's not quite time to sit down for dinner, and Mama lets you take the edge off by dipping a chunk of bread into the simmering sauce. It was great.

After the "appetizer course" we all sat down and Mama and J.D.'s mom started bringing stuff in. I can't remember every detail but of course there was pasta, spaghetti that day, tossed in sauce in a huge serving bowl with meatballs and sausage and peppers piled on top and more sauce in a separate bowl. There was a plate of J.D.s favorite, meat rolled up with something in the middle, then browned and simmered in sauce. This was the famous "brazhole" or "brazhool" that J.D. was always raving about. Much later I found out it was actually spelled "braciola." And sure enough, Mama looked at us and put out her hands, and smiled, and said, "Mangia! Mangia!" We all looked at each other and smiled. She was so happy to see us enjoying her food. A big basket piled high with crusty bread was passed around the table. It was from Amato's, which anybody from our area would recognize immediately. Everybody's place setting had a small water glass. Mr. Palmisano filled his glass with red wine from a big bottle that had no label on it and passed it along to Rocco, who poured himself a glass too, then passed it on to J.D.'s mom, and then to Mama. When it got to J.D., he started to pour himself some. His mom looked at him and made some kind of face and gesture that seemed to say,

"Hey, what are you doing?" J.D. hesitated and stopped pouring when the small glass was about half full. Mr. Palmisano, said, "Carmella, what? Whatsa matta?"

She said, "These boys aren't eighteen. What if their parents find out they had wine at our house?"

"It's a couple ounces of dago red, for God's sake," said Mr. Palmisano. "They're not babies anymore. A little wine, which, by the way, boys, I made myself, is not gonna hurt anybody. This whole thing about eighteen years old is crazy. You let kids have a little wine and they develop good habits. You make it a big crime, and they're just gonna sneak around and they don't have any good examples and they don't know how to handle it and they go out and get drunk and get into trouble. Go ahead, boys, just a little sample taste."

Mrs. Palmisano glared at him but didn't say anything more. We all took a little dago red, which I remember thinking was a pretty disrespectful name because we knew it was rude and frowned upon to call people dagos and polacks and things like that. But then I realized that sometimes people in Wittenberg would refer to their neighbors as stubborn krauts. So I thought, Well, I guess if you're an insider, it's all right. All the food got passed around and we ate until we were totally stuffed. We all thanked Mama and Mrs. Palmisano and said how delicious everything was and how we couldn't eat another bite, and they seemed really pleased that we enjoyed the meal so much. But it wasn't over yet. Mama went into the kitchen and came out with a huge tray of cannoli, and even though our stomachs truly were bulging, we had to try at least one cannoli. But there were several kinds, with different fillings, and most of us had more than one.

Mr. Palmisano said, "How d'ya like those cannoli, boys? Those are from Amato's bakery, just like the bread. And Palmisano's Market is the only place you can get Amato's products other than the bakery itself. You get it at Palmisano's or you have to go all the way to Ironton to the bakery."

"Yeah, for now, anyway," said Danny. "You know The Union is trying to work a deal with them to sell their stuff. That would be the last straw, if you ask me. They're already trying to run us and the other smaller groceries out of business. They have a shitload of money for ads and they undercut our prices on everything. Our business is down, right, Rocco?"

"What do you mean 'our' business is down?" asked Rocco. "You never worked in the store a day in your life. And anyway, how do you know The Union is trying to work a deal with Amato's?"

"Well, I'm married to your sister, for chrissake. Doesn't that make me a member of the family?"

"Watch your language, Danny," said Mrs. P. Also, Marie gave him a look.

"Well, excuse me," said Danny. "I'm trying to be concerned about the family business and if you can't see what's going on, then the hell with it. Go ahead and sit back and let The Union run you out of business."

"So, what do you propose to do?" said Rocco. "They're a huge company. We can't compete with them on prices. We have to rely on our loyal customers, and our personal service, and the things you can only get at Palmisano's, like Amato's bread."

"Well, I've got news for you," said Danny. "We don't have many things you can't get at The Union. And if by personal service you mean delivering groceries for free to little old ladies in the neighborhood who can't get out of the house, well that's great, but it's a money loser, not a money maker."

"Ah, bafongool," said Rocco. "So, you tell me what we're supposed to do. Yeah, you come up with a plan to solve our problems."

"Oh, yeah, you wouldn't listen to any of my ideas any-way. You got your head so far up your ass."

"OK, that's enough," said Mr. P. "We got guests here, and besides, we don't need no fights within the family. And yeah, Danny, you are part of the family. And don't forget that I own the store so if you tell Rocco he's got his head up his ass, what does that say about me? Don't answer that. So let's all enjoy our dinner and talk about something else."

Danny's family owned a construction company and he worked for them doing something, but we never knew exactly what. He was also related somehow to the Angelo Rizzo family that ran Angelo's bar. It was impossible to keep straight who was related to who. J.D. would always be talking about this cousin or that cousin, and they may have been first, second, or third cousins, or maybe not really cousins at all. There was a lot of intermarriage among the German families in Wittenberg too, but it just seemed like the Italians were more into the cousin thing.

We hung around talking about sports, mostly, until probably four o'clock, then somebody made a move to

get up and get going, and we thanked Mr. and Mrs. P. and
Mama for a great time and a great dinner, and they said we
would have to come back sometime, and we said that would
be great.

15

THE WEEK AFTER THE LOSS TO ROOSEVELT, practice was intense
heading into the Parsons game. We had to be tough. Take it
to 'em. A-gile! MO-bile! HOS-tile! Blocking, hitting, hus-
tling, tackling. We couldn't let Parsons hand us another loss.
That would be really bad. Win our next three games and
we'd have a 7-1 season and that was very respectable and
would put us back on top of the conference. Back where
Ganaway belonged. Make the critics shut up. Parsons was
a home game and as usual, the stadium was packed. Fumb
started at center. He had really stepped up after Nelson got
hurt and even though Nelson had pretty much recovered
from his injury, it looked like Fumb now had the job. That
happened sometimes. A guy got hurt, missed a few games,
and the guy who replaced him turned out to be pretty damn
good, maybe better than the original starter. Those were the
breaks. Life is unfair.

Parsons should have been an easy win. The school was
in a well-to-do suburb farther out from the City than we
were. They were more into tennis and marching band. They

were the Parsons Pirates but we called them the Parsons Pussies, or in mixed company, the Parsons Pansies. They had a lacrosse team, and lacrosse is a pretty tough sport, but not many schools even had lacrosse, and if they did it was a club sport, not a varsity sport. The Parsons band was pretty damn amazing. The Ganaway band had uniforms that looked like Humphrey Bogart would have worn them, and they had to march in ten-yard increments, stopping at the white yard lines so they wouldn't get all mixed up and out of line. The Parsons band, on the other hand, would execute complicated moves and cuts and patterns, with lines splitting off here, and marching over there, and coming back together again here, all the while playing music that was definitely not John Phillip Sousa stuff. You get the picture.

We should have beaten Parsons; we almost always did. But not this year. We ran the Helwig offense, but we weren't running over them. Somehow the Pussies managed to shut us down. They were smart, and they knew exactly what we were going to do on just about every play. According to Helwig, that shouldn't have mattered. But in this game it did. You could see the frustration on the sideline, as Coach Carpenter kept going up to Helwig and talking to him. I'm sure he was trying to convince him to mix it up, throw some passes, do something unexpected, surprise them somehow. Carpenter, an assistant coach, was getting more and more frustrated with Helwig's inability—or refusal—to modernize our game. This was looking way too familiar. We lost to Parsons 21-19. Humiliating.

So now we were 4-2 going into the Norfolk game. Norfolk Academy was definitely the most high-class, exclusive school in the whole area. They had a lacrosse team too, and they played lacrosse against Parsons and St. Iggie and a couple of other schools. Same with hockey. Norfolk was all boys, like St. Iggie, but this was a boarding school with a good reputation, and had students from a fairly wide geographic area, some from out of state. It certainly wasn't in the same class as places like Andover and Exeter and Choate, but back then we didn't know anything about Andover and Exeter and Choate, so we thought Norfolk was pretty damn hoity toity. They had a cheer like St. Iggie, not as crude and blatantly obscene, but still a bit off-color and actually quite clever. It went like this: "We don't smoke, we don't drink, Norfolk! Norfolk! Norfolk!" Get it? I guess you had to be pretty secure in your masculinity to get behind a cheer like that. We had a cheer too. It went: "Go Ganaway go! Go Ganaway go! Hit 'em high, hit 'em low! Go Ganaway go!" Very original. Very imaginative. We also had a song, which we would sing to the tune of "Notre Dame Victory March." It went:

> *Beer, beer, for Ganaway High,*
> *You bring the whiskey, I'll bring the rye.*
> *Send those freshmen out for gin,*
> *And don't let a sober sophomore in.*
> *Da da da, we never stagger, we never fall,*
> *We sober up on wood alcohol,*
> *While our loyal sons go marching*
> *On to the next bar room!*

This was a pretty ignorant song. I think a lot of us didn't realize that rye is a type of whiskey. I think that most people knew that wood alcohol was poisonous. I hope so. At least I never heard of anyone who had actually tried to drink wood alcohol, but anything is possible. The song certainly does indicate that drinking was a popular activity among high school kids in our town.

Losing to Norfolk would be bad, because you really didn't want to lose to the spoiled brat rich boys, any more than you wanted to lose to the privileged Pussies or the unholy Saints. It was an away game, played at the very nice Norfolk field. It was always a bit odd playing at Norfolk, because their home crowd was pretty small, owing to the fact that a lot of the parents lived somewhere else, and anyway probably would have been too busy or tied up at the country club to sit through a football game against the commoners of Bell Island, or Ganaway, or God forbid, Ironton or Roosevelt.

If you knew anything about football and were paying attention, the Norfolk game provided some prime examples of how Helwig's thinking was causing problems. The game was close. We weren't moving the ball as easily or consistently as Helwig insisted it should move if we just executed our fundamentals flawlessly and dominated the defense with our strength and power, and all the usual rah rah. We were staying in the game, but we were not "running over them" and we were not "unstoppable." The game was close, and I think we were down by a touchdown in the fourth quarter with a few minutes to play. We were not in a great position, had the ball on maybe our own thirty-five-yard line. Third down, maybe four yards to go for a first down that would keep us in the game, give us a chance to score a winning touchdown. So, what would be a reasonable call to make in that situation? Many teams would try a pass. The defense might be expecting that, given the situation, but a short pass, enough for a first down, would still make sense and have a decent chance of success. Especially in our case, a pass would make sense, because the defense definitely *wouldn't* be expecting it from the three-yards-and-a-cloud-of-dust Ganaway Rivermen. But not only did Helwig rarely call a pass play, he had a rule that you never threw a pass if you were behind your own forty-yard line. Why? Just really, really old school thinking. You might get intercepted and then the opposing team might run it right into the end zone. Or they'd have great field position. I don't know if we were the only team that never threw a pass from inside its own forty-yard line. Probably. But I'm sure it was generally known by all our opponents that we followed this outdated rule.

To no one's surprise, we ran the good old 46 Power. That meant that the 4 Back (the tailback) would get the snap and run through the 6 Hole (off the strong side outside tackle). This was a play we ran over and over and over, a fundamental mainstay of our offense. All of our opponents had seen it many times. And even though we could run it with power, and reliability, and precise execution, we simply could not always dominate the defense with it. And that's what happened against Norfolk. We ran our old standby play, and they stopped us short of a first down. So we had to punt. It was a good punt, and we stopped them from having much of a runback, but they managed to move the ball, and make a couple of first downs, and run out the clock, and win the game. We were crushed, and so pissed. We had really wanted to win that game and be on a positive roll heading into the BI-G game the next week.

When the clock ran out, Helwig just looked down and

kicked the turf and shook his head. I had managed to sidle up next to him and man, he did smell like booze. Carpenter was fuming. I didn't really know what to think or feel right then. Was it Helwig's fault that we lost because he was so stuck in his ways and so conservative? I know that thought crossed my mind. And there was so much talk like that going around town. But we were the players. It was up to us to execute and to take it to 'em. It was up to us to win! We were Ganaway out there on the field, no excuses.

It was another silent bus ride home. After we got showered and dressed, we headed for Gino's, as usual. After a bit of a wait—the place was crowded like most nights after a game—we managed to get a table where we could all sit, and we ordered our pizzas. A lot of the people there had been to the game, and the ones who knew us tried to come up with something to say but what could you really say? "Close game," or "You almost had 'em." And what could you say in return? Our friends and acquaintances were trying to be nice, but it was just awkward. J.D. had carried the ball the most, and had thrown a few passes, not many. ShiThead had done a good job blocking and plowing up the middle to make a few first downs. Fumb's snaps had been good. He'd improved a lot in just a couple of weeks.

We really didn't want to talk about the game, so the conversation moved to talking about girls. J.D. definitely had his eye on Peggy Harrison. ShiThead had been to the movies once or twice with Sally Summers, a sophomore at Bell Island who was the sister of Dale Summers, the Bell Island quarterback. G was seeing Linda Gregg, mostly at work at the Tate. I was fantasizing a bit about Karen Reinhardt, although the thought of having to deal with her father was not a pleasant one, so at that point my amorous exploits were still all in my imagination. If Fumb and Scourge were having wet dreams about some young beauties, we didn't know who they might be.

At that point in our junior year, all the members of the Backfield were sixteen, except Fumb, who was seventeen. So we all had our driver's licenses, but only Fumb could drive at night. Scourge's family had two cars, nice ones. Fumb had his car. G's family had two cars because both of his parents had jobs, although his mom probably could have walked to the Ukrainian Club for her part-time job there. But, no, that would have been rough in the winter, or in the rain, now that I think about it. And now the Simpson family had become a two-car family, thanks to my mom getting the job with the Stenzel Insurance Agency. Plus, we had my sister's car, but that really didn't count because she wasn't inclined to let anybody else use it. With all the people in J.D.'s family, he could usually find a car to use if he needed it.

The beer supply line from Palmisano's Market was flowing smoothly without a hitch. We would chip in cash to J.D., who would look for the right opportunity to ring up the beer and stash it away until time to imbibe. And imbibing was happening both in G's basement and at the boathouse, depending on the situation. G's basement was good for playing pool and listening to records. At the boathouse we were careful not to make a lot of noise, but it was sort of isolated, and we found that if we exercised a reasonable amount of caution, we could hang out there and drink and shoot the shit and nobody seemed to know or care that we were there.

Our pizza came and we dug in like ravenous dogs. Damn, that pizza was good! I know I've said this before. To this day I can't figure out just what was in that crust. I like to cook, and I've made lots of bread and homemade pizza, but I just can't even get very close. I know it had to have something in it like lard or shortening, because it was just so pastry-like. Anyway, as we were sitting there talking and enjoying our pizza, the door opened and we saw G's brother come in. He looked around and we waved to him, and he came over to our table.

"What's up, Tommy?" said G.

"Pete, Dad's been in an accident. A bad one. At work," Tom said.

"An accident?" G sounded very concerned. "What do you mean? What kind of accident?"

"His foot got caught. His foot got crushed. His ankle too. It doesn't sound good."

"Wait, wait," said G. "Slow down. How did this happen? How did you find out about it? Where's Dad now?"

"The foreman at Cooper called. He talked to Mom; she was home; she's not working tonight. He said they took Dad to the hospital. Mom told me to come find you and let you know."

"Shit!" said G. "Did this have anything to do with that kettle thing? Where they cook resin or whatever? J.D.'s brother Tony told us about that. Sounded dangerous. Damn! Well, where's Mom?"

"I took her to the hospital. They've got Dad in the emergency room or surgery or something. I thought you'd want to go over there."

"Of course I want to go over there," said G. "What do I owe for the pizza?"

"Forget it!" Fumb said. "Go see what's up with your dad. And let us know when you know something."

Tom and G left and the rest of us sat around for a while longer. If G's dad was going to be out of work that would be really tough. We didn't know much about workmen's comp or disability insurance or anything like that. Maybe we assumed the union would somehow step in and provide support for the family. I said something about Tom being drafted and when would he have to go to basic? That would make things even worse for G and his mom. Nobody knew anything about when Tom would have to go into the army. We stayed for an hour or so but it was a pretty down atmosphere, what with the loss to Norfolk and the news about G's dad. We were all tired anyway, so we split up and headed home.

16

I CALLED G THE NEXT DAY, SATURDAY, TO ASK ABOUT HIS DAD. It was really bad. He had, in fact, been working in the resin room. He was down inside the kettle scraping the dried resin off the sides of the kettle, when the agitator, or stirring blade, started moving and shoving G's dad around the kettle. He yelled as loud as he could to try to get somebody's attention and get the blade to stop turning. But by the time somebody heard him yelling and climbed up on the kettle and looked through the hatch, it was too late. G's dad's foot slipped through the hatch in the bottom of the kettle, and the blade kept turning and just crushed his foot and ankle. Somebody quickly managed to get the blade stopped, but the damage was done. G sounded pretty upset as he was telling me about all this, and I asked him if there was anything I could do. He said he was going to visit his dad in the hospital, and he'd call me later, maybe we could get together or something.

Caldwell Memorial Hospital was in Bell Island, just over the bridge. I don't know how good it was, but local people seemed to think it was good enough for having babies, or having your tonsils out, or if you came down with pneumonia. They had an emergency room that handled the usual stuff, and that's where they had taken G's dad. When G called me back a couple hours after we talked, he said his dad had been transferred to St. Elizabeth's, which was a much larger hospital in the City, about forty-five minutes away. G and his mom and brother were heading up there. I asked him if I could do anything, or if I should come to the hospital. He said no, not right then, but he'd keep me posted. I told him I'd stay near the phone in case he needed to get in touch with me. I decided I should call the other guys and let them know what was going on. I reached a couple of them and asked if they would try to get in touch with the guys I hadn't been able to contact. Over the course of a few hours, we managed to get word out to everybody and we were all really concerned about G and his dad. We didn't know Mr. Gorlukovich very well because he was usually not around when we were at G's house. But from the few times we'd talked to him, he seemed like a really nice guy. We agreed to meet at Gino's so we could talk to G and give him support. Not sure what that would mean, but just be there for him.

The group all got to Gino's before G, who came in about ten minutes later with his brother Tom, who sat down and ordered a takeout pizza and said he needed to take it to their mom. G said maybe he should be with his mom too, but Tom said no, G should hang out with his friends for now and their mom just needed to rest. When Tom left with the pizza, we started asking G questions about the accident and how his dad was doing.

J.D. said, "Hey, G, I told my brother Tony about what happened to your dad and that we were going to get together tonight. He asked if I thought it would be OK if he joined us so he could hear about it too. I didn't think you'd mind so I told him to come. Hope that's OK."

"Yeah, of course, that's fine," said G. "That's him coming in right now, isn't it?"

Tony Palmisano came in and spotted us immediately and came over to where we were sitting. "Hi, Peter," he said, "I'm really sorry about your dad. As you know, I'm very familiar with where he was working. So what the hell happened?"

I think we had only met Tony in person on two occasions; first when we went to the market that one day, and he was telling all about the resin room at Cooper and the kettle and the crazy shit you had to do when you worked there. The other time was when we had Sunday dinner at J.D.'s.

"Thanks for asking, Tony," said G. "All I know is what my dad told us, and he said it happened so fast he's not sure he even remembers everything."

"Yeah, yeah," said Tony, "I can just imagine. But hey, why don't we go over to Angelo's? There's more room over there where we can have a little privacy. What do you think?"

Angelo's! Hell, yeah, we'd go to Angelo's! I know that's what we all were thinking because we'd heard other guys talk about it. And we kept saying we were going to go over there but we had never done it. It was only a few blocks away on the other side of the street. From the outside it looked like all the other bars around town. Fake brick asbestos shingles, front entrance, a side entrance near the rear. Apartment upstairs. Alley in the back. Inside it looked a little classier than the average gin mill. There was nice woodwork, wood floors, front room with a pool table and quite a few tables opposite the bar, which ran parallel to the long side of the room and then took a right angle toward the wall, so you had a long line of barstools and then a few more forming a little *L* shape up near the front of the room. Facing the bar you looked into a big mirror, which was above the shelves holding the liquor bottles. The beer taps were installed in the bar, so the bartender would be facing you as he drew your beer. If you looked to the left, way down the bar, there was a short partition sticking out from the long wall. There was a space between the end of the bar and the partition, and there was a hinged shelf that the bartender would lift up to get behind the bar, and then lower it behind him. On the partition was a wall phone, which we soon noticed was ringing a lot.

There was also a back room that you could see from out front that had more tables and had a door into the kitchen. We sat down at a table in the back room and ordered pizzas. The kitchen was the domain of Mama, or Nonna, Rizzo, who took our order and waddled back into the kitchen. While we waited for the pizza, we just made small talk and told Tony something about ourselves, and asked some questions about what he was studying in college, just the usual chitchat.

Mama brought the pizzas out, one in each hand, set them down on the table, and went back in the kitchen and came out with two more. Those damn pans were *hot!* After that we always said that Mama had asbestos hands, so maybe she was moonlighting at Cooper. We soon discovered that Mama made a pizza that was every bit as amazing as Gino's. It had some of the same pastry-like qualities, but

the crust was thicker, chewier, in a way even more myste-
rious than Gino's. It was crisp on the outside, and sort of
thick around the edge, where Gino's was flaky and thin and
puffy and very light. The crust on Angelo's pizza looked
like it kind of climbed up the side of the pan it was baked in.
Gino's was probably baked directly on the floor of the oven.

After she delivered the pies, Mama said, "Now whadda
you boys wanna to drink?"

There was a short hesitation and then Tony said, "We'll
have some beers."

Mama looked us over and said, "You boys eighteen?"

Tony was probably twenty, but the rest of us were sixteen and Fumb was seventeen. Now what to do? Lie to
Mama's face? Tony looked over at Sal Rizzo, who was
behind the bar, and made a little questioning look, raising
his eyebrows, as if to say, "What do you think?"

Sal looked over at Mama and waved his hand in kind
of a dismissive gesture and said, "It's OK, Mama. I got it."
And he proceeded to bring bottles of Genesee for everyone.
Wow, that was easy.

Tony knew Sal because Marie, his older sister, was married to Danny Rizzo, and Danny was Sal Rizzo's cousin or
something. I know I've mentioned that before but it can be
hard to keep all the connections straight. Sal seemed quite a
bit older than Danny, but again, when you had large families
with siblings born maybe ten or fifteen or more years apart,
it was tough to keep everybody straight. And sometimes
you'd have a situation where a person had an aunt or uncle
who was younger than they were. Sal had a kind of world-
weary, careworn look on his face, like his life was slipping
by and he was stuck behind the bar at Angelo's.

"So Peter," said Tony, "what the hell happened?"

"We call him G," said J.D., "but sorry, I didn't mean to interrupt. Go ahead."

G described what had happened at Cooper just like he had told me on the phone. "And that's about all I can tell you," he said.

"Shit," said Tony, "this really pisses me off. I knew something was going to happen in one of those fucking kettles one of these days. They don't give a shit what happens to the workers at that place. Or any of these goddamn factories around here. You should hear some of the stories guys tell."

"Like what?" said Scourge.

"Well, for instance, the dust that blows around that whole place constantly. You guys saw me that day at the market when I got off work and you were eating your subs. You saw that dust just coming off my clothes in a cloud. Who knows what kind of nasty shit is blowing around in that dust? And I know a guy who works at Empire Paper. When the ten-foot-wide sheets of paper are going through the drying rollers, up and down and threading back and forth between six or seven rollers stacked one above the other, sometimes the wet paper breaks and starts piling up in the pit underneath the rollers. Those rollers are blazing hot. This guy I'm talking about works as a fifth hand. A fifth hand's job is to get down in the pit and roll up the damp paper, which is hot from the rollers, into huge wads and shove it up out of the pit, where another guy throws it into a cart and takes it back to the beater room. Meanwhile, another guy is working to get the sheet of paper, which is still piling up in the pit, back onto the rollers. Anyway, this guy I know showed me this nasty six-inch burn on his back where he bumped up against one of the rollers. He said he could hear his skin sizzle. He'll have one hell of a scar from that. And listen to this. A few years ago, there was a guy who came to work drunk, and he worked in the beater room, and he fell into the fucking beater pool and got sucked in and ground up. Seriously, that's a true story. Really happened. Sorry, I'm getting off the subject."

"Do you know if anybody else has had an accident like G's dad?" said Scourge.

"Not personally," said Tony, "but I'm not surprised something like this happened. Like I said, they just don't give a shit about anybody."

"Why don't you ask around and see what you can find out," said Scourge. "See if this kettle agitator has ever started moving with someone in the kettle."

"Yeah, good idea," said Tony, "I will."

"So G, what's the situation with your dad?" said ShiThead. "How's he doing?"

"I guess it doesn't look very good," said G. "They transferred him to St. Elizabeth's where they have specialists, because Caldwell didn't think they could handle it. They've got his foot and ankle all wrapped up and they're giving him some strong painkillers. I think we should know more tomorrow."

Tony got us another round of beers and we sat around talking about football, and girls, and how we didn't want to get stuck working at Cooper, or Empire, or International Bolt, or Rollins Boat Co. for the rest of our lives. I was hoping that Sal at the end of the bar couldn't hear us, because that topic would have hit home with him and hurt.

17

I TALKED TO G ON SUNDAY, AND HE SAID they were going to do surgery on his dad's foot and ankle, but they weren't making any promises. Apparently, the damage was really severe, some of the worst the surgeons had ever seen. And it wasn't just the smashed bones and tendons, but they were also worried about blood circulation and whether they could make the repairs needed to save the foot. He said his mom was a wreck and that Tom would be going to basic training at Fort Polk in about a month. I told him I would pass this information along to the other guys.

Practice on Monday was intense, as we expected it would be. A lot was riding on the Bell Island game. Of course, that was always the case, but it would be really bad to lose to them three years in a row, really humiliating. Plus, we were going in with a 4-3 record, so we needed a win to give us a winning season. And to add even more pressure, some guy had written a letter to the editor of the *Courier-Tribune*, with a title something like "Has Ganaway Lost Its Swagger?" Just what we needed.

At lunch one day that week, J.D. told us that Tony had been asking around, as he said he would, about whether there had been other accidents in the kettles at Cooper like the one that had crushed G's dad's ankle and foot. There were accidents, he found out, but nothing major—maybe a cut or poke from a chisel, or a knock on the head from a slip down the side of the kettle, or a twisted ankle or sprained wrist. But there had been some reports of the agitator blade starting to move when it wasn't supposed to. It had never happened when someone was down in the kettle, until G's dad. At least nobody that Tony talked to could remember that happening before.

"That's really interesting," said Scourge. "Tell him to find out as much as he can about that, OK? About the agitator moving when it wasn't supposed to."

"OK, I will," said J.D. "So are you thinking lawsuit?"

"Well," said Scourge, "that's a little bit premature. But yeah, in a situation like this you shouldn't rule anything out. If you can show a pattern of negligence, of ignoring warnings, that leads to some bad thing happening, you've got to take a look at that."

"Spoken like a true ambulance chaser," said ShiThead.

Scourge flipped him the bird. "Up yours, asshole."

"Well said, counselor," said Fumb. "Seriously, I think we should sue the shit out of them. What do you think, J.D.? Should we sue your girlfriend's old man for all he's worth?"

"Why would you sue Peggy's father?" said J.D. "What does he have to do with it?"

"He's the general manager, for chrissake," said Fumb. "Scourge, couldn't you sue his ass?"

"OK, slow down, guys," said Scourge. "All I'm saying

is that G should get as much information as he can about the situation surrounding his dad's injury, that's all. It's just smart to do that. And since we've got someone close to the situation, with access to information—that would be Tony—it makes sense to use that inside connection."

"So G, what happens if your dad can't work?" said Fumb. "I mean, eventually he'll go back to work, but what happens while he's laid up?"

"I'm not exactly sure," said G. "I guess he'll get unemployment, or workmen's comp, or something. I really don't know how that works. My mom is really worried, I can tell that. And now Tom is heading for Fort Polk in about a month. That's going to be weird: Tom gone, Dad laid up at home. I don't think Mom will be able to get any more hours at the club. So I don't know, we'll just have to see, I guess."

"Well, that's bullshit too, with Tom getting drafted," said Fumb. "Why are we sending guys to Vietnam, for chrissakes? That's such bullshit. Why do we give a shit about Vietnam?"

"It's the commies," said G. "If we don't stop them in Vietnam, then they'll keep advancing and take over other countries."

"What other countries?" said Fumb.

"Well, I don't know. Whatever countries are over there. At least that's what I've heard."

"Yeah, well I don't buy that bullshit," said Fumb.

"OK, OK," said Scourge, "this isn't the time to be talking politics and military strategy. G, is there anything we can do to help you out in any way? Let us know."

"Yeah, that's right, absolutely," said ShiThead.

"OK, thanks guys," said G. "I can't think of anything right now, but if I do I'll let you know."

———

GOING INTO THE BI-G GAME, Bell Island had a better record than we did. Their young coach was getting a lot of attention in the region for how he'd moved the team from a middle of the road, respectable, competitive team, to a team to be reckoned with. Ganaway had always been the team to be reckoned with, and now it seemed like we were slipping back, almost trading positions with Bell Island. It was up to us to put a stop to that shift, and we were pumped up for it. On the practice field there was a lot of energy, a lot of spirit, and a lot of noise—grunts, claps, shouts, helmet bumps—everybody really getting into it and getting psyched up.

It was a home game, so on Friday when we got to the locker room there were already some people there, milling around and giving us encouragement as we walked down the sidewalk and down the stairs. The cheerleaders were there to greet us, and the pep club members. Peggy Harrison was a cheerleader; Karen Reinhardt was in the pep club and so was Linda Gregg. I'm sure we were feeling like pretty hot stuff. At Ganaway, if you were on the football team you had a certain status and level of recognition and it was easy to start thinking of yourself as pretty special. Of course, my experience when the cheerleaders didn't know my name helped me to avoid getting an outsized ego.

We went into the school and down the stairs to the locker room. We weren't the first players there, but we were on the early side, and we started getting dressed at a leisurely pace. As more players arrived, the noise level rose and the room began to feel charged, alive. Guys were talking and giving each other bumps and punches. It was a very upbeat, high-spirited atmosphere. We finished dressing, and as always, gathered in a large group, all standing, in the large open area near the showers. The coaches came in and stood together in front of us, waiting for Coach Helwig to come in. It wasn't long before he came out of his office and took his place between the coaches and the team, pacing back and forth and looking down at the floor. He stopped abruptly and turned so he was facing us. He looked us over, back and forth, not saying anything for what seemed like a long time. Then he started to talk, quiet at first, then getting louder and more dramatic.

"Boys," he said, "I don't have to tell you what this game means. We've had our rough spots, we've made mistakes, we haven't done all the things we know we need to do to win. But all that's behind us. We don't look back. We will not look back. We look ahead. The only thing we focus on is this game. THIS game. THIS game against Bell Island. Bell Island. The boys from over the bridge would like nothing better than to hand us a loss on our own field, in front of our parents, our friends, our neighbors. All our fans who have always believed in us, always supported us, always cheered us on in every game. Yeah, they'd like that. But they're not going to get what they want. Because we are the Ganaway Rivermen. And in about two minutes we are going to go out there on that field and we are going to send Bell Island back across the bridge knowing what it feels like to get run over by a steamroller. To know what it feels like to take a pounding from Ganaway. We are gonna go out there and take it to

'em! We are gonna give 'em everything we've got, and that
means we are gonna win this game! We are gonna win this
game for us, for this team, for all the Ganaway teams that
have gone before us, for Ganaway High School! Now let's
go out there, and let's win this one for Sarkovits! GO!"

The room erupted in yelling and whistling and hooting,
and soon a chant started, as it always did at this point before
a game: "Go Ganaway! Go Ganaway! Go Ganaway!" And
with that the guys nearest the door started running out of the
locker room and up the metal stairs. Metal cleats on metal
stairs. Crashing, clanging, banging. The noise was deafen-
ing, and it got us fired up beyond what you could believe.
Up the stairs and out the door, we turned to our right and
ran through the open gate in the chain link fence that surrounded the stadium, then through the double line of jumping and waving cheerleaders and across the running track
into the end zone, then to the sideline area on the home side
of the field in front of the large concrete stands that were
flanked on each side by bleachers that stretched down in
both directions to the goal lines. There we gathered again
and waited. Soon the captains of each team were called to
the center of the field for the coin toss. I don't remember
who won the toss or who kicked off. The captains returned
to their teams, and then we gathered around Helwig again
for a final mini-pep talk. The stadium was full and the noise
was so loud that I couldn't really hear what he was saying. After a minute, he leaned over and stuck out his hand,
and the guys closest to him reached in with their hands and
everybody gave one last shout of "Go Ganaway!" and the
kicking team—or maybe it was the receiving team—took
the field as the stands erupted in cheers and the band erupted

in our fight song: "Ganaway High, Ganaway High, run right through that line! Run the ball around Bell Island, touch-down sure this time…" to the tune of "On Wisconsin."

I was standing next to G and was thinking about Helwig's pep talk in the locker room. I said to him, "Hey, who the hell is Sarkovits?"

He said, "I have no fucking idea."

As is turned out, no one else knew who Sarkovits was, either. Probably some player on a team many years ago, was what we concluded. Maybe Helwig had spent a little too much time at Kramer's Tavern before the game. Maybe he'd watched the Rockne movie too many times.

The game was pretty close in the first half, thanks to our defense. Our offense wasn't doing much of anything. In the second half they pulled out some plays that we hadn't seen before, and we weren't prepared to deal with that. We lost the game 21-6. It was bad.

18

THE LUTHERANS WERE FANATICS WHEN IT CAME TO GOING TO CHURCH.
Well, they were fanatics about a lot of things, but going
to church was a real specialty. I suppose some Catholics,
the ones that went to mass every day, had them beat, but
let's just say that among Protestants, the Lutherans had
all other denominations beat hands down when it came
to going to church every time you turned around. Church
on Thanksgiving Day, church on Christmas Eve, church
on Christmas Day, church on New Year's Eve, church on
New Year's Day. Church every Wednesday evening during
Lent, church on Maundy Thursday, church on Good Friday.
Church on Easter Sunday, of course. Seriously, it was
insane. One year when Christmas Day fell on a Saturday,
we did practically nothing but go to church. Friday—
Christmas Eve church. Saturday—Christmas Day church.
Sunday—church, of course. The next Friday—New Year's
Eve church. Saturday—New Year's Day church. Sunday—
church, of course. And at each and every one of these
church services, we would go through the same order of

service and have to listen to another sermon. You can see why the minister really couldn't come up with anything new or interesting to say, so we had to listen to the same stuff we had heard a thousand times before. But I suppose that's pretty much the same with all religions and denominations. Yeah, come to think about it, the Catholics had to sit there and go through the mass over and over and over, and they couldn't even understand what the hell the priest was saying. But like I said, for the sheer number of church services, the Lutherans had it hands down over the Methodists and Presbyterians and whatever.

It seemed like Dad was getting more and more fed up with the whole Lutheran thing and also with the Lindke family fixation. We were always expected to show up at Grandma and Grandpa Lindke's for every holiday. Plus they were always inviting us for picnics in the summer and Sunday dinner in the winter. Grandpa Lindke owned a lumber yard, Lindke Lumber, and was pretty well off. The business had been started by his father. My mom had two older brothers, who both had families and lived near Grandma and Grandpa in a kind of family compound. Both of my uncles worked for the business and would inherit it one day, I assumed, but I was never clear on how my mom fit into this little lumber empire. Would she get a share, or some kind of inheritance from the business when the patriarch eventually went to be with his lord and savior in the big lumber yard in the sky? Or did my uncles already own all or part of the business?

The Christmas after we lost to Bell Island for the third year in a row was not very merry. Dad had been coming home from Volcker's more plastered than usual, and he seemed to be getting more belligerent. Not abusive. He never threatened any of us physically and he never got verbally abusive, but he just seemed less patient, and more annoyed and aggravated about everything. One night the week before Christmas Mom said something like, "Bill, you're getting home later and later every night from Volcker's. And I can tell you're drunk. And I know for sure you're spending more money because I pay the bills and I balance the checkbook. What's wrong? What's bothering you?"

And he let loose with a pretty angry reply. "What's bothering me? Lots of stuff is bothering me. Your father is bothering me. Always wants us over at his place every time you turn around. When's the last time we saw my father? Yeah, I don't remember either. And Reinhardt is bothering me. With all his talk about everybody but the Lutherans going to hell, and so we've got to give money to missions, so we can go out and teach all nations and convert the heathens so they won't go to hell. Tell them the 'good news' and bring them into the fold of the good shepherd. I'm just sick of so much shit. I'm sick of working my ass off and having nothing to show for it. Your brothers sit over there and they're lining their pockets off Lindke Lumber. What are you getting out of it? No, don't bother, it's none of my business. And I'm sick of Volcker's too. Same old krauts sitting around playing euchre night after night. I don't think any of those assholes were in the service. It was their Vaterland that started two world wars and killed millions of people and they just sit down there at Volcker's and act like nothing happened. I'm gonna start going uptown to the VFW. At least there you got guys who served their country and fought the goddamn krauts and japs and stopped them from totally destroying the goddamn world. I'm going to bed."

On Christmas Eve we were getting ready for church and Dad was dragging his feet, drinking his coffee and reading the paper. Mom ignored him as long as she could and finally said, "Bill, hurry up, we're going to be late."

"I'm not going," he said. "I don't feel good."

"What do you mean you don't feel good?" said Mom. "What's wrong?"

"I don't know. I've got a headache, and my stomach hurts," he said.

"Well, you're probably still hung over," said Mom. Maybe not the best thing to say.

"Yeah, well if I am, it's my own business, nobody else's," he said. "You guys go, I'm staying home."

Mom was furious but didn't say anything more. We finished getting ready and drove down to the church, even though it was a short walk, because it was freezing cold. I have to admit that there was something very familiar and comfortable about the church on Christmas Eve, with the candles flickering on the altar and along the side aisles, and the organ playing and the choir and congregation singing the old familiar hymns. It was tempting to think that, yeah, this gathering of God's chosen people, the anointed ones, the saved ones, had nothing to worry about. We had the keys to the kingdom, we had die einzig richtige religion, we were home free. Joy to the world, the Lord is come! Yeah.

After church we headed over to the Lindke homestead to do the usual Christmas Eve stuff, like drink eggnog and open presents. It was a large, rambling clapboard house, probably seventy or eighty years old already back then. Grandma and Grandpa and the uncles and aunts and cousins had been at church too, and we'd seen them and wished

them Merry Christmas and said see you later and everything was very jolly. We got there just about the same time
as everyone else, and we all went inside and stomped the
snow off our feet and took off our coats and piled them on
a big bench in the front hall. We all walked through the living room and into the dining room, where Grandma had set
out some snacks and Christmas cookies. It didn't take long
for someone to ask, in a surprised, sort of concerned tone,
"Where's Bill?"

"He's not feeling well," said Mom.

"Oh? What's wrong?" asked Grandma. I always thought
that Grandma liked Dad more than the rest of the Lindke
clan. She was the nicest, the kindest, the most accepting one
of all of them. She really didn't seem to care that Dad wasn't
a Wittenberger, and she wanted him to feel like he was part of
the family, and she knew that this would make Mom happy
too. She wanted peace, and love, and kindness. Like you're
supposed to want if you're a good Christian, right?

"He may be coming down with some kind of bug," said
Mom. "He'll be OK. He said to say Merry Christmas to
everyone." Which, of course, he definitely had not said.

We sat around and had snacks, and the grownups—
pretty much everybody except my brother and me, because
my cousins and my sister were all quite a bit older than us—
had spiked eggnog, or Tom & Jerries, or shots of whiskey,
or beers. We followed the tradition, which was: Christmas
Eve—go to church, go to Grandpa's, exchange presents
between the households; Christmas Day—go to church,
go home, see what Santa brought, i.e., exchange presents
within the household, go to Grandpa's for Christmas dinner. We followed the tradition, except for Dad, who that

year said screw the tradition. He not only skipped church and Grandpa's on Christmas Eve, he also skipped church and Grandpa's on Christmas Day. We worried that he might actually be sick, but I don't think so. When we got home from Grandpa's on Christmas Eve, Dad was in bed. I'm sure he'd gotten shit-faced and decided to hit the sack before we all got home.

Things around the house were pretty tense the week between Christmas and New Year's. I guess Dad decided to wind down the hostilities because he went to church on New Year's Eve and New Year's Day and attended the festivities at Grandpa Lindke's without a whimper. He did stop going to Volcker's every night, but he started driving to the VFW, which was worse because it wouldn't be good to have him driving around after he'd been tossing down beers and shots of Kessler's. Mom was not pleased with this new routine, but she didn't say much about it, other than to comment regularly on the cost of the old man's nightly entertainment. He was getting home later from the VFW than from Volcker's, which he said was because he had to drive uptown instead of taking a short walk down the street. This didn't really add up, because he used to get home from Volcker's by 10:00 or 10:30, and now he was getting home closer to midnight, sometimes later. Mom found this especially annoying since she wanted to get to bed because she had to get up and go to work, and he would wake her up when he came stumbling into the bedroom. And why did she have to get up and go to work? Because he was spending so much money drinking. It was not a good situation.

19

AFTER THREE SURGERIES, G'S DAD HAD TO HAVE HIS FOOT AMPUTATED.
Saving it was a long shot, and the doctors couldn't pull it
off. We talked about G's situation one night at the boathouse. We had decided that it really wasn't too risky to hang
out there. It was in a pretty isolated spot and in the winter, nobody was ever around. There were a couple of space
heaters, and they warmed the place up pretty quickly. Our
Palmisano's beer pipeline provided ample refreshments.

G said his mom was beside herself, trying to figure out
what this meant for the family, for their income, for her husband's future. It was all too much for her to get her head
around. Mr. Gorlukovich was stressed out too, of course. He
had been working his job at Cooper for maybe fifteen years.
It paid pretty well, it was steady, dependable work, and
along with what G's mom earned part time at the Ukrainian
Social Club, provided an income the family could count on,
could live on, certainly not lavishly, but comfortably. He
had no idea what kind of job he could do with one foot

missing. He certainly wouldn't be able to climb down into the damn resin kettle, even if he wanted to.

G said his parents had no idea what was going to happen in the future, and they were worried. He said his dad had been told he'd get workmen's comp, but he didn't really understand what that meant. He'd also been told that he might be able to get disability payments, but he didn't understand that, either. G himself didn't know anything about this stuff, and he felt really bad that he couldn't be of some help to his dad.

Fumb was convinced that Cooper would do whatever they could to screw G's dad and dump him on "the trash heap of expendable workers," as he put it. "Watch out for those bastards," he said. "They don't give a shit about you, and they'll do anything and everything they can to cut you loose and forget about you."

Fumb had the strongest opinions about this, but I think we were all in agreement that the big companies were out for one thing and one thing only, and that was to make money, and the workers be damned. The unions had their own issues—we heard stories from Tony about some of the shit that went on at Cooper, and ShiThead told us that his old man would bitch about guys sitting on their asses if they could and refusing to screw in a light bulb if it wasn't officially part of their job. But overall, we all thought that the unions were needed to keep the companies from totally exploiting and mistreating workers.

Somebody asked J.D. if Tony had been able to find out anything more about the problem with the resin kettle. J.D. said that Tony hadn't found out much new. Just what he had said before, but he did find out that safety reports had been filed about the agitator starting to move when it was supposed to be turned off. And supposedly this had been investigated and any issues had been resolved.

"Does your dad have a lawyer?" Scourge asked G.

"I don't think so," said G. "Why, does he need one? I think they told him that he would get paid somehow while he's off work. The money is what he's really worried about. If we'll have enough money to live on."

"Well," said Scourge, "my dad's a lawyer, so you may think I'm just saying this because of that, but it sounds to me like your dad really should have representation in this. For some work injuries it's not too complicated. Maybe it was a total accident. Guy trips on his own shoelace, falls, breaks his wrist. He gets his wrist set, put in a cast, he's off work while it heals. Nobody's fault, just a stupid accident. Workmen's comp pays the medical bills and pays him his regular wages while he's off work. Wrist gets better, cast comes off, he has no permanent disabilities, goes back to his regular job, end of story. But in your dad's case, you have some more complicated issues. For one thing, losing your foot is a lot bigger deal than breaking your wrist. You don't just recover from that and go back to the way things were before you got hurt. No, your whole life is going to be different. You won't be able to go back to your old job. You may not be able to get any kind of job that's anything like you had before. Your earning power may be seriously diminished. Plus, in your dad's case you have the real possibility, I think, of some liability for his injury on the part of Cooper. Even if this agitator thing had never been observed before, the company has an obligation to provide a safe work environment. There is no way in hell that something like that kettle should ever malfunction and injure someone. It's obviously a very dangerous operation they're asking workers to do. There should be triple, quadruple levels of inspection, safety checks, all that stuff, to prevent what happened to your dad. I really think he should get an attorney. Doesn't have to be my dad's firm, of course. But this incident has changed his life, and the life of your whole family. You need to make sure your interests are represented and protected."

"I'm impressed," said ShiThead. "You sound like a real live mini-lawyer."

"Yeah, I'm impressed too," said Fumb. "And I totally agree that your dad should get a lawyer, G. You've got too much at stake with this situation. There's no way you should let those bastards at Cooper get away with anything."

"So, what do you think I should do?" G asked.

"Well," said Scourge, "I'd say talk to your dad about what we're saying here. Sound him out. See if he seems agreeable to getting legal representation, or at least is open to it. Like I said, he doesn't have to work with my dad's firm. There are lots of good firms out there. But if he feels more comfortable working with somebody where he's got a connection, like through you and me, I can talk to my dad about his situation and see what he says. I'd keep the discussion with your dad pretty theoretical at this point. He may not put any credence at all in the opinion of one of your dipshit high school friends. But if he shows some interest in getting more information, just let me know. I know that if he did decide to use my dad's firm, they would send an attorney out to your house to talk to him. And there wouldn't be any pressure. I know personal injury lawyers all have the reputation of being ambulance chasers, as our dear friend ShiThead here has alluded to. But they're not all slimeballs."

"Yeah," said G, "sounds like he really does need to talk to a lawyer. Why don't you talk to your dad and I'll talk to mine and then you and I can talk?"

"Sounds good," said Scourge.

We sat there talking and drinking our beers, supplied by the Palmisano's Market pipeline. Out the windows you could see the night sky turned fiery red from the molten metal that had been poured at the Oneida Mill across the river on Bell Island. There were three steel mills along that stretch of the river, two on the Ganaway side, and they belched smoke and soot that filled the air and combined with the outpourings of the paper mills to create the familiar stench that permeated our environment. If you weren't used to it, the smell might make you gag. The locals said, "Smells like money."

20

THAT WINTER, THE WINTER OF OUR JUNIOR YEAR, J.D., ShiThead, and
I were playing basketball, Fumb and G were wrestling, and
Scourge was swimming. ShiThead and J.D. were starting
most games, and I was warming the bench. I had quite a following in the stands, however. Fumb, G, and Scourge would
always be at the games, and sometimes they'd have girls
with them. ShiThead was getting pretty tight with Sally
Summers, and she would come and root for Ganaway, which
was generally frowned upon by her Bell Island friends but
tolerated as long as it wasn't a Bell Island-Ganaway game.
G was getting pretty serious about Nancy Gregg, and even
though Scourge didn't have a main squeeze, he was popular enough so that he never had trouble getting a girl to
sit with him at a basketball game. During the pregame
warm-up, when we'd be shooting layups, my little cheering
section would stand up and scream at the top of their lungs,
"Simpson! Simpson! Simpson!" whenever it was my turn
in line to shoot the layup. Didn't matter if I made the layup
or not. And in the final minutes, sometimes seconds, of a

game, they would start yelling "We want Simpson! We want Simpson!" trying to convince the coach to put me in for a brief appearance. Sometimes I would acknowledge my fans with a glance up into the cheering section and an elegant flourish and bow, although I knew the coach didn't like this whole Simpson thing, so I had to be discreet.

After the games we would go to Angelo's, where we had become regular customers. I think a couple of us had turned seventeen by then and Fumb was either eighteen or close to it. For some reason, and I really don't recall why, we established a strict rule about not knowing each other's birthdays. To this day, I don't know the birthday of any of the guys. The whole thing was just another of our stupid inventions that made the Backfield fun and exclusive. Totally pointless, totally ridiculous to anyone but one of us. And that's why we loved it. Regardless, the birthday didn't really matter, because ever since our first visit to Angelo's, we had always been served our beers. Sometimes Mama Rizzo would still ask us, "You boys eighteen?" Maybe she just felt the need to pretend she was obeying the law. We'd just nod our heads and say, "Oh yeah, yeah," and that was it. We had gotten over our aversion to lying through our teeth, I guess.

As I've said before, Mama made unbelievably good pizza—I have never had anything like it before or since. She used tomatoes, not sauce, and the crust had somewhat of a pastry-like quality, although not as light and puffy as Gino's. It was more dense and chewy, but still flaky. Hard to describe but once you ate it you would never forget it. I know I'm repeating myself, but I can't help talking about it. She would also make us wonderful ham sandwiches on crusty Italian bread cut in thick slices. God, those were good!

There were some interesting characters who would drop in regularly, like the old lady who sold flowers, and an old drunk that everybody called "Johnny Vino," or just Johnny V. We found out that Johnny V was not only a drunk but also a numbers runner. I guess he had done it long enough that being shit-faced didn't impair his ability to keep his bets straight. He'd make his rounds going up to different guys who must have been his regular customers. I don't recall him ever approaching us. Probably wasn't sure he could trust a bunch of young assholes. Angelo's was also a favorite hangout for older guys who never quite grew up—guys in their twenties and maybe even their thirties who had hit their peak in high school and spent their afternoons and nights at Angelo's reliving the glory days and trying to impress the girls who came to drink their sloe gin and Squirts. That was another thing we learned about at Angelo's. Sloe gin. I had never heard of it before the night I heard a girl at the bar order a sloe gin and Squirt. I noticed over our next few visits that guys never ordered them, so it was quite a while before I ever tasted one. I think that time was one night when J.D.'s sister Marie was there with Danny. We had gotten to know Danny and Marie a bit and I screwed up my courage and asked her if I could taste her drink. She was really nice and happily slid her glass over and said, "Here, help yourself. They're really good. Very refreshing." It actually was damn good. I probably would have started ordering them instead of beer except it was definitely not cool for guys to like sloe gin and Squirt.

I think this was the same night that I asked Danny why

the phone at the bar was ringing all the time. He looked at me with an expression that seemed to say, "Where the hell have you been all your life, kid?" My Wittenberg naivete and innocence were showing, apparently.

"Take a guess," he said.

"No, really, I have no idea," I said.

"You mean your old kraut friends down in Heinietown don't like to gamble?" he said.

"Well, yeah, I see guys playing poker sometimes," I said. I was really showing just how clueless I was.

"Well, there's other things you can bet on other than poker," he said.

"Oh," I said.

He didn't go into a lot of detail, but he explained that the phone was always ringing because guys were calling to place bets on sporting events or horse races or other stuff. He said you could get in over your head with that and you didn't want to mess with bookies unless you were sure you could pay up when you lost.

Sometime after this conversation at Angelo's, maybe one day at lunch, J.D. and I were talking, and I mentioned about the old man's drinking getting worse. I felt kind of disloyal or something talking about family stuff. But J.D. and I had become such good friends that I really trusted him—and the other guys too—plus I think I needed to get some of this off my chest. I told him about the switch from Volcker's to the VFW, and the concern about driving home drunk, and all the money he was spending.

"What's he spending all the money on?" said J.D.

"Booze, I guess," I said.

"Seriously?" he said. "I hate to say this, but it sounds like he might be into more than booze."

"What do you mean?" I said.

"Well," said J.D., "if he's spending the kind of money you're talking about, I'd be concerned that he's into some kind of big-time gambling shit."

"Where, at the VFW?" I said. "They have big-time gambling at the VFW?"

"Are you sure he's going to the VFW?" J.D. said.

"Well, that's where he says he's going," I said. "But yeah, we have no way of actually knowing what he's up to, I guess. He takes off in the car and, yeah, we really don't know. Shit."

J.D. said that I should consider the possibility that the old man was gambling a lot. You could lose a lot at poker if that's what he was into. And you could lose a lot betting on the horses. He also told me about an old, nondescript warehouse down on Crozier Street that not too many people knew about, pretty shady, where supposedly some serious kinds of gambling went on. J.D. said that he'd heard there was a card game called Siganette, or Ziginat, that got into some really high stakes and guys could get way in over their heads. He didn't really know much more than that about it and said he didn't want to know. According to J.D., the Palmisano family had nothing to do with the local mob. The Rizzos were another story. He said that Danny, for example, knew a lot more than he did about how the bookie thing worked, with the phone ringing all the time at Angelo's.

I asked him if he thought that Dad could be involved in this warehouse gambling thing, and he said of course he couldn't know, but just the idea of the old man spending so much money, which was causing some really serious problems with Mom, not to mention the whole family budget, made him suspicious and worried. Now he had me worried. I said I supposed that I could follow the old man some night when he left for the VFW and see if that's really where he was going, but I hesitated to do that. I probably wouldn't be detected following him, but I'd have to tell Mom what I was doing and why, and that would just open up a whole new can of worms.

"So, who runs this place on Crozier?" I said.

"I really don't know," said J.D. "It's a very secretive thing."

"Do you think Danny would know anything more about it?" I asked him.

"It's possible," he said, "but I don't know exactly how I'd bring this up with him. Basically, you want to know if your old man is gambling at this place and if he's losing a lot of money. Even if he knew stuff like that, I doubt that he'd be able to say anything about it. I guess I could talk to Marie about it first, see what she thinks, see if she knows anything. But would you want me talking to her about your family business?"

"We could trust her, couldn't we? To be discreet?" I said.

"Oh yeah, for sure, no problem with that," he said. "I just don't know what…well, let me think about it. Let me think about it."

21

NOT LONG AFTER THIS DISCUSSION WITH J.D., we had another blowup at home about the very thing we had talked about. It was on a Saturday morning. I had been out with the guys the night before, driving Mom's car, and got home around midnight. The old man wasn't home yet and I went to bed. Everybody else was in bed. I woke up early Saturday to a lot of yelling going on downstairs. I got up and went to the top of the stairs and I could hear Mom and Dad going at it, mostly Mom.

"Bill, this has just gotten completely out of control! What in the heck is going on? You didn't get home until almost three o'clock in the morning. I know because I couldn't sleep, I was lying awake worrying about you, wondering where the heck you were and what you were doing."

"I told you I was at the VFW," he yelled.

"And what were you doing there until 3:00 a.m.? Are they even open that late? I'm sorry, but I don't know if I can even believe what you tell me anymore."

"Yes, they're open. A lot of guys hang out there. They

talk about stuff that they can't talk about with anybody else. They know stuff, they've seen stuff, that other people don't know anything about. It helps to talk about stuff with people who understand."

"Well, OK, I'm sure you saw some terrible things in the war, but why can't you share your feelings with your own wife? I'm supposed to be the one who is with you for better or worse, all the stuff we said in our vows. And yet you don't feel like you can talk to me about things that are troubling you? That's what a wife is for. Why do you leave me out?"

"Goddamn it! Goddamn it! You just don't get it. How can I explain it? I just need to deal with some shit and not talk about it to people who can't understand it."

She wasn't completely buying his story. "So how much does it cost to sit at the VFW and talk about stuff to your veteran friends that you can't talk about to anyone else? I'll tell you how much, because I pay the bills and balance the checkbook. It costs *a lot*. I'm sorry, but I'm having a real hard time believing that you're telling me the whole story. I want to know where our money is going. You used to deposit your whole paycheck in the bank. Now it seems like every week you're taking more cash and putting less into the bank account. So far you haven't touched the savings account, which I've been trying to build up with my earnings from my job, and you had better *not* take any money out of that account, I swear."

"OK, OK," he said. "Look, a few things have come up and I needed to take care of them. We should be good now, so stop worrying about the money. Everything's OK. Now, how about just get off my back for once and I'll take of everything."

"Well, if you're spending all that money on booze, you had better knock it off *now*. And whatever the 'things' are that have come up, they had better not come up again. I feel really bad that I don't feel I can believe what you're telling me. Are you playing poker or doing some other kind of gambling? You know what Pastor Reinhardt thinks of gambling. It can ruin families; it *has* ruined families. Look at the Papkes. I'm worried that's what may be happening to us."

"Oh, here we go with Saint William of Reinhardt again. Mr. Perfect. Jesus, Jr. Wears his halo everywhere he goes. Reinhardt should talk. He's got plenty of flaws himself, but don't ever expect him to admit it. No, Mr. Holier than Thou is above all worldly temptations. Pompous ass! So you're going to model your life after a self-righteous, cold, overbearing, egotistical jerk who never shows one hint of understanding or forgiveness for anybody? Nice role model. I don't give a shit what he thinks about anything."

"Well, this conversation is going nowhere," said Mom. "Let's just say that whatever you're wasting *our* money on, it had better stop. And maybe get home at a reasonable hour once in a while. Like the old Volcker's days. As long as you have to keep going out and drinking every night, I'd rather have you going there."

"OK. All right. Enough. You don't get it, you don't care to get it. I'm a piece of shit. I'm ruining our family. I get the message. Fine." He put on his hat and coat and went outside to shovel the driveway, even though the driveway didn't need to be shoveled, actually.

By this time, Donna and Sam had heard the commotion

and the three of us ventured downstairs to find Mom crying in the kitchen. When she saw us, she immediately tried to pull herself together and act upbeat. She said, "Hey, good morning, what would you like for breakfast?"

I said I wasn't hungry and that I'd heard her and Dad going at it. I asked her what was up. She tried to downplay it and said she thought he just needed an outlet, a break from work, some time to himself, and that talking to guys at the VFW was probably good for him because a lot of them had been through the same kinds of things he had. She said he was probably just going through a phase and that he'd get over it. Donna and Sam seemed to accept this explanation, but privately, I wasn't buying a word of it. I did, I think, have some appreciation of the fact that guys who had been in the thick of the war had seen and done things that they found hard to forget about. And that even after twenty years, some of them still felt the effects of those experiences, and that those experiences had changed them in some fundamental, irreversible ways. But, having talked to J.D. about Dad recently, I was convinced that whatever he was into was about more than war nightmares or whatever you wanted to call it. Or maybe the war experience had changed him and led him to do things he otherwise wouldn't have done. I needed to talk to J.D. and see if he had been able to find out anything from Marie. Actually, he called me that same day, and said he had some information for me. We agreed to meet at Palmisano's the next day when the market would be closed as usual on Sunday.

We all went to church on Sunday, including Dad, which I took as a good sign that he was at least trying to patch things up from the big fight of the day before. When the collection plate came down our pew, Mom put the envelope in and leaned over to Dad and said, "That's what we should be doing with our money, not wasting it at the VFW or wherever you're going." Oh boy, here we go again, I thought. The old man just glared at her and didn't say anything. I tried to tune out Reinhardt's sermon, as I always did, because I didn't want to get annoyed by all his usual drivel. When we got home, we all changed our clothes and Mom started making lunch. Dad didn't say a word, didn't sit down to eat, and just went down in the basement, supposedly working on something, but obviously just avoiding Mom.

I took one of the cars and drove up to Palmisano's to meet J.D. as we had arranged. J.D. let me in the back door, and we sat down at the table in the back room. He offered me a beer from the hidden stash but I said no, better just talk about what he'd found out. So he told me that Marie had shared with Danny—in complete confidence, so she said—the stuff about the old man supposedly going to the VFW, but spending way more money than seemed logical, and getting home later and later, and all that.

"OK, so here's what Danny was able to find out," said J.D. "First of all, this is very delicate information. Nobody is supposed to know about this or where it came from. You can't say that Danny told you this stuff, or he's gonna be in a world of hurt. He really stuck his neck out for us on this, and he had to be very careful and discreet about who he talked to and what questions he asked. So, here's the situation. Basically, your old man's got himself in some deep shit. He's been gambling, probably sports, horses, the old warehouse, doesn't really matter that much what kind of gambling he's doing. The main thing is that he owes some people a lot of money. And these are not people you want to owe a lot of money to. They don't mess around. If you don't pay up, well, you're gonna feel some serious pain. You do not want to get yourself in that situation. No way."

I was having a hard time getting my head around exactly what J.D. was telling me. So, the old man was lying about going to the VFW, that was pretty clear. And he was losing a lot of money gambling on something or other, or maybe multiple things. And he owed money to some bad people. But why did he owe money? If he was gambling and losing, his money was going down the shitter, for sure. But then it was gone. I said something like that to J.D.

"Think about it," he said. "You're big time into gambling. You're hooked on it. You're losing more than you're winning, which is always going to happen if you keep at it long enough. You don't want to quit gambling. You're behind and you've got yourself convinced that if you can just bet another race, or another card game, you can win back what you've lost. Because you need that money back. You can't afford to lose it. But you're out of money and don't have any to bet with. You need to get more money. Where are you going to get more money to bet with? You have to borrow it. From where? From the bank? No, the wife will find out, and she's already pissed that you're spending too much money—on something. So somebody tells you about where you can borrow some money. The interest rate is ridiculous, but it won't be too bad if you pay it back right away—right after you win a whole shitload on the next horse race, or card game. You find the guy who will give you a loan. You take the loan, but instead of winning back your money, you lose it all. You're screwed."

What he was saying all made sense. The old man had really fucked up big time. "Jesus Christ," I said to J.D., "the old man's really got himself into a mess, hasn't he? What should I do? Should I talk to him? Even if I did, would he admit it? And what would he do about it? I wonder how much he owes. And where would he get the money to pay it back?"

"No, you absolutely cannot talk to him about this," said J.D.

"So, what the hell are we gonna do?"

"Well, let's think about this," said J.D. "If your old man doesn't pay what he owes, he's gonna get hurt. And I mean really hurt. Like broken bones and shit. We have to avoid that at all cost. My thought is that if your mom were to find out what's going on, that would create an unbelievable shit-storm in your family, but it would force your old man to face the issue and they would find some way to pay off what he owes. It might be the end of your parents' marriage, but your old man might come out of it in one piece, at least."

"Yeah, I see what you're saying," I said, "but we can't tell my mom either. So how do we force the issue, like you said?"

"I've got an idea but I think it's better if you don't know anything about it," said J.D. "In fact, this whole conversation we're having here—that never happened, right?"

"What conversation?" I said.

22

THE NEXT WEEK WAS REALLY STRESSFUL. You could feel the tension between Mom and Dad. After supper he didn't drink his coffee and read the paper as usual, and he didn't head out for Volcker's or the VFW or wherever. Instead, he went down in the basement to do, what? We didn't know and nobody asked. Maybe he was working on some kind of woodworking project—he did have quite a well-equipped wood shop down there. Or maybe he was drinking. It was very awkward because nobody said anything, and he stayed down there until the rest of us went to bed.

This went on for a few days and we all wondered how long he would keep it up. There couldn't possibly be enough down there in the basement to keep him occupied indefinitely. Then one night, probably around 3:00 a.m. I think it was, everyone was jolted awake by a huge crash. My mind did the usual "What the hell was that?!" and I'm sure everyone else had the same kind of reaction. In a matter of seconds, all five of us were out in the upstairs hallway, with wild-eyed expressions on our faces, looking at each other and peering down the stairs into the darkness, probably wondering if we should arm ourselves with a lamp or a hairbrush or some kind of weapon. There were no guns in the house that I knew of. Dad ran into the bedroom and came out with a heavy work boot, the best weapon he could find, I guess, and whispered, "Everybody stay here."

I whispered back, "I should come with you."

"No, I'll check it out and call you if I need you," he said.

He started down the stairs, slowly, trying to scope out as much as he could as he descended. At the bottom of the stairs he turned left into the living room, and we couldn't see him anymore. After maybe a minute or so, he yelled, "What the hell?!" and turned on some lights. We didn't wait for him to tell us to come down; we just ran down there and found him standing by the window, with broken glass scattered all around him on the floor, holding a brick in his hand.

"Don't come over here; there's glass all over the place," he yelled. I looked and saw that he was in his bare feet and was bleeding from a cut on one foot. Mom went and put some shoes on and went to the kitchen and got a broom and dustpan and started sweeping up the glass. She said, "Bill, you've cut your foot. Don't move until I get this glass swept up." As she worked at cleaning up the glass, Donna, Sam, and I just stood there, kind of in shock, wondering what the hell had happened and what was going to happen next.

"Bill, go sit on the davenport. Be careful, you may have some glass stuck in your foot." Mom was taking control of the very crazy situation. Dad did as he was told, walking a few steps with his bleeding foot pointed up, trying not to get blood on the carpet. I should say any more blood, because there was already a spot where he'd been standing. He sat down on the davenport, still holding a brick in his hand.

"Let me see that brick," said Mom. "Did someone throw that through our window? I guess someone did. What in the world is going on?"

Dad acted funny, like he didn't want her to have the brick, but he didn't really have any way to avoid giving it to her. He hesitated and she went over and took it from him and saw that there was a note tied around it with string. "What?!" she shouted. "What is this all about, for heaven's sake?"

"What does the note say?" I think I was the one who asked the obvious question. She handed me the brick, which had this message written on a piece of heavy paper and wrapped around it, held on with a thick rubber band. It said, "Pay up or say goodbye to your kneecaps. And if that doesn't get you to pay up, your family will be next." All I could think of was holy shit, holy shit! I must have had some crazy shocked look on my face. Donna looked stunned, like she might start to cry. She said, "Well, what does it say, Chris?"

Mom now regretted that she had let me see the brick. She tried to grab it back from me but I had already handed it to Donna. Mom said, "We're not talking about this now. We're not talking about this, do you hear me? All of you, do you hear me? You kids go back upstairs and go to your rooms and try to get back to sleep. Your dad and I will take care of this. You boys have school tomorrow, and you have work, Donna. Bill, you've got to get something to cover that broken window; it's freezing cold outside. Maybe this is somebody's sick idea of a joke or something. Or maybe juvenile delinquents. Some of those neighborhoods uptown have some pretty bad people."

We did what she said, but I thought, The cat's out of the bag now, I'm afraid. We had all seen the note, except maybe for Sam, and we couldn't keep it from him. The old man took the opportunity to exit the scene and went down to the basement to start working on fixing the window. I really wanted to eavesdrop somehow on the discussion that I knew was going to happen out in the kitchen once the broken window was covered up. But I didn't want to make a terrible situation worse by going against Mom. What a fucking mess the old man had gotten himself into. And us too. I went into my room but I just couldn't resist. I went back out into the hallway and to the top of the stairs. Sam and Donna both came sneaking out of their rooms too. You could hear that Dad was working on the window and Mom was talking, trying to keep her voice down as much as possible.

"Bill, what in the world is going on? Does this have something to do with your nightly visits to the VFW? If that's really where you're going? You've been lying to me, haven't you? For all this time, you've been lying to me! I can't believe it. I just can't believe it. What have you done? You have to tell me!"

"Goddammit, Doris, keep your damn voice down! Just shut up! I've got to get this window fixed. Then we can talk. In the basement! Not here where the kids will hear us."

So that was all we got. We looked at each other, didn't know what to say. Finally, I said, "OK, well, Dad's obviously got himself into some kind of deep shit. We'll have to see what happens tomorrow. So just try and get some sleep." And we all went back into our rooms.

Needless to say, the next morning, actually just a few hours later, was an extremely uncomfortable, awkward time. The old man was gone when the rest of us got to the kitchen for breakfast. We kids didn't know what to say or how to act, and Mom wasn't sending any helpful signals. I didn't think there was any way that she and Dad could just gloss over this thing. I figured that she had extracted some details from him about what was going on, who he owed money to, how much he owed, when it was due, all that kind of stuff. I couldn't see any way that he would have been able to stonewall her. I knew it must be terrible for her, and unbelievably embarrassing. She would be desperate to keep people from finding out the truth about what the old man had done.

For myself, I felt like I had definitely done the right thing. Without getting Mom involved, there would have been no way to prevent the old man from getting in even deeper shit. I had to hand it to Danny. He'd come up with a crazy but effective way to force an intervention. It was going to be a real shitshow, but that's what the old man needed to save his ass, even if he didn't realize it.

Usually, Dad got home from work around 5:00, Mom and Donna a little later. Sam took the bus home right after school. I usually got a ride with somebody after basketball practice. The day after the crash, everyone was home except Dad. I figured that there was a planned reason that he was late getting home on this particular day. Mom had us all come and sit at the kitchen table.

"Kids," she said, "I need to tell you a few things and

this is to stay right here in this room, you understand?" We all nodded.

"You know that your father is a very honest man, a very trusting person. Sometimes too trusting. Your father has made some bad investments, and he has lost some money and he needs to pay it back to the people who got him into these investments. I can't go into a lot of detail. Your dad feels terrible about all this. He was taken advantage of. But all that doesn't matter now. He's straightened everything out but we still owe some money, quite a lot of money. We can handle it, and I don't want there to be any talking about the situation. I certainly don't want you asking Dad any questions, and I don't want you to say a word to anyone outside our family. Just this family, the five of us. Nobody else is to know anything about what I'm talking about now. Understood?"

We all shook our heads and mumbled, "Sure, yeah, right, exactly."

"But what was that brick thing all about?" asked Sam.

"She told you not to talk about it, stupid!" Donna snapped at him.

"OK, OK," said Mom. "No rudeness or arguing. I'll just say this and then we're going to drop it. That was a very dumb thing to do and whoever did that is going to be in trouble with some people. Like I said, your father is an honest man, and he will pay what he owes. He made a mistake, but other people have made similar mistakes. We will take care of it. OK?"

We all nodded "OK." I thought this was a pretty good approach for Mom to take, and probably the best she could do. Total bullshit, but what else could she do? It might work. I knew there would be some very ugly discussions between our dear parents behind the scenes. It would be interesting to watch how it all played out, knowing what I knew about the real situation. And I would probably be able to get more information through J.D. if I wanted to. At that point I wasn't sure if I wanted to know more.

23

AFTER THE MEETING WITH MOM, things went along pretty well for several weeks. At least there was no drama. No more bricks through windows, and Dad's kneecaps were intact, so I assumed Mom had figured out some way to pay whatever he owed to the people he owed it to. She had referred to the savings account that she was trying to build up with earnings from her job at Stenzel Insurance, so it was likely that she had used some of that money, maybe all of it, to bail his ass out. This hunch was confirmed when she announced that it was time for Donna to start paying rent. She was an adult, said Mom, and should be chipping in something toward household expenses. It didn't have to be a lot, but it was important for everybody to play their part. There was the mortgage, and property taxes, and besides, Donna should start putting money aside for future needs. It was never too early to start saving for your future. I could tell that Donna did not like this turn of events, but I never heard her say anything about it. No doubt she had figured out that the "bad investment" story was a pile of shit. She and I never talked about it, but she wasn't stupid, and the whole brick through the window thing made it pretty obvious that something fishy was going on and Mom was covering it up.

I didn't escape the fallout from the old man's folly, either. Mom told me that the Stenzel agency was looking for a part-time person to do clerical work, like filing, and mailing out bills, and making copies, that sort of thing. I thought that's what Mom was doing but I guess she was learning more about the nuts and bolts of the insurance business, and the agency was doing well and needed a little more help. She said it would be great experience for me, and I could put half of my pay into the family savings account, and that would be a good way to save for college, which was just a year or so away. At first, I was kind of irritated, because I knew that this, and Donna's paying rent, was all about paying the old man's loan shark or whatever. But of course I didn't object, and the more I thought about it, I liked the idea of an office job where I could get some "business" experience and also earn some beer money. I wouldn't be able to play tennis, but that really didn't bother me much. I liked being an athlete, but I didn't mind the prospect of being a two-sport rather than a three-sport man. Sam pretty much escaped, wasn't asked to contribute from his grass cutting and snow shoveling revenue.

The most shocking announcement was that Dad would be working Saturdays at Lindke Lumber. Mom said that Grandpa "needed some help" and that Dad's woodworking skills made him a great fit. I wondered how much Mom had actually told Grandpa about Dad's situation. I'm sure she would have tried to avoid telling the actual truth, but she had to tell him something, why we needed the extra money.

Just thinking about the old man's humiliation at having to work for Grandpa Lindke made me shudder. I felt really bad for him. The whole mess was his own fault, but having to work over there on Saturdays, doing who knows what, and knowing that the whole Lindke crowd, Grandpa and Grandma, and the uncles and the aunts, had to know something was really wrong, even if they didn't know the whole story, had to be just awful for him.

The latest we'd heard about G's dad's situation was that he had agreed to talk to a lawyer, somebody from the Bullshit Law Firm, and had decided to discuss a personal injury suit against Cooper. Scourge thought they had a pretty good case, and they'd be talking to people they thought could be of help. I reminded Scourge that my sister worked in the office at Cooper and said he should let me know if they thought she could be helpful.

J.D. was all for suing Cooper. At a rendezvous at the boathouse Scourge told him that he'd overheard Paul Harrison at the marina talking about Peggy, saying something like, "Yeah, and my daughter is going out with some dago kid named Joe Palermo or Joe Palmolive or something. We should have sent her to a private girls' school like we wanted to. Maybe she would have met some boys from Norfolk. But no, she threw a big fit, insisted she wanted to go to Ganaway, be a cheerleader, always talking about the famous Bell Island and Ganaway rivalry, the BI-G game. So now she's running around with dagoes, polacks, hunkies, who knows what."

J.D. obviously was not pleased. "I knew her old man was a jerk," he said. "Peggy tells me stuff about him but I never paid too much attention to it. What a pompous asshole. He couldn't care less about the dagoes and polacks and hunkies who work in his shithole factory. That's why we need unions, guys, because of assholes like him. If you let selfish, greedy bastards like him run things with nobody keeping an on eye on them, they're going to walk all over people and not give a shit what happens to them. Just like the robber barons. They made fortunes by exploiting and murdering working people and never blinked an eye. And you know what? People like them will still do it if they can get away with it." He was pretty wound up. You couldn't blame him.

This rendezvous had actually been called to celebrate Fumb's eighteenth birthday. Of course, we didn't know exactly when his birthday was. That would be a violation of Backfield law. But when Fumb suggested that we have a rendezvous and that he would bring the beer, we knew his big day had arrived—not precisely when, but we knew that it had happened—and that our beer supply would hence-forth be assured and simplified. We met at the boathouse and Fumb brought a lot of beer and we drank it all. Way too much. Scourge kept telling everybody to keep the noise down. We would quiet down for a while and then the noise level would climb back up. Finally he said, "Look, assholes. If somebody hears us partying in here, and my old man hears about it, we're going to lose our headquarters. Now SHUT THE FUCK UP!"

That got our attention and we toned it down. We talked about G's dad and how Cooper needed to get seriously fucked over and made to pay. Same for Paul Harrison, who was in charge of what went on there and should learn a lesson he wouldn't forget. We didn't stay real late, but when we left, every one of us had sucked down way too much beer. It wouldn't be the last time we got behind the wheels of cars when we were in no condition to drive.

24

THE BACKFIELD DIDN'T ALWAYS DO EVERYTHING TOGETHER. One time, Fumb, Scourge, and I had decided to take the boat and go get a sub at our favorite sub place, which was in Bell Island. Mac's was the name of the place, and it was right on the river and you could dock your boat and get your sub and just relax and look out at the river. After we had our subs we decided to take a walk and check out a place that we had heard a lot about, a place called Nick's that was supposed to be very cool and sometimes had a live band. It was a few blocks in from the river, and then you turned left and went maybe another six or eight blocks. It was late afternoon, I think, so there weren't many people there when we went inside to check it out. One of the first things we saw was a large sign that said, "Photo ID Required to Purchase Alcohol." That wasn't a good omen, but we sat down at a table and looked the place over. It wasn't huge, and there were a lot of tables crammed into one open room. There was a long bar that stretched along one wall, and it had short "wings" on each end. It looked like it had a total of maybe thirty barstools, the kind that were attached to the floor, and swiveled, with no backs. There was a spot with no stool where you could walk up to the bar and order a drink. Up on the wall behind the bar were all kinds of banners— local high schools, lots of colleges, and professional sports teams: baseball, football, hockey. Off in the corner was a low platform, what passed for a stage, obviously where the bands played. It was quite dark, with only a few windows and some ceiling lights, which were either not turned on or were dimmed.

Since Fumb was eighteen, we decided to send him up to the bar to see if he could get us all beers. No such luck. Apparently, they were very strict about the ID thing. Maybe if the place was really crowded, and the bartender was swamped, you could get away with one guy buying beers for a group, one at a time, and not one right after the other, but it definitely wouldn't be as smooth as at Angelo's, where we had become "anointed" and could get served, no questions asked.

Fumb came back to the table with his one draft beer, in a mug with a handle, sat down, and said, "Jesus! This place is expensive!"

"Why? How much was that?" Scourge said.

"Eighty-five cents," said Fumb.

"You gotta be shittin' me!" said Scourge. "Well, I guess this isn't gonna be our new favorite place, even if we could get served, which obviously we can't. Damn, I can't believe that. What makes this place worth that much for a beer?"

"Well, they probably charge that much or more at the Commercial Club, right?" said Fumb.

"Hmm. Never thought about that," said Scourge.

"Everything you buy there goes on your monthly statement, so I never thought about it. Damn, my old man's bar tab must be off the charts."

"That's why the Bullshit Law Firm screws the hell out of their clients, right?" said Fumb.

Fumb finished his beer and we left Nick's and headed back to the boat. We crossed the street and started walking back up the street and we noticed a place we hadn't seen on the way to Nick's. It was a classic Bell Island-Ganaway gin mill—nondescript, two-story, fake brick shingles, front door, rear side door, no driveway, gray, drab, with a dull, almost invisible sign above the front door—"Striebig's." We stopped in front of the building and Scourge said, "Whaddya think? Should we check it out?"

"Yeah, why not?" said Fumb.

We went up the two low steps to the front door and went in. On each side of the front door was a picture window with a square table with four chairs in front of it. Some old guys were playing euchre at one of the tables. Looking straight ahead there were a few more tables, then the typical L-shaped bar on the left, with a few barstools on the L, then more barstools along the long section of the bar, then a wall with a doorway leading from behind the bar into another room, maybe a kitchen. Behind the bar was an old guy in a long white apron, the kind that has a cloth neck strap and covers your chest, and a cloth strap that you wrap around your waist and tie in the front. When we came in he turned and faced us but it seemed like he wasn't looking at us, but was looking over our heads. It almost seemed like maybe he was blind, but that didn't seem likely.

"Can I help you?" he said in a high-pitched, raspy, hoarse-sounding voice.

"Just checking it out," said Fumb. "Never been here before."

"Make yourself at home," said the old guy. "Let me know if you want anything."

"Thanks," said Fumb.

We walked past the bar and past more tables, and then you veered to the right and walked past what looked like a takeout counter, and behind that was the kitchen. So the kitchen was between the bar room and a good-sized back room with more tables, some of them round ones with six or eight chairs. There was a door from the kitchen to the bar room and to the back room.

"Should we try to get a beer?" said Scourge.

"Nothing ventured, nothing gained," said Fumb. He headed back out front to the bar and we sat down at one of the tables in the back room. We were the only ones there. In a minute Fumb came back with two huge stemmed glasses of beer.

"Look at this," he said. "I gotta go get the other one. Couldn't carry all three at once."

Scourge and I looked at each other. "Whoa!" he said. "That's some major league beer, right there."

Fumb came back with the other one and sat down.

"So, no problem, I guess," said Scourge.

"No, not at all," said Fumb. "The old guy didn't ask me for proof or anything, and he didn't hesitate when I told him I wanted three. All he said was, 'mug or schupper?' I said, 'What's a schupper?' and he just reached under the bar and pulled one of these out and showed it to me. Actually,

I don't think he can see very well. It looks like he's got his eyes taped open with Scotch tape or something. I couldn't tell if he was looking at me or looking over my shoulder."

"So how much does a schupper of beer cost at Striebig's?" said Scourge.

"You're not gonna believe this," said Fumb. "Forty-five cents."

"You've got to be shitting me!" said Scourge. "Seriously?"

"Seriously," said Fumb. "So I guess we've found our new favorite gin mill, eh boys?"

"A toast!" I said. We all raised our schuppers. "Here's to Striebig's and to old guys with Scotch-taped eyelids!"

Later we learned that the old guy with the Scotch-taped eyelids was, in fact, Mr. Striebig, who obviously had some pretty serious problem with his eyes, and actually did need tape or something to keep them open. What assholes we were, making fun of that decent old guy, who gladly served us beer and provided a place where we could hang out together and laugh and dream up stupid shit, and where we made some great memories. We finished our beers and decided not to press our luck by ordering another round. And anyway it was getting a little late and we needed to get the boat back to the boathouse. But we knew we'd be back.

25

THAT SUMMER OUR STUPIDITY LEVEL REACHED A NEW HIGH. We were hanging out at the boathouse and going out on the boat as much as we could, working around everybody's summer job schedules. Of course, Scourge was always the key player, and he was working quite a few hours at the marina. Looking back, it's probably a good thing that we couldn't be on the boat more than we were. It improved our chances of survival.

Usually, we made a point of not drinking when we were on the boat. How we managed to be that sensible I don't know. But the common sense ended there. Some of the stuff we did was truly insane. Like the depth charge thing. Two guys would climb out onto the gunwales of the boat, one on either side of the cabin, and lie down, facing the bow. The captain, usually Scourge, would hit the throttle and get the boat screaming across the water. Somebody would yell, "Fire One!" and the guy on the port side would roll off the boat and slam headfirst into the water. Then on the command of "Fire Two!" the guy on the starboard side would do the same. Scourge would swing the boat around in a tight arc and go back and pick up the two depth charges. They'd climb up the ladder at the stern and two other guys would get in position for the next depth charge launch.

I have to admit that the first time I tried this I almost shit my pants. But it really was a blast and after you did it a few times, not scary at all. I can't believe how easy it would have been for somebody to break his neck. But when you're that age, you're invincible and don't think about stuff like that. It wasn't long before we started launching four depth charges, two at a time. One port and one starboard depth charge would fire, then the other two would go.

We did a lot of water skiing too. After a while, I managed to get up on the skis every time with no problem. We did some swerving back and forth, jumping over the wake, nothing too fancy, but ShiThead and J.D. learned how to go on one ski, and that was pretty impressive.

I wore contact lenses. I talked my parents into letting me get them to play football, because I was blind as a bat and there's no way I could have played QB and thrown passes without them. But I never wore them on the boat. One time I was on the skis and whoever was driving the boat, probably Scourge, thought it would be funny to run me near a buoy to test my skill and see how I managed to swerve around and avoid hitting it. Unfortunately, he forgot that I couldn't see a damn thing without my contacts. I was screaming across the water when all of a sudden something flashed by my face on the left side. I heard a loud whoosh sound and ducked my head, for all the good that would do. The guys on the boat were a big blur but I could tell they were all gathered in the stern, which was strange because we hardly ever all stood together like that. I kept skiing for a few minutes, then waved to the spotter. The boat slowed down and I dropped the tow rope and they circled back to get me.

When I got up next to the boat and started to climb in, somebody said, "Hey, dickhead, how close did you think you could get to that buoy? We thought you were gonna wipe out on it. You could have killed yourself trying to impress your friends."

"Impress my friends? What are you talking about? You know I can't see shit without my glasses. You assholes could have killed me! I came about two inches from hitting that goddamn thing!"

"Ooh. Sorry," said Scourge. "I forgot about that."

For a minute I wanted to kick his ass across the boat. But then somebody started to laugh, and then everybody started to laugh, and then I started to laugh, and for some reason my near death became a hilarious thing, and we literally could not stop laughing. And every time we ever brought it up years later, we laughed our asses off.

We normally didn't go out at night and, like I said, we didn't drink on the boat. One time we made two exceptions. We had been at the boathouse in the evening and were drinking a lot of beer. As the sun was going down, we were all pretty ripped and I guess feeling exceptionally stupid, which for us was pretty damn stupid. G in particular was really smashed, and he was the one who started saying we should go for a boat ride. "Look what a beautiful night it is," he slurred. "Look at the sun going down over the river. Beautiful. Let's just go for a ride. It's so beautiful."

Scourge really didn't want to take the boat out. By the time we got out on the river it would be getting really dark, and he knew it was a bad idea. But the fact that something is a bad idea to a bunch of intoxicated adolescents doesn't mean you're not going to do it. We all ganged up on Scourge and started nagging and bugging him until he finally gave in and said, "OK, but we're not going out for long and we're not going very far."

"Yes!" we all chimed in.

"Yay, Scourge. Way to go, Captain!"

"Cast off!"

"All hands on deck!"

We pulled out of the boathouse and out into the river, turned north, and the wide expanse of the river opened up to us. The sun was down over the horizon and there was just the faint glow of sunset. It had been an unusually clear day; maybe the wind was in a good direction and blowing the smoke and soot away. Someone, probably G, had made sure that we had plenty of beer aboard, and we cruised out into the middle of the river and dropped the anchor and passed the beer around. We sat there drinking and enjoying the beautiful night, the steady breeze, and the waves lapping on the boat. We talked about girls, who was getting a titty feel or a hand up the crotch. J.D. and ShiThead claimed they were getting hand jobs from their steadies, which made the rest of us jealous.

The conversation drifted to other topics, like G's dad's lawsuit and Palmisano's Market losing their deal to carry Amato's bread. It looked like the Bullshit Law Firm was putting together a pretty good case claiming that Cooper management had been irresponsible and negligent in the resin kettle incident. G's dad was struggling with mobility and adapting to life with only one foot. His brother was at boot camp at Fort Polk, and his mom was having a pretty hard time with all of it. J.D. said that Danny had been right about The Union trying to make a deal with Amato's to carry their products, which would mean that Palmisano's would no longer be able to carry them. This was going to happen, and it would be another blow to business for Palmisano's, which was struggling, like a lot of small local businesses, to compete with the big chains that were opening stores everywhere.

All this talk about his dad and the little stores getting screwed seemed to get G really worked up. We had all had a couple of beers since we anchored the boat, on top of what we'd had at the boathouse, but maybe G had scarfed down even more, because he seemed pretty plowed. He started going on about how he was fed up with all these assholes who didn't give a shit about anybody, and whatever happened to common decency, and how we should line these bastards up and give them a taste of their own medicine and kick the shit out of them and see how they like it. He was really worked up. And then, all of a sudden, out of the blue, he said, "Fuck it! I'm goin' for a swim," and he jumped off the back of the boat with all his clothes on, even his shoes.

It took us all completely by surprise and at first we were all kind of frozen in place on the boat. Then we woke up and ran to the stern and looked for G, but we couldn't see him. By now it was pitch black on the river, and the current was really strong. We looked and looked and didn't see him and we started to panic. Scourge and ShiThead took off their shoes and stripped down and jumped in, and just about that time G came to the surface, but he was already at least ten yards downstream from the boat. We could barely see him but we could tell that he was struggling to stay afloat, probably because of his clothes and shoes. J.D., Fumb, and I were left to figure out what the hell to do next.

Somehow, I had the presence of mind to open the locker at the stern and get out three life preservers, and I threw them out as far as I could. Fumb yelled to J.D., "Pull up the anchor! They're drifting away on the current really fast!" I was trying to keep my eye on the guys in the water so we didn't lose them completely, but they were rapidly floating far away from the boat, and I couldn't tell if any of them had managed to get hold of a life preserver.

I heard J.D. yell from the bow, "I can't get this damn thing loose! It's stuck on something on the bottom."

I said, "Fumb, can you help him? I don't want to lose sight of these guys. I can hardly see where they are now!"

Fumb ran forward and the two of them yanked and strained, but as big as Fumb was, they couldn't manage to get the anchor dislodged. I heard Fumb yell, "Just untie the damn rope!" He pulled with all his might on the rope to create a little slack so J.D. could untie it. When they got the rope untied, they tossed it in the river and the boat started to drift downstream. But by now the guys in the water had floated so far from the boat that I couldn't see them.

"I don't know where they are!" I yelled.

Fumb got in the driver's seat and started the engine. I didn't know if he'd ever driven a boat before, but he seemed to know what he was doing, or at least was doing a good job faking it. He swung the boat around in a really tight circle, trying to keep it more or less lined up with the direction that the current was taking the guys in the water. He gunned the engine and we jolted forward, then he slowed it down so that we wouldn't run over the guys by accident. J.D. and I were on the bow, staring out into the darkness, trying to see where they were. Pretty soon, J.D. spotted them ahead of us on the starboard side. "There they are!" he said. They had managed to grab one of the life preservers, and they were all holding onto it.

Fumb maneuvered the boat so they could climb up the ladder at the stern, and when they were all back on board, we all just stood there looking at each other, like, "Now what the fuck just happened?" But it didn't take long before we started giving G massive shit for his stupid move.

"What the hell were you thinking, asshole?" said ShiThead.

"You could have gotten yourself killed, and all of us too, idiot," said Scourge.

"Nice going, moron," I added.

"You're lucky I took that boating course at the yacht club," said Fumb.

"What? What boating course? What yacht club?" said J.D. "You're so full of shit."

So, in a matter of seconds, G's idiocy was forgotten, forgiven, and added to the growing corpus of Backfield lore. We cruised back to the boathouse and the swimmers dried off in the warm summer breeze. Well, not G; his clothes were not going to get dry in the breeze. We docked the boat, took inventory of the equipment, and adjourned to our upstairs sitting room, where we popped some more beers. One anchor gone, two life preservers gone. We agreed that Scourge should buy replacements, discreetly, at the marina, and we would all chip in to reimburse him. We even said that he didn't have to contribute, since we shamelessly and

regularly exploited him by using the boat and the boathouse. It was a rare gesture of courtesy and fairness on our
part, and we told him not to get used to it.

26

AFTER FUMB, SCOURGE, AND I DISCOVERED STRIEBIG'S, it didn't take us long to introduce the rest of the Backfield to this gem of a gin mill. The main attraction, of course, was that you didn't need proof to buy beer. A close second was the schupper, that enormous goblet of beer that was incredibly cheap, even by our miserly standards. And then the roast beef sandwiches. Oh my God, were they good. Both the beef on wick and the hot roast beef and gravy. In our area, these sandwiches were served in lots of bars and restaurants, and different places had their own versions and their own dedicated fans. Beef on wick is thin-sliced roast beef with lots of juice, piled on a hard roll with coarse salt and caraway seed baked into the top. Most people eat it with horseradish on it. The hard roll is called kimmelwick. Or sometimes you see it spelled kummelweck. So then it's beef on weck. Doesn't matter how you spell it, it's delicious. The hot roast beef and gravy sandwich is just what it sounds like—a piece of white bread covered in sliced roast beef in a tasty gravy, then another slice of white bread on top of that, then more gravy over the whole thing. Oh my God. Almost every time we went to Striebig's we would get one or the other of those.

Another reason we liked Striebig's was that there weren't any other kids around. I don't know why Striebig's hadn't been discovered by other underage tipplers. Probably other kids didn't appreciate the same things we did. We liked being in there with the old guys drinking shots and beers and playing euchre. It was usually fairly busy but never really crowded. We had a table that we kind of claimed for our own in the back room up against the wall. We could fit three guys on each side of it, very cozy. It was almost always waiting for us, nobody else sitting at it, when we came in. On the wall above the table was a fairly large, framed photo of three racehorses crossing the finish line at the same time. Printed on the photo was a caption, "Triple Dead Heat," and then underneath the framed picture there was a little sign that read: "First triple dead heat photo finish in a stakes race. Carter Handicap at Aqueduct Racecourse, June 1944." Why do I remember this? I've been asking myself that question for many years, even as I forget to buy milk at the grocery store or forget the name of the guy who's been cutting our grass since forever.

Mr. Striebig was always behind the bar, staring out into the room with his taped-open eyes. Usually Mrs. Striebig was in the kitchen, making roast beef sandwiches, and sometimes she would relieve him at the bar. She wasn't as pleasant as he was, maybe not too happy about spending her whole life in the bar or in the apartment upstairs. We'd sit at Striebig's and drink our schuppers and talk about BTU, and the Quelt House, and about trying to get laid, and about The Bat, and Helwig, and Freckles Kramden, and about all kinds of crazy shit that made no sense whatsoever. Somehow, we got on a tangent about balsa wood, and how balsa wood was a very underappreciated material, and how the engineering department at BTU had discovered that balsa wood could be used to build transmissions for cars, so that they would be much lighter and would get great gas mileage. I know this sounds totally ridiculous, because it is, and probably not even funny to anybody but us, and I almost hesitate to mention it, but this kind of insane foolishness was the stuff that only we could invent, and it belonged only to us, to the Backfield. Nobody else was in on it. It was our world, our parallel universe.

A lot of times we'd top off an evening at Striebig's with a short walk across the street to Nick's, the cool place. We could get a good buzz on at Striebig's for not much money, and then cruise on over to see what was shakin' at Nick's. Of course, first we'd have to settle up our tab. Whenever the time came for that, Scourge would always have to use the john. I think maybe one time he got away with it and the rest of us chipped in and paid the bill, and he thought he was very cagey to have gotten off without paying. He knew perfectly well that we weren't going to fall for that stunt more than once, but he did it every time and it became another of the Backfield legends. Good old Scourge, Scrooge—Tyler Lewis Barrett, TLB, Tight Little Bastard. One night at Striebig's we presented him with a filthy old sock from the football locker room, and told him he could use it to keep his precious treasure in. And son of a bitch, the little bastard did just that. Every time we went anywhere, he brought his sock with his money, and we knew from the smell that he never washed it.

One night, after an especially long and lusty session at Striebig's, we were headed out the door on our way over to Nick's to check out the scene. Scourge went out first, and he looked kind of unsteady, sort of swaying and weaving like he was losing his balance. All of a sudden, he took about five quick steps over the sidewalk and toward the street, and then he leaned way forward and tossed his cookies. Several schuppers of beer were launched into the gutter. It was more than just barfing. It was a classic projectile heave, and the sight of Scourge, silhouetted in the glow of the streetlight, blowing lunch in the street in front of Striebig's, will be forever etched in the memories of all Backfielders.

Striebig's was rivalling Angelo's as our favorite gin mill. Well, maybe that's not the right way to put it. Each place had its special charms. Striebig's was guys only; we never took girls there. And like I said, those cheap schuppers were hard to beat. At Angelo's you'd see a more varied clientele: young guys like us, older guys sitting around drinking and playing pool and reliving the glory days, girls in groups or with guys, old timers playing cards and drinking shots and beers and placing bets with Johnny V.

Whenever we got together, we would usually be at Gino's, Striebig's, Angelo's, or the boathouse. We didn't hang out at G's house anymore. With his father being laid up, it just didn't seem right or comfortable. But then we found that G's job at the Tate gave us another place to hang out. There we could see free movies and take advantage of make-out space in the balcony. If you wanted to go to the movies, all you had to do was find out from G when he would be there working as an usher and Linda Gregg would be working the ticket booth. You'd wait until no other customers were around, give Linda a nod, and head inside to the lobby. G would be taking tickets at the door, or in our case, not taking tickets, and you'd just walk into the theater. If you were by yourself, or with the guys, you'd find a seat on the main floor since the balcony was reserved for making out. It was weird, but even the adults seemed to recognize and honor this unwritten rule. If you were with a date, you'd head up to the balcony, find a spot as far away from other people as you could, and settle in. We would always avoid the smoking section, where the seats had built-in ash trays that always smelled bad.

I had taken Karen Reinhardt to the movies several times, but I wasn't getting anywhere in the make-out department. She'd do some French kissing, and I could get an occasional boob squeeze through her blouse and bra, but that was about it. I was getting really frustrated. One night I took her to see *Thunderball*. I figured she wouldn't be very interested, so maybe she'd be more susceptible to my amorous advances. I could always go see the movie again on my own. But no such luck. All of a sudden, she was really into James Bond. On the way home in the car I said something like, "Hey, we've been dating for quite a while now but you don't seem to want to get a bit more familiar," something stupid like that. She acted kind of offended and said,

"If you're talking about making out, or sex, you need to know that intimacy is supposed to be between a husband and a wife. I don't even feel right about what we're doing up there in that balcony. It seems like you just keep pushing me to do more stuff, like that's all you're interested in. You know it's immoral but you keep on doing it."

"What we're doing is immoral?" I said. "We're hardly doing anything at all."

"Well, Second Timothy says, 'Now flee from youthful lusts and pursue righteousness, faith, love, and peace, with those who call on the Lord from a pure heart.' My father says it's sinful to give in to lust before you're married. Even thinking about it is sinful. You should get your mind onto other things."

Did she just say that? Could she possibly believe that? Had she actually memorized that?

"Wait a minute," I said. "You mean that we're going to hell because we did some very minor making out in the balcony of the movie theater?"

"Well, we could be forgiven, but that's what the Bible says. Don't you believe what the Bible says?"

"Well, actually, if you really want to know," I said, "no, I really don't think I believe what's in the Bible. Who wrote the Bible? We have no idea. I know what we hear in church and confirmation class, I know all that. But it's all a lot of illogical stuff that isn't even consistent and goes against common sense. Like my dad says when my mom is going on and on about how we need to give money to missions so we can spread the Word to the heathens. You mean to tell me that millions, probably billions, of people are going to hell because they haven't accepted JC as their lord and savior? And they haven't even heard about him? And that's why we have to spread the Word, to save all these people from hell? Come on, give me a break. What about all the people who died before JC was even born? This stuff just makes no sense at all."

"I can't believe what I'm hearing from you, Chris," she said.

"I'm sorry," I said, "I don't want to offend you, but I think you've just been brainwashed for so many years that you can't even think objectively about this stuff. It goes against common sense; it's like fairy tale stuff."

"Well, there are many brilliant scholars and theologians, not just today, but for centuries, who have studied this and believe it's true. Not just my father, many many brilliant people. People smarter than you."

I knew I wasn't going to get anywhere arguing with her. We drove the rest of the way to Wittenberg, I dropped her off at her house, and that was the last time we went out together.

27

AFTER BREAKING UP—IF YOU WANT TO EVEN CALL IT THAT—with
Karen Reinhardt, I was in the market for a new female
friend. G was tight with Linda Gregg, ShiThead really had
the hots for Sally Summers, J.D. and Peggy Harrison were
going strong. Fumb had recently taken a liking to a girl
named Amy Strickland, whose family was in the funeral
home business. Scourge was still playing the field but
seemed to be quite interested in the daughter of a local den-
tist. Her name was Jill Long. We started describing her as
a "toothsome lass," of course. And later, when we found
out she was having a birthday, we told her that she was getting "Long in the tooth." We thought we were hilarious. The
girls just rolled their eyes. They did that a lot. Jill introduced
me to her friend, Lilly Stewart, who was the daughter of one
of the partners in the Bullshit Law Firm. Lilly was very cute
and seemed quite adventurous, so I felt pretty good about
my prospects.

Most romantic activities took place either in the balcony
of the Tate or in the back seat of somebody's car. There were

places you could park along the river that were fairly remote, and even if the cops saw a parked car or two, they would usually leave them alone. I guess they figured if nobody was causing any trouble, why not just leave well enough alone? But after a while we started bringing girls to the boathouse on occasion. We had discovered that nobody seemed to be paying any attention to us when we were there, just with the guys, so why not include the girls too. We were still careful to keep the noise down. We started playing some records, but not real loud. It did get a bit crowded if all six of us were there and we all had girls. We always made a point of having as few cars parked outside as possible, so we would meet somewhere and cram twelve people into two cars, three at the most.

None of the girls liked beer, so when they came to the boathouse, we had to expand the bar selections. Sloe gin and Squirt was an option, but after some taste trials we settled on the good old 7 and 7 as the girls' drink. Seagram's Seven Crown and 7-Up. That was a bit pricey, so we were thrilled when Fumb discovered Guckenheimer Reserve at State Street Liquors. Guck, as we soon came to call it, actually wasn't bad, even though it was on the bottom shelf in the liquor store, right next to the Kessler's. And it was even cheaper than Kessler's, if you can believe that. However, the girls objected to being served what they considered to be rotgut, so we had to keep a bottle of Seven Crown around so that we could refill it with Guck. Nobody ever knew the difference.

Date nights at the boathouse consisted of drinking, listening to records, talking, and making out. One of our favorite records was *The Freewheelin' Bob Dylan.* Lots of great songs on that album. The talking part would start out with guys and girls talking together, and then gradually separate into guys talking to guys and girls talking to girls. After a while, we would check the time, and realize that it was getting late, and we needed to get in some make-out time. Couples would match up and find spots in the main room where you could do some cuddling and kissing. For more privacy and more advanced levels of making out, you had to get creative. There was the bedroom, of course, which was the prime spot, but that would only serve two people. So we had to keep track of who had used the bedroom, so that next time somebody else could take a turn. Some romantic activities could happen in the main room with the lights off, because it was pitch dark in there. When the boat was in the water, you could sneak down there and climb onboard and snuggle into the cabin. And there were also the cars parked outside.

One of the first nights when all twelve of us were at the boathouse, we were sitting around drinking our beers and 7 and 7s, and just shooting the shit about this and that, kind of getting to know the girls, and the girls getting to know each other and all of us. I was a little surprised when J.D. said to Peggy, "So, your old man doesn't like you going out with a dago, eh?"

"What are you talking about?" she said.

"Well, Scourge heard your old man talking to some-body down at the marina, and that's what he said."

"Doesn't surprise me," she said. "My dad is a jerk. He thinks he's a real big shot, and that because he's the general manager at Cooper, he's really upper class. Even though he grew up down the street from a steel mill in Pittsburgh.

That's where my grandpa worked. My dad is ashamed of his background, which I think is really disgusting. My grandpa worked his tail off to send my dad and his two brothers to college, and now he walks around with his nose in the air, acting like a snob. Before we moved here, he wanted my brother to go to Choate, and he made him go, even though he didn't want to. And he said that when I was old enough for high school, I was going to Rosemary Hall."

"What? Wait a minute," said G. "He wanted your brother to choke?"

"No, asshole," said Scourge, "Choate is a boarding school. All boys. In Connecticut, I think. And Rosemary Hall is a girls' school."

"Well, that's a pretty stupid name," said G.

"So how did you manage to get out of going to Rosemary Hall?" ShiThead asked her.

"I just told him NO! I told him I wanted to go to high school with my friends. I didn't want to go off to some prissy place with a bunch of spoiled little brats. And when we moved here, which I didn't want to do, I told him if he was going to make me move, then I was going to go to high school in our new town. He backed off of Rosemary Hall, but then he started talking about Miss Turner's School, which is at least local but I still said no, I'm not going to school with a bunch of privileged, stuck-up little princesses. I threw such a fit about not wanting to move and leave my friends, and having to fit in to a totally new place, that I finally wore him down and he shut up about Miss Turner's School and said I could go to GHS."

I liked Peggy. She was pretty, and fun, and had a mind of her own. I was glad to hear that she wasn't tight with her old man, because that could have made things awkward with the lawsuit going on, especially since my new girl's father was heading up the lawsuit for G's dad. But at this point it was too early to say anything about the lawsuit with all these girls there. We had to make sure that we could trust everybody to understand that what was said in the boathouse, stayed in the boathouse.

When the new TV show *Get Smart* started, it was great because it was on Saturday night, and that's the night that we were usually at the boathouse. We'd gather around the portable black and white TV with its rabbit ears antenna. We loved *Get Smart*. At least the guys did. The girls thought it was stupid and not funny at all. But we got so much great material from observing the adventures of Smart (Agent 86), and 99, and the Chief, and Siegfried, and Shtarker, and the rest. We loved Smart's phrases, and we used them every chance we got, much to the girls' annoyance: "Would you believe...," "Missed it by *that much*," "Sorry about that, Chief," "...and *loving* it." And the Cone of Silence. Hilarious.

One Saturday night, Lilly brought a bottle of Drambuie that she had lifted from her old man's liquor cabinet. None of us knew what the hell it was or how you were supposed to drink it. All we knew was that it said "liquor," well, actually "liqueur," so we figured it was booze and that was all that mattered. Probably at that point none of us had ever tasted scotch, so when we sampled the Drambuie it was kind of a shocker. Somebody had a large orange drink from McDonald's, so we mixed the Drambuie with that, if you can believe it. It tasted pretty bad, but that didn't stop us from drinking the whole thing. Drambuie and McDonald's orange, and beer, and 7 and 7s. We got pretty wasted that night, and Lilly earned a spot in the Backfield Hall of Fame for introducing us to such a sophisticated drink. More things to drink. As we were always fond of saying, "Too much of a good thing is not enough!"

28

AS ALWAYS, THE SUMMER WAS GOING BY TOO FAST. The only good thing was that summer football practice was starting up. But the pressure was really on. This was our last chance to beat BI. Three losses in a row was unheard of. Of course, as members of the freshman and JV teams we didn't really have anything to do with two of those losses, but that didn't matter. We were on the varsity last year and we lost that one too. It was up to us to put an end to this losing streak, and everybody knew how much was riding on this season, for the team, for the town, and surely for Helwig.

Talk about Helwig had intensified. It seemed like the mutterings that had been going on for a couple of years had come more out into the open. Some people were even saying that maybe it was time for him to go. As players, we really didn't know what to think or how to react. Hey, he was our coach, he was a legend, he was the leader of our team. We had to believe in him and follow him. We needed to have passion, to be all in, to believe that we could be the best, that we were the best, that we could win it all, damn it! We talked about this at the boathouse a few days before practice started.

"I think we need to tune all this shit out," said ShiThead. "All these assholes in town are shooting their mouths off about stuff they don't know anything about. Most of them have never set foot on a football field. They read stuff in the paper and they sit around at the bar and just throw around all kinds of bullshit. We gotta stop listening to all this shit and focus on the game. We gotta run our plays with *precision*. No mistakes. Take it to 'em. Every time. I know I sound like I'm giving a Helwig pep talk. But basically, that's what I think we gotta do. Do it the way we've been taught and the way we know how."

"I think you're right," said Fumb. "We have to focus, and we can't be listening to all the gossip all the time. We should tune that out. But I wouldn't be honest if I didn't admit that Helwig's got some issues going on. He's obviously drinking. Sometimes a lot, I think. And let's face it, he's totally stuck on the single wing. Nobody, nobody else runs it anymore. OK, we're good at it, Ganaway has been running it forever. But seriously, isn't it time to modernize? I don't know. I don't want to cause problems. We need to stick together. We need to stick with Helwig. Yeah. Whatever."

"I totally agree with all that," said Scourge. "I think we just need to focus, like both of you guys said. Yeah, Helwig's not perfect, but there's no way we can win consistently if we're going to be second guessing everything. We can't let ourselves get distracted with griping and complaining about this or that. Too many cooks spoil the broth. We've got to kick ass, stick with the program, and do absolutely the very best job we can every game, every play." That seemed to sum up the feelings of the whole group.

———

ON OUR FIRST DAY OF SUMMER PRACTICE, everybody was in high spirits. We were seniors now, and we relished being the leaders of the team. Of course, you felt a lot more like a leader if you were a starter and not a bench warmer. I would have loved to beat out G for starting QB, but that wasn't going to be an easy thing to accomplish. He was still bigger, stronger, and quicker than me, and a better blocker. I had to be honest with myself and admit that. I did believe I was a better passer, and probably had more finesse on some plays from the wing-T. But that wouldn't matter unless we made some significant changes to our offense.

The locker room was noisy and alive, everybody excited to be there. The first few days of practice we wore just shorts, shoulder pads, and helmets. We got dressed quickly, and once we were all out on the field, Helwig gathered us all around and directed us up into the bleachers, where we sat maybe ten guys to a row, starting about the third row. Once we were all settled in, the coaches came up the steps and stood in front of the first row facing us. We were all surprised, maybe even shocked, to see Coach Tim Parker walk up the steps with the others. What was the JV coach doing here at varsity practice? Helwig walked in front of the other coaches and looked up at us and started talking.

"Boys," he said, "we are about to embark on a mission. A mission to answer the question that someone asked in a letter to the editor of the newspaper last year. That question was, 'Has Ganaway lost its swagger?' The person who wrote that letter suggested that the answer to that question was, 'Yes, Ganaway has lost its swagger. Ganaway has slipped. Ganaway football is not what it used to be. The Ganaway Rivermen are no longer feared by their opponents. The Ganaway Rivermen are no longer the team to beat, the team that will run over you, will crush you. The Ganaway Rivermen have had their day.'

"Is that true, boys? Do you believe that?"

We weren't sure if we were supposed to answer that or what. Helwig said it again.

"Do you believe what that person said in the newspaper? Do you?" he yelled.

"NO!" we screamed, "NO!"

"That's what I want to hear!" said Helwig. "No, Ganaway has not lost its swagger! And we're going to prove it this season! We're going to work our tails off to be the BEST at our game. We're going to play Ganaway football. We're going to be tough and we're going to run over them on offense and we're going to be a brick wall on defense. We're going to be unstoppable, and we're going to be impenetrable. And in order to do that, it's going to take every man on this team to work harder than he has ever worked before. When you think you can't run another drill, you're going to run five more drills! When you think you can't run another wind sprint, you're going to run five more wind sprints! We are going to be the toughest, meanest, best prepared team this conference has ever seen.

"But we're going to be one more thing. We're going to be smart. We're going to do what we've always done, and do it to perfection, and we're also going to be making a few changes. You'll notice that Coach Tim Parker is with us today. As some of you know, Mr. Parker was a standout quarterback at Bucknell. In addition to heading up the JV team, he's going to be working alongside Coach Rudnik, Coach Carpenter, and me this year. His main responsibility will be the JV team, so he won't be working full-time with the varsity, but he's going to be working with our offensive backfield to change things up a bit."

Holy shit! To most people, what Helwig said would probably not make much of an impression at all. But if you knew anything about Helwig, and Ganaway football, this was quite a shocker. Was Helwig getting the message, waking up? Did he really believe we needed to make some changes in our approach? It sounded like it. But only time would tell. For me, a move to more plays from T formation would be great. Maybe I'd get more playing time. I could only hope.

After Helwig talked to us, the other coaches each had a short message, and then with a huge "Go Ganaway!" we headed out onto the field. We never practiced in the actual stadium, but we did use the track to run conditioning laps sometimes, and that's what we did that day. After running a mile, we trooped across the street to the practice field and started running through all our usual drills. Then we split into offense and defense, Coach Rudnik heading up the defense, Carpenter and Parker working with the offense, Helwig overseeing the whole thing. I was excited when Parker took Fumb and me aside and had us practice snaps, with me under center in T formation. Then he had me take some snaps, go back to pass, and throw some passes to various receivers. We did this for quite a while, and he told me to do different things and critiqued me on my moves and technique. It felt great to get that much attention. He brought G over too and had him do the same stuff. G still had the inside edge, both for single wing and T, but I was obviously being taken seriously. We also worked on handoffs. The time went by very fast, and before I knew it, Helwig was blowing the whistle and calling the whole team together.

"OK, boys, looking good, looking good. Good energy out there, good fire. But we've got lots of work to do. We don't win the conference without every man putting out his best effort, every practice, every game. We've got to be smart, and disciplined, and tough. We've got to take it to 'em, and run over 'em, and run through 'em."

Uh oh, I thought, this sounds awfully familiar. What happened to the "making a few changes" that he had talked about before practice started? He did say we've got to be smart. Maybe that was something to hold onto. But I was thinking that Parker was going to have his work cut out for him.

Helwig finished his talk and we headed for the locker room, and I tried to put negative thoughts out of my mind. This was just the first day of practice. We had two weeks before our first game against Eastport. Senior year. This was my last chance to show what I could do—if I could manage to get off the bench and onto the field.

29

ON THE AVERAGE DAY, THERE WASN'T A LOT GOING ON in the Twin Cities, nothing very exciting, no BI-G news. You'd open the *Courier-Tribune*, which even back then didn't amount to much, and turn to the sports page, then the comics, then maybe "Keglers Corner" for bowling news, then scan the stories about the school board meeting, or common council meeting, see a picture of a little kid with a cute dog, or a kid holding up a fish he'd caught in the river, that kind of stuff. But one Saturday the headline, in large type like it might have been talking about the end of World War II, was "Fire at The Union." Subtitle: "Cause Unknown, Being Investigated." Holy shit! That really was big. My first thought was that I hoped nobody got hurt, like G's girl-friend's sister, who worked there. Or anybody, of course.

The story in the paper said that a fire, which may have started in a dumpster behind the store, had burned a fairly large section of the store, mostly in the behind-the-scenes area. Firefighters had battled it for several hours before bringing it under control. Nobody was hurt. Damn, pretty serious. I finished reading the story, flipped through the few remaining pages, and was just about to fold it up and put it away when I saw a small headline in the "News from Around the Area" section. It said, "Vandals Hit Ironton Bakery." It was just a short blurb, and it said that overnight, someone had thrown a brick through a window of Amato's bakery in Ironton. Nobody was present when it happened, and the incident was under investigation by police.

My first thought was, oh my God, this sounds mighty fishy. I had to talk to J.D. I called him and asked if he'd seen the paper. He had, but he couldn't really talk about it on the phone. We decided that I'd pick him up and we could go somewhere and talk. We went to McDonald's, which had opened a location in town just about a year ago, near our only strip mall. We ordered our usual, the 3-2-1. That was three cheeseburgers, two fries, one Coke. I wish I could eat like that now. We sat in the car, chowing down on our healthy lunch, and talking about the stories in the paper.

"I don't know," I said, "when I saw that second story about a brick getting tossed through the window at Amato's, it was just too much of a coincidence. Or not a coincidence. You know what I mean."

"Yeah," said J.D., "I do know what you mean. You're thinking Danny. Me too. I'm absolutely sure that my old man would not have had anything to do with this. You know he doesn't want anything to do with the mob, or whatever the hell it is anymore. But Danny, he's always talking about how he's part of the family. He really wants to be thought of as part of the family. And the Rizzos definitely do have some shady connections, shall we say. I wouldn't put it past him to think that if he could mess up The Union deal with

Amato's, that he'd be doing the Palmisano family a huge favor. I'm worried about what Rocco might do. As you may have noticed, he doesn't have a lot of love for Danny. I just hope he doesn't blow his cool and get this whole thing out in the open."

"Do you think Danny has the right connections that he could orchestrate this?" I said.

"I don't know. I didn't think so, but then he pulled off the thing with your dad. So maybe he does have some influence somewhere. Or maybe he's just doing this shit on his own. I imagine that brick that got tossed through the window at Amato's had a note on it. And I'm sure the Amato family hasn't forgotten about their place getting burned down almost fifty years ago. Danny is fucking nuts to do this. I mean, a brick through your window is one thing. But starting a fire at a major grocery store, part of a big chain? This is another one of those things where it's going to be best for nobody to say anything about anything. That's why I said I hope Rocco can keep his mouth shut. And I hope Danny doesn't get all pumped up and brag to somebody about it. Jesus."

We finished our lunch and I dropped J.D. off at his house. He said, "I'll call you later if I find out anything."

I went home and talked my brother into running some pass patterns for me. He was a good athlete, had a lot of natural athletic ability, and even though he was in grammar school he could catch the ball and run some pretty good patterns. We did this for about a half hour and then my mom came out of the house and yelled, "Chris, telephone for you!"

"OK," I yelled back. I thanked Sam and said he'd done

a good job, told him we'd do it again someday soon. I went into the kitchen and picked up the phone.

"What's up, J.D.?"

"Hey, Croc. We're going to the boathouse tonight, aren't we?"

"Yeah," I said, "I assume so. That's the usual plan."

"Well, I'm afraid there's some shit I have to tell everybody about. Obviously about what you and I talked about. But they have to keep everything a complete, total secret. We can't have any girls. Can you help me contact everybody and tell them to show up, but no girls? If they can't ditch the girls, then they can't come, and I'll have to find another time to talk to them."

"Sure," I said, "yeah. What time?"

"How about 9:00? But call Scourge first, and if there's any problem with the boathouse, call me right back, OK?"

"Will do," I said.

As soon as I hung up, I called Scourge. His mom said he was working at the marina. I got the phone book and looked up the number, called the marina. When somebody answered, I said, "Can I please talk to Tyler Barrett?"

The guy said just a minute and I heard him yell, "Ty—telephone!"

"Can I help you?" Scourge asked when he picked up the phone.

I gave him a quick summary of what was going on, without getting into any of the details. He said nine o'clock at the boathouse was fine. I called J.D. back and told him I would call the other three guys, and let him know if there were any problems. It took me a couple of hours to track everybody down, but we got it set up and the meeting was on.

When the group was assembled at the boathouse, we cracked some beers and J.D. laid out what we were there for.

"Guys," he said, "did everybody see the story in the paper about the fire at The Union?" Everybody grunted or nodded.

"How about the little short article about vandalism at Amato's?" he asked.

I think a couple of guys had missed that, and J.D. filled them in.

"Here's the thing, guys," he said. "There's going to be a lot of talk about this. And I've got some information I'm going to share with you, but you must absolutely swear on your oath as members of the Backfield to keep everything that is said here tonight absolutely confidential."

Everybody nodded their heads. Then Scourge said, "Everyone, raise your left hand, grab your balls, and repeat after me: 'I do solemnly swear, upon fear of castration, that I shall not reveal to any creature, living or dead, a single word that is spoken here tonight, so help me Batshit Baxter.'"

"All right, asshole," said J.D. "Very funny. OK, so listen up. I'll get right to the point. I think there's a good chance that my dipshit brother-in-law, Danny Rizzo, had something to do with both the fire at the Union and the brick through the window at Amato's. And here's why I say that. I'm going to be perfectly frank. Danny is a pretty stupid fuck and he thinks that he is not totally loved and accepted by our family. The Palmisano family. My brother Rocco gives him a hard time once in a while but regardless, Danny is married to my sister and he is definitely part of the family. He's just insecure or something. Remember when we all had dinner at our house and Danny was talking about how The Union was going to get a deal with Amato's to sell their bread, and so Palmisano's would lose one of its main attractions? Maybe its only attraction? Well, I have no idea how he might have known about that, but the Rizzos have some connections that we don't talk about, so maybe he does have some kind of inside information. And even though it seems pretty far-fetched, I think it's possible that he could have had something to do with the two things you read about in the paper. In his twisted mind, it'd send a message to both The Union and Amato's that they'd better cancel the bread deal."

"Is he really that stupid?" said Scourge. "Commit arson over a bread deal?"

"Yeah, he's definitely stupid enough to do something like that," said J.D. "Now I'm not saying he actually did it. Just that he's capable of it."

"Well, remember when I was asking about 'protection' and you told us about Amato's getting burned down back in 1920 or something?" said G. "Would Danny know about that?"

"Oh yeah, I'm sure he would," said J.D. "Hey, look, the reason I'm telling you all this is because if the stupid fuck did do something like what we're talking about, even though he's an asshole, we don't want him to get caught. So I had to let you guys in on this. So if anybody says anything about it, you guys just gotta act totally clueless. You know what I mean?"

Everybody nodded and mumbled. "Yeah, right, sure."

"OK, good," said J.D. "That's all I wanted to say. So yeah, we're cool."

"So what else is new?" said Fumb.

"I don't know what's new, but I've got a question," said ShiThead. "How many bars are there on Samuels Street?"

"Geez, I don't know," said Fumb. "All I know is there's a shitload. Why do you wanna know?"

"Well, I was just thinking, maybe we should see how many bars we could drink a beer in. Set some kind of Guinness World Record."

Everybody's ears perked up at that. "Actually, that's a pretty cool idea," said G.

"Well, not all of us are eighteen yet," I said.

"I know," said G, "but why not just go in and order beers and see what happens?"

"Yeah," said ShiThead, "seriously, let's do it. What have we got to lose?"

So, that's what we did. I don't remember how many cars we had, or who drove from the boathouse. We parked, hit a few bars within walking range, drove down the street a little farther, parked, hit some more bars. I also don't remember how many bars we chalked up that night. I do remember that almost all of them served us, no questions asked, and that we hit enough of them to get pretty shit-faced. This wasn't the only time we tried to conquer Samuels Street. We came up with a song about it, which we sang to the tune of "When Johnny Comes Marching Home." It went like this:

> *We're out to conquer Samuels Street, Haroo!*
> *Haroo!!*
> *We're gonna get blitzed before we're through,*
> *Haroo! Haroo!*
> *Oh, our fame will grow both near and far*
> *As we drink a beer in every bar,*
> *And we'll all feel proud when we conquer Samuels*
> *Street!*

Seems to me we never made it past the Polish Eagle, and truthfully, we really didn't try it that many times. But truth was never a big thing with us, and the quest to conquer Samuels Street became a legend. And if trying to conquer Samuels Street wasn't stupid enough, we added another challenge. Every once in a while, when the spirits moved us, we'd all pile into Fumb's Chevy and drive into the City and see how many times we could drive around Hollowell Circle. This was a traffic circle where several of the beautiful old parkways converged, and there was a very classy, small old hotel right there on the circle, and usually there was a doorman or some employee standing out in front. We would make laps around the circle until it looked like the doorman was going to yell at us or maybe call the cops, and then we'd screech away down one of the parkways and head back to Ganaway, safe in our familiar blue-collar world, and we'd get in our cars and weave our way home to our respective houses, where we'd try to sound sober to any parents who might be waiting up for us. And then pass out in bed.

30

LEADING UP TO OUR FIRST GAME OF OUR SENIOR YEAR, I was feeling pretty fired up. Coach Parker was working with the offense, concentrating strictly on the T formation. G and I were both running plays from the T in practice, but I felt that I actually had the edge. He was still the clear lead guy on the single wing. With only a couple weeks for practice, we had a lot of ground to cover, but we were making progress. My passing was good, I was getting back in the pocket quickly, and finding my receivers, and throwing hard and with good accuracy. We were running handoffs, pitch-outs, options, all the stuff that went with the T. It seemed like Parker must be making some headway with Helwig, but until we got into a real game, we wouldn't know for sure.

A couple days before our first game against Eastport, Parker took G and me aside during practice. "Simpson, Gorlukovich," he said, "you've probably figured out by now that you're going to be sharing the QB duties this year. As you know, my main job is JV coach, so when summer practice ends, I'm not going to be able to spend as much time working with the varsity offense. But I am going to try to be at varsity practice, at least for a part of it, as often as I can. And I'll be on the sidelines with Coaches Helwig, Carpenter, and Rudnik at all the games. Gorlukovich, you're going to be running the single wing, Simpson, you'll run from the T. Mostly you're going to be calling your own plays, based on what you see on the field. But you can expect plays to be sent in too. We're going to mix it up, keep our opponents on their toes. Coach Helwig has let me have a lot of input, but he's still the coach. What he says, goes. OK? You got all that?" We told him that, yes, we got it. This was going to be a season like nothing we had seen before in our high school career.

In the locker room after practice, I had a chance to ask G how things were going with his dad, how he was doing with rehab, what was up with the lawsuit. He said he thought things were going as well as could be expected. His dad was working hard trying to adapt to having just one foot. He didn't know a lot of details about the lawsuit, said he thought they were trying to determine if they had enough evidence to make a case that there had been willful negligence.

When I got home, Donna was just pulling into the driveway. My sister and I didn't talk much, even though we lived in the same house. We made a point of not talking about the old man situation, but I knew she felt bad for him, and that day she broke our silence.

"I know Dad is really hurting," she said. "We're not supposed to talk about it, I know, but I can tell how humiliated and depressed he is, having to work for Grandpa Lindke and everything. He must have really gotten himself in some serious trouble. I guess the only good news is that things seem to be going OK overall now. I just hate to see him looking so sad all the time, and not talking, and going down in the basement every night. I saw that he's building some really beautiful cabinets or furniture or something down there. I don't know what he's going to do with it. I wish I could talk to him but everything just feels so weird."

"I know," I said, "I feel that way too. But seriously, it's best if we just let him work it out. Him and Mom, I guess. I think I heard him say something to her about making those cabinets for specific people. Like he's taking orders for custom stuff and selling it. If that's true, then that's a really good thing, I think. Even if he's basically miserable, that's something he's really good at, and if he can make some extra money doing it, that would make Mom happy, for sure. And he sure has access to a huge supply of top-grade lumber for whatever he's making."

"Yeah, that's true," she said.

"On a different subject, you ever hear anybody at Cooper talking about what happened to Pete Gorlukovich's dad?"

"Well, I did hear some talk, but nothing very specific. Just basically that he hurt his ankle real bad. We're not supposed to discuss stuff like that."

"Well, you do know that his 'bad' accident resulted in his whole foot being amputated, right? I'm sure I told you about that."

"That's really terrible," she said.

"Yeah, terrible is right. Now he's out of work and he doesn't know if he'll ever be able to find any kind of decent job. I'm sure something like that would generate some kind of report that's filed away somewhere. Would that be something that your office would get involved with?"

"It's not something that I would personally get involved with, but yes, the personnel office would get reports of safety issues and accidents, that sort of thing," she said.

"Well, could you ask around, or maybe not ask but look around, and see if you can find any reports or anything about resin kettles malfunctioning? Not just about Mr. Gorlukovich's accident. Any reports of problems that may have happened over the last year, or two or three years, even? Involving the kettles."

"Gee, I don't know, Chris. If I start snooping around in files and stuff I could probably get in some big trouble."

"Yeah, but you could be really careful. You do work in the personnel department. Aren't there times when you're alone, or nobody's paying attention to what you're doing, when you could see if you could find files with accident reports and that kind of stuff?"

"Chris, I don't want to get fired!"

"I'm not asking you to do anything that would get you fired. Just casually look around, see if you can find out where accident or safety reports are kept. And how many reports there are. And how hard it would be to find things. Maybe it's not even possible. I'm just asking you to do that much right now. How dangerous could that be?"

"Well, let me think about it, and see what I think after I look around the office. I feel like some kind of spy."

"All we're trying to do is make sure G's dad gets a fair shake, gets what he deserves. If that machine had problems with malfunctioning, and if the company knew about it and did nothing, then that's not right. Accidents happen, sure.

And there's workmen's comp to pay people when they get hurt. But if it's something that could have been prevented, and the problem was just ignored, then that's more than just an accident. Anyway, that's what Tyler Barrett says. You know his dad's a lawyer and his firm handles this kind of stuff so they've seen lots of cases and they know what they're talking about. You want to do what's right, don't you?"

The reason I knew as much as I did about workmen's comp was that Scourge had explained some stuff to us. Like there was actually a schedule that laid out what you get if you lose a finger, or a hand, or an arm, or a foot. It seemed really disgusting to think about a price list for amputated body parts. But the whole workmen's comp thing was supposedly designed to cut down on lawsuits and all that expense and avoid all kinds of delays so that injured workers didn't have to wait forever to get some kind of settlement. But there were exceptions, if you could make the proper case, and of course that's where the lawyers came in. The workmen's comp law was written to make it very hard to bring a lawsuit outside of the scheduled settlement. That didn't mean it was impossible, but it was a high bar to prove that there was intent or willful neglect that caused an injury.

You can say what you want about ambulance chasers, and no doubt there are lots of shady lawyers who will push the limits every chance they get. But the case with G's dad just seemed to have some real possibilities that it was more than an unavoidable accident. Was that actually the very first time that agitator blade started turning when it shouldn't have? When the kettle was empty and a person might be inside it?

———

I TOLD G ABOUT MY CONVERSATION WITH DONNA as we were suiting up for the Eastport game. He said he really appreciated it but didn't want her to get in any trouble. I said not to worry, I didn't even know if she'd do anything, and anyway, she was the careful, cautious type.

It was nice to have the Eagles as our first game of the season. All reports indicated that they were going to be their usual mediocre, uninspiring selves. Of course, you didn't want to get overconfident and underestimate them, or any team, because that's the way you get your ass handed to you and look like fools. But this would be a logical game for us to try out our new modernized offense, and if that happened, I'd be getting quite a bit of time on the field.

The first time we had the ball, G was sent out onto the field. That was disappointing. Maybe Parker hadn't made that much headway with Helwig after all. And when we scored on our first possession, I didn't know if that meant we'd stick with the single wing, or if that would give us a chance to give our new stuff a try. I got my answer pretty fast. We kicked off, our defense stopped them, and they didn't get a first down. As they lined up to punt, Helwig grabbed me by my shoulder pads and said, "Simpson, get in there. Show me what you can do." Holy shit! I was going in on the second possession of our first game. Man, the pressure's on, I thought.

I was nervous as hell as I watched their punter set up for the kick. The center snapped the ball, not a good snap, almost over the kicker's head. He managed to catch it, but it threw his rhythm off and it gave our defense a little more time to come at him. He managed to get the kick off, but it was blocked by one of our guys and we recovered the ball on maybe the thirty-yard line. What a great break! I ran out onto the field and we huddled up. I think the first play I called was a handoff, something safe, nothing fancy. Then another running play. We were something like third and five. OK, here goes, I thought. Fake handoff to ShiThead, I go back in the pocket, spot Scourge open right over the middle, uncork a classic spiral, and he's got it! He breaks a tackle, turns upfield, then heads for the corner with another guy right on his heels. The guy trips him up just as he reaches the goal line, but he falls into the end zone. Touchdown! Yes! Oh my God, I'll never forget that feeling. Senior year, first game, first pass, complete! Touchdown!

It was a home game and the hometown fans loved it. I trotted off the field feeling like a total hot shit. I don't know if I've ever felt better than that in my whole life. Dudek went out and kicked his second extra point of the game. By halftime we were ahead 28-0. Dudek missed the extra point on the third touchdown, and we ran for a two-point conversion on the fourth touchdown. In the locker room, Helwig was fired up. He was also drunk. Not too drunk, but when you're around people who drink a lot, you get to know the signs, even if they're subtle. I'm not sure if everyone on the team knew it, and right then it really didn't matter. We were riding high, and if the coach was a bit high, that was just fine and dandy.

After a rousing pep talk—Helwig was seriously good at that—we gathered around him, put in our hands, and yelled "Go Ganaway!" at the top of our lungs, and then ran clanging and banging up the stairs and back out onto the field.

We ran away with that game. It actually got a little embarrassing, we were running up the score so bad. Helwig put G in for a while, and we ran the good old 46 Power stuff all over them. One of the plays I called when I was in there was a razzle dazzle deal that we'd worked on just a few times in practice. I took the snap from Fumb, handed off to ShiThead, who turned around and flipped it back to me, I passed it to J.D. on my left, and he let loose a bomb to Scourge running down the right sideline. It was a perfect throw and Scourge trotted the last fifteen yards into the end zone. The home stands erupted! People were jumping up and down and hugging each other and screaming and hooting at the top of their lungs. Wow. Talk about swagger! Has Ganaway lost its swagger? Hell, no!

The score got so lopsided that Helwig put in the entire second string for most of the fourth quarter. I don't think we scored again, and Eastport did score a touchdown, but it was a complete blowout. Final score: Ganaway 53, Eastport 7. The locker room was a madhouse, everybody yelling and slapping each other and going nuts. Helwig said a few words and everybody cheered and pumped their fists in the air and started chanting, "Yay, Coach! Yay, Coach! Yay, Coach!" Definitely a high point of our football career up to that time.

We didn't go to the boathouse after the game, because we wanted to be seen and soak up the love and admiration of our classmates and fans. We hit Gino's first, which was packed as usual on a Friday night, and got some pizza. After a little while, we headed across and up the street to Angelo's for some more slaps on the back and some beers. Didn't have to pay for a single beer that night. Everybody there wanted to buy us a beer. And everybody was talking about the razzle dazzle play. Every one of the Backfield had been in on that one, all except G, because you can only have one QB on the field. But G got his share of praise and worship for running over Eastport like a steam roller. Ganaway had its swagger back.

31

THE SATURDAY AFTER THE EASTPORT GAME I really wanted to sleep in and sleep off the previous night's revels. But because it was football season, I couldn't work at the Stenzel Agency after school, so I would usually go in on Saturdays. Mr. Stenzel was almost always there, for at least part of the day. Mostly I was doing filing, but sometimes he'd have me type up some policies or correspondence. I was actually a pretty good typist. I'd taught myself touch typing from a manual that my mom had at home. When I got home from work I had a message that J.D. had called. I called him back and he said that we were all going to meet at Striebig's at such-and-such a time to continue the celebration of our blowout victory.

I don't remember if I took my mom's car or if Fumb picked me up, but he and I were the first ones there, and we ordered schuppers. The other guys dribbled in and pretty soon everybody was there except Scourge, enjoying their schuppers and talking about the Eastport game and the Summit game coming up. After about twenty minutes,

Scourge came busting in and came over to the table—our regular table—and sat down, all excited.

"Guys, guys, you won't believe what I found up in our attic," he said.

"In your attic?" said Fumb.

"Yeah, I was up in the attic looking for some old serving dishes for my mom, and I was digging around in all this shit and I got started looking through some old pictures and clippings and files and boxes, and I came across some old records and this was in there with them. Look at it." He held it up so all of us could see it. It was an old 33 rpm record and on the cover it said, "TRILLBLOW RECORDS. BATTLE AT THUNDERBLOW. WINDESMEAR vs. BOOMER. PART 1."

"What the hell is that all about?" said ShiThead.

"Oh my God. You won't believe it! It is so hilarious! It's about a farting contest. We've gotta go to the boathouse and listen to it. Seriously. You won't believe it."

"Well, have a schupper and we'll have another one and then we can go over, OK?" said Fumb.

"OK, OK. But I can't wait for you to hear this."

So we all got a schupper and sat around talking and drinking for another fifteen or twenty minutes, then we paid the tab. We did not let Scourge escape to the bathroom. He was just itching to have us listen to this record.

"C'mon! C'mon! Let's go. You gotta hear this!"

"OK, calm down," said ShiThead. "It can't be that funny."

"Oh my God, yes, it is! You won't believe it. It's so hilarious!"

"Yeah, I think you said that before."

So we piled out of Striebig's, got in our cars, and headed
for the boathouse. Once we were settled in and had popped
some beers, somebody said, "OK, now what the hell do you
have here to show us?"

"OK, here we go," said Scourge. "Just wait. Here, listen." And he took the record out of the sleeve and put it on
the turntable. Transcribing the record doesn't begin to do it
justice; you have to listen to this hilarious thing. But here's
how it starts:

> *Announcer*: How do you do, ladies and gentle-
> men. It is our privilege to bring you an eyewit-
> ness report of the first international crepitation
> contest. We are speaking to you from the ring-
> side of the great Maple Leaf Auditorium, which
> is packed to the rafters with spectators, eager
> and curious. For the benefit of my listeners who
> are not acquainted with the facts relating to this
> event, it might be well to describe the two contes-
> tants. Lord Windesmear, from Wopping Foghole
> in Devonshire, is of course the champion of the
> British Empire. The challenger is Paul Boomer,
> native of Australia, who, I understand, worked
> his way to Canada on an ocean freighter carry-
> ing a load of Melbourne cabbage, upon which,
> so it is stated, Boomer trains exclusively. Ah, I
> see now there is a bit of a flurry around Lord
> Windesmear's entrance, and yes, here he comes,
> Lord Windesmear. I'll see, I'll see if I can get
> him to come to the microphone and say a few
> words. Joe, Joe, so will you see if you can get his

lordship to come over here for a few minutes? Tell him it's for the radio.

Joe: Ok, I'm gonna get him for ya.

Announcer: Thanks. Well, Lord Windesmear seems to be in good spirits. He's smiling and chatting. Thrown about him is a beautiful silk dressing gown of purple velvet, upon which is worked what I imagine to be the coat of arms of the House of Windesmear. It's a beautiful thing. Uh, good boy, Joe! In just a minute, ladies and gentlemen, I think we're going to have his lordship himself come to the microphone and say a few words. Right over here, please, right over here. Yes, right here. Yes, folks, here he is. Right in the microphone, the champion himself, Lord Windesmear. Your Lordship, how did you come to take an interest in this unusual art?

Lord Windesmear (*aristocratic British accent*): Well, I suppose you could say it all started over Lady Windesmear's fan.

Announcer: I see.

Lord Windesmear: Yes, I noticed she was constantly waving this fan in front of her face, so I asked her why the deuce she did it. And so she retorted that if I constantly insisted on crepitating, she had to fan away in pure self-defense, you see. So my friends were drawn into the controversy, and persuaded me to capitalize on my proficiency and sort of, eh, sort of go in for it and all that. That, that's all.

Announcer: Thank you very much, Your Lordship. Thank you, and good luck to you. That was Lord Windesmear, the champion crepitator of the British…oh, and here's the challenger, here's Paul Boomer from Australia. Paul, over here please. Please ask Mr. Boomer to come over here, please. The radio, we want him to speak on the radio. Just a moment, ladies and gentlemen, I think we'll have Paul Boomer for you right away. Yes, here he comes. His attendants have just pointed us out. And, heh heh, howdy Paul. Heh heh heh. He just waves his hand in greeting and starts walking over to the microphone. And here, ladies and gentlemen, is Mr. Paul Boomer. Uh, will you say hello to our audience, Mr. Boomer?

Paul Boomer (*working man's Aussie accent*): Hello, Canada!

Announcer: Uh, now tell me sir, when did you first realize that you were proficient enough to take a, uh, 'shot' at the empire championship?

Paul Boomer: Well, ever since I was a little nipper I liked to fart. I remember I used to make me mother and father laugh their bleedin' 'eads off when I used to let one go in church during the announcements of the Ladies' Aid.

Announcer: Eh, excuse me, Mr. Boomer. On the radio we call it, eh, crepitating.

Paul Boomer: Now, look here, copper. What I always says is, a fart's a fart, whether you raise up on one cheek and sneak, or whether you give it a full blast like I do.

Announcer: Heh heh, very well. As long as the BBC has no objection, I personally find the four-letter word much easier to say, and uh, more descriptive than the longer and more academic crepitating.

From here the record goes on to give a vivid "blow by blow" account of the farting contest, complete with hilarious sound effects as the two contestants take their turns at the "farting post." Different farts have specific names, like "fundesbreak," "sissler," "fudgiefart," "triple flutterblast," "fragrant fuzzy," and "little freep," and each one counts for a certain number of points. Seriously, this thing is hilarious. As many times as we listened to it after that first day, we always laughed our asses off. As you might imagine, we couldn't wait to play it for the girls, who were, surprise surprise, totally appalled. They couldn't believe what immature, stupid idiots we were. Well actually, they could believe it, some of them having hung around with us for a year or more.

As you might imagine, it didn't take us long to try to set up our own crepitation contest, but we found that, unlike Lord Windesmear and Paul Boomer, we really couldn't crepitate at will. But we didn't want to let this great opportunity for more insanity go to waste, so we just pretended that we were all great crepitators, and established a new society. This was my brilliant idea. We would be known as the Fraternal Order of Competitive Crepitators, or FOCC. Our motto would be "What the FOCC?" The guys liked it.

Somebody said, "Hey, if we add to it a little bit, make it the Fraternal Order of Competitive Crepitators United, then it'd be FOCCU. Get it?"

I came back with, "How about Fraternal Order of Competitive Crepitators of North America? FOCCNA. Fuckin-A! Or we could use the Odd Fellows model. The organization my dad belongs to. Independent Order of Odd Fellows. IOOF. Except we'd be the Indecent Order of Odoriferous Flatulists. The Od Fartists. Or, the Od Farters. No, just the Od Farts. What do you think?"

Lots of heads nodding. Yeah, yeah. But this was all a bit too much for us to come to a consensus on right then. The names were all good, everybody thought so. We decided we'd give it a little time and see if one of the names seemed to emerge, to rise above the others. Maybe we had too many names to consider? No, because, as we all know, too much of a good thing is not enough!

Later, Scourge would come up with a writ, which would be awarded occasionally to a member who had demonstrated actual crepitational competence. This was the *Writ of Crepitatum Flatulentum Superiorium with Oak Leaf Cluster.* The person receiving this award would be designated the

"Grand Exalted Crepitator," or GEC, for the month. I've said it before and I'll say it again: it really didn't take much to amuse us.

32

COMING OFF THE ASS KICKING THAT WE GAVE EASTPORT, the coaches were trying hard to strike a balance between pride and wild enthusiasm and possible overconfidence. At every practice we heard, "Boys, we did a great job against Eastport. We played hard and we executed well. But we can't get complacent. We can't let up. Seniors—this is your time. This is your last year at Ganaway. Make yourselves and Ganaway proud. Juniors, sophomores—you have the honor to play on a team that changes the trajectory, that launches Ganaway to new heights." We heard some version of that just about every day.

Our second game against Summit was another home game. Usually, it was pretty much a given that we would beat Summit. But last year we had almost blown it, so we couldn't take anything for granted. Coach Parker showed up toward the end of practice every day, after the JV team practice, to work with us on offense. G and I were having a great time sharing QB duties. The entire Backfield—or were we the FOCC now, or the FOCCU, or the FOCCNA, or the Od Farts?—whatever we were, we were now first team, and that was great. Everybody was a starter, nobody was a scrub.

This was going to be a very full week, with the game on Friday night and then the wedding of ShiThead's sister on Saturday. Paula was in her early twenties and had been engaged to Steve Frankowski for a year or more. I forget where he worked, but I guess he had a decent job in one of the plants. Paula had a job somewhere too, and I don't know what the plan was for after they were married. It really wasn't something that concerned us much, and we were just looking forward to the reception at the Polish Eagle. All of ShiThead's friends had received invitations, which said "and guest," but we discussed it and decided we didn't want to bring girls to the wedding. With the exception of ShiThead's squeeze, Sally Summers, none of the other dates knew Paula or maybe had even heard of her.

Practice that week went well. I think the whole team felt that we were really clicking, working hard, feeling confident, excited about the game coming up. G and I were getting the message that the game plan would be much like the Eastport game, running from both the single wing and the T.

Friday couldn't get there soon enough. We were itching to get out on the field, running through the double line of cheerleaders jumping up and down and yelling and waving their pom-poms, and past the band assembled in the end zone and playing our fight song, "Ganaway High," to the tune of "On Wisconsin." I don't think we knew the tune was actually "On Wisconsin" back then. It was our song, and the words went like this:

> *Ganaway High! Ganaway High! Run right through*
> *that line.*
> *Run the ball around Bell Island, touchdown sure*
> *this time.*
> *Rah! Rah! Rah!*
> *Ganaway High! Ganaway High! Fighting for her*
> *fame.*
> *Come on let's fight, fellas, Fight! Fight! Fight!*
> *We'll win this game!*

One of the things I will always remember about that game is that, believe it or not, we threw a pass from inside our own forty-yard line. It may actually have been more radical than that, like inside the thirty-five-yard line. In any case, I was the one who called that play. Summit's defense had been surprisingly tough. We had third and long, and normally we would have been forbidden to call a pass. We would have run a 46 or 48 Power, probably failed to get a first down, and had to punt. But I called a pass play, a pass to be thrown over the middle, a more conservative call than a down and out pattern. But even then, unheard of. And by God, it paid off! I dropped back, got good protection, saw our tight end slanting over the middle, pretty much open, and I rifled him the ball, perfect spiral, perfect lead. He caught it, turned upfield, and picked up maybe five or ten yards before he was stopped. Damn! We had a first down, and great field position, and man, did I feel like a hot shit!

Going into the half, I think we were ahead by two touchdowns, and we were feeling confident. Maybe overconfident, because in the second half they came out and scored right away. And their defense had tightened up. I got sacked a couple times, and when I called a razzle dazzle, like we had run against Eastport, I fumbled the ball when ShiThead pitched it back to me, not a great pitch, and Summit recovered. Worse yet, I had called the razzle dazzle inside our forty-yard line. I guess the inside-the-forty pass completion had gone to my head. When I got to the sideline, Helwig was waiting for me.

"Simpson! What do you think you're doing? What kind of a call was that? Way too risky. WAY too risky! You've got to use your head, son. Now, go sit down!"

Oh shit. Oh shit. What had I done? Helwig was pissed. Really pissed. And I could smell the booze on him. Damn, he was going to have my ass for this.

Luckily, our defense stopped them and they had to punt. G went in and we ran mostly power plays, maybe with a reverse or a tailback pass thrown in. We kept possession and moved the ball, chewing up a lot of time.

Pretty soon after my chewing out by Helwig, Coach Parker came and leaned over in front of me where I was sitting on the bench. I thought, oh boy, here comes another reaming out. But Parker didn't yell at me. He lifted my chin with his fist and looked me right in the eyes and said, "OK, Simpson, look at me. OK, that razzle dazzle was probably not a great call. But that fumble on the pitch from Hanuszewicz was not your fault. He messed up that pitch. Your handoff to him was perfect. Stuff like that is gonna happen. OK? You gotta leave that behind. If you go back in there, don't think about that. Be smart. Think about field position. Look over their defense. Look for weaknesses. Call plays based on what you see out there. OK?"

I nodded. He said, "Say it. Tell me. OK?"

"Yes," I said. "OK. Got it."

"Awright," he said, "that's what I want to hear."

He straightened up and I saw him walk over and say something to Helwig. Maybe he said something about me. Probably. It didn't look like Helwig was concentrating much on what Parker was saying.

For most of the second half, G was in there. But I didn't get completely benched. Helwig—probably at the urging of Parker—put me back in for a couple series of downs once we had it pretty well locked up, and we did move the ball. I even threw another pass. And we scored a touchdown while I was in there, right at the end of the game. It was an option play, where I faked a handoff to ShiThead, kept the ball, then flipped a lateral to J.D., who broke a couple of tackles and sprinted into the end zone.

We won the game. It wasn't a complete blowout like Eastport, but it wasn't really close. It seemed like the fact that we were showing some new looks from our offense was having a positive effect. Our opponents couldn't be so sure, as they had been in the past, of what we were going to run at them. I felt like I'd been pulled back from the precipice. It looked like I hadn't totally messed up my first-string status, but I may have come close.

Like we did the week before, after the game we hit Gino's, and then Angelo's for some beers and praise and slaps on the back. For most people, the game was all positive. For me, I kept thinking about the razzle dazzle gone wrong. I tried to concentrate on what Parker had said. That it wasn't my fault, that ShiThead had messed up the short pitch back to me. I told myself that I needed to put it behind me, move on, think ahead. As we sat and drank our beers and talked at Angelo's, I gradually stopped dwelling on the fumble, and Helwig's chewing out. We won, I told myself, now on to the next game. Ironton. They would be much tougher than Eastport and Summit.

On Saturday I worked at Stenzel Agency until noon or so, then headed home to get ready for the wedding. I took a shower, put on my church clothes—the one suit I owned—and waited for Fumb to come pick me up. We decided that we'd all ride with Fumb, so we wouldn't have multiple cars on the road being driven by guys who'd been partying all night. The weather was perfect, actually warmer than normal for that time of year.

The wedding was at four o'clock, and we got to St. Casimir's Church in plenty of time. ShiThead was in the wedding, one of five groomsmen. I don't think he knew Frankowski that well, but I suppose Paula wanted him to be in her wedding. This was the first time I'd been inside a Catholic church, and I was fascinated to see all the statues, and flickering candles, and the very large and gruesome version of the crucifix. I started to make mental comparisons with our Lutheran church, which had some similarities but was not nearly as ornate, but then it was time for the wedding, and the organ struck up a tune. I don't think it was the usual "Here Comes the Bride" thing.

I was surprised at how long the wedding took. In fact, I was wondering if it would ever be over. I didn't realize that there would be a full Mass, complete with communion and all the trimmings. Lutherans did a fair amount of standing up and sitting down, but we couldn't come close to all the standing, kneeling, sitting, and standing that these Catholics went through. And of course, the genuflecting. In fact, it wasn't entirely clear to me exactly when the happy couple became married to each other. I was getting really impatient and wanted the whole production to be over. My stomach was growling and I wanted to get over to the Polish Eagle and start drinking beer and chowing down on some pierogi and kapusta and golabke and those amazing breaded pork chops.

Finally, the bride and groom headed down the aisle and out of the church. Then the guests filed out, confetti or rice or whatever was thrown, and we headed for Fumb's car to take us the few blocks to the Polish Eagle. We couldn't wait to get to the open bar, where the beer was flowing like Niagara Falls, and shots of whiskey—maybe Seagram's Seven or Canadian Club, and not Kessler's—could be had for the taking, as they were lined up on the bar, and anybody could grab one. Or two. Or three. Or more. Soon the bar was stacked three or four deep and everybody was getting down to the business of celebrating the joyous occasion. ShiThead was obviously eating up being a guest rather than a scullery hand, and he looked very dapper in his rented tux.

After a while everybody found a seat and dinner was served—all the fabulous Polish food that the Eagle was famous for. Then there were the toasts—slurred and barely comprehensible sentimental rantings and lame attempts at humor by friends of the bride and groom. As always at these affairs, the microphone worked like shit and you couldn't really get people to shut up and pay attention, but it didn't matter. Everybody was getting totally hammered and having a great time. Then something started that I hadn't seen before.

The band, which was a great polka band led by ShiThead's uncle, did a drum roll, and Paula and Steve were seated on the dance floor in chairs facing the guests. People were going around handing out sheets of words to a song. The band started playing, and everybody started singing— most of the guests had been to Polish weddings before. Then a bunch of guys surrounded Paula and Steve, picked up their chairs, and lifted them up above their heads. Holy shit! They staggered around and the bride and groom wobbled and bounced around up there on their chairs, and the guys carrying them went prancing around the dance floor with them until the song was over. And it wasn't exactly a short song. Then came the old favorite song:

In heaven there is no beer,
That's why we drink it here,
And when we're gone from here
Our friends will be drinking all the beer.

After that was the dollar dance. You paid a dollar and got a shot of whiskey and a dance with the bride. Or the groom. Both men and women were supposed to participate in the dollar dance, and the groomsmen worked the crowd to make sure everybody chipped in. Some of the dollar bills were pinned to Paula's dress. Obviously, the dollar dance took a while, but nobody cared because everybody was drunk on their ass and having a great time. After the dollar dance, the band just kept playing polka music and everybody was out on the dance floor, whether they knew how to dance the polka or not. It was a riot to watch Fumb bouncing around dancing the polka with Mrs. Hanuszewicz.

At some point, the bride and groom did the thing

where the bride throws her bouquet to the single girls, and the groom takes off the bride's garter and throws it to the single guys. Then the happy couple took off and the wedding guests hung around, still going at it. Probably around midnight we decided we'd better get the hell out while we could still walk. G lived close enough that he decided to walk home. The rest of us staggered out to Fumb's car and fell in. No way in hell Fumb should have been driving that car. But he was a big guy, and we stupidly figured that no amount of alcohol could possibly impair his judgment or driving ability. We were laughing our asses off and reliving the wedding reception, but then somebody had to take a pee. Real bad. We were just coming up to Forest Park, so Fumb pulled the car over to the curb and everybody got out and found a tree to piss on. Man, that felt good. Like gallons of beer streaming and steaming in the fall air. It was a beautiful night. Getting cool, but the sky was clear, not even any paper mill smell blowing our way.

"Let's sit down a minute," said Scourge. "It's so beautiful out tonight." Nobody had a problem with that, and we all picked a big, thick tree to lean against, not any of the ones we had pissed on, and we just sat there, feeling happy, and lucky to be together. We'd had so much to drink that it only took a couple of minutes before we were all asleep. We rested in blissful slumber until we heard someone's voice.

"Hey, what do you boys think you're doing?" the voice said.

Slowly, one by one, we woke up. Groggy, but awake. More or less.

Oh shit, I thought, when I realized that the person with the voice was a Ganaway cop.

"Uh, hi, officer," somebody said.

"You boys been drinking?"

"Uh, well, a little bit," said Scourge. "We were at Paula Hanuszewicz's wedding. Mostly we were eating way too much great food." It was good to have the lawyer talking.

"Sure," said the cop, "I can just imagine." He was looking at J.D. "Hey, aren't you Rocco Palmisano's brother?"

"Yeah, yes, I am," said J.D.

The cop looked us all over and then he said, "Who's driving?"

Fumb stood up so the cop could see how large he was. "I'm driving, officer."

"How drunk are you?"

"I'm actually pretty good," said Fumb. "I was taking it easy because I'm driving." He actually sounded coherent. Even believable.

"OK," said the cop, "I'm going to follow you home, and that's as far as you're going. These guys will have to stay at your house and sleep it off until tomorrow. And believe me, if you try to get cute, you're going to really regret it. You hear me?"

"Yes, sir," said Fumb.

"Officer?" said J.D. "I can actually walk home from here if that's OK."

"Yeah, OK," said the cop.

"Uh, I live close too," said Scourge. "Is it OK if I walk?"

The cop looked skeptical, but we all chimed in politely and confirmed that Scourge was telling the truth. I guess we convinced him.

"OK," he said. "You two guys get your asses home.

Big guy, you'd better not mess up. I'm gonna be right on your tail."

We all followed orders and when Fumb and I got to his house, the cop turned on his gumball machine and flashed his lights just for a second, then he pulled away slowly and headed down the street. If anybody heard us come in at Fumb's house, they didn't let on. I called home and Mom answered. "Chris, what's the matter?" she said. I gave her some bullshit story about Fumb having car trouble and we made it to his house but I was going to have to stay over and I'd be home tomorrow and don't worry. Naturally, she wanted to know if I'd be home in time for church. I told her I doubted it because Fumb would have to work on the car. I don't know if she believed me. Most likely not. She wasn't that naïve.

33

THERE REALLY WASN'T TOO MUCH FALLOUT FROM THE BIG DRUNK at the wedding. I slept in my clothes on Fumb's bed, and when I showed up at breakfast, Fumb explained that he'd heard a funny noise in the engine and decided he'd better not drive any farther than necessary until he checked it out. And he was going out right now to do that. I excused myself and said I was going to go out with him and try to learn something about cars. If his parents thought this story sounded fishy, they didn't say anything, and Fumb and I went outside and he raised the hood and messed around with some things, and solved the "problem." He knew so much about cars that he could make up something plausible about what he was doing.

When Fumb dropped me off at home everybody was at church. I enjoyed the little bit of solitude to read the Sunday paper. There had been nothing more in the paper about the fire at The Union or the vandalism at Amato's. I decided to call J.D. and see if anything had developed at his house. At first I hesitated, because I thought maybe it would be better if nobody knew anything more about that whole situation. But then I thought, well, I was more in the know because of the brick through the window thing at our house, so if I brought up the subject and J.D. thought it was best not to talk about it, he'd just tell me that.

When I got him on the phone, I didn't specifically say what I was calling about, but a few subtle hints were enough for him to figure it out. Apparently, he wasn't alone in the room with the phone, because he just said, "Yeah, let's do that. 3-2-1 sounds great. Meet you there in about half an hour?" I said sure.

We got to McDonald's about the same time, got our 3-2-1s, and sat in the car with our favorite lunch. "So, what's the deal?" I asked him.

"OK, well, this is just between you and me, right?"

"Absolutely," I said.

"Well, just like I was afraid of, Rocco went bullshit on Danny. Fortunately, he didn't do it in front of the whole family. Just dad, Tony, and me. An Italian guys-only thing. Actually, I was surprised they let me in on it. We met in the store after it closed. I'm not going to try to quote you what all was said. But after getting threatened with having his balls ripped off, Danny admitted that he did both the fire and the brick. The brick had a note on it that said, 'You better know which side your bread is buttered on.' Clever, huh? He said the fire was intended to be just a 'warning' and it was started in the dumpster, but then it got out of control before the fire department got there.

"Of course, Danny is so fucking stupid that he didn't think about what this was going to look like and what the fallout would be. My dad had an initial impulse to call

Mr. Amato. But if he called him, what would he say? He couldn't admit that he knew anything about the brick or the message on it. So what could he say? 'Hey, sorry my son-in-law is a stupid chooch. You go ahead and sell your bread to The Union. We're fine with that. We know you gotta make a living.' No, he couldn't do that. He couldn't admit he knew anything about any of it. Wait for the cops to call him? Probably that's all he could do. And they're sure to call him. And then just say he had no idea about anything, including that Amato's was talking about a deal with The Union.

"So, to make a long, ugly story short, the decision was just to do the usual. 'Omerta.' Anybody asks you anything about any of this? You know nothing. By the time our 'discussion' ended, I think Danny was really shitting his pants. Just because the Rizzos have some connections, that's not going to help him any if the heat is on. In fact, if the Rizzos actually knew what he did, it could be a lot worse than anything Rocco could throw at him. So, now, as far as the Backfield is concerned, same thing. Nobody knows nothing. That's it. No discussion, no speculation. Just nothing."

I told him that I got it completely. And as far as the brick at our house, that, too, had been buried. We never talked about it. I wished I could thank Danny for saving my old man's ass by getting my mom involved. The brick had worked great for that. But he should have left it at that. This was the perfect time for the "Cone of Silence" to descend upon all of us. And as for the meeting here today at McDonald's? What meeting?

When I got home, Donna was in the living room folding clothes. I took the opportunity to ask her if she'd been able to find out anything about what we had talked about.

She said, "Well, I overheard Connie Klein talking to Debbie Mason the other day. I was going to tell you about it but we really haven't had a chance to talk. So anyway, Connie—she works in our department, mostly handles retirement stuff—I heard her talking to Debbie Mason about Mr. Gorlukovich."

"What were they saying?"

"I couldn't hear everything, but I did hear something about how the thing in the kettle happened. Debbie was saying that she had heard the assistant plant manager talking to Mr. Harrison about liability. Not sure what that actually means. But apparently Mr. Harrison blew his top. He said that the thing with Mr. Gorlukovich was an accident. He said probably the stupid hunkie or polack or whatever he is—those were the words he used, according to Debbie— was drunk. That those stupid hunkies and polacks and dagoes are lazy bastards and they don't pay attention and they don't do things the way they're supposed to. No wonder the stupid bastard got hurt. It's his own damn fault for being a stupid polack."

"What else did she say?"

"That was about all. Somebody came into the office and they stopped talking."

"Well, that's very interesting. Kind of confirms what I've heard about Harrison. What do people in the office think of him?"

"I'd say he's not exactly well loved," said Donna. "He has a reputation for being rude and unfriendly, very high and mighty, very full of himself. And always talking about polacks and dagoes and using other offensive terms. I heard that he once said he was happy there aren't any colored people in the plant. And even the union was happy about that. And that one good thing about this 'shit-hole town' is that there are no colored people here. But he didn't use that term. You know the term he used."

"Jesus," I said, "what a shitbag that guy is. Guess his daughter is right."

"His daughter? What about his daughter?" Donna asked.

"Oh, his daughter just said some things about what a pain in the ass he is. Don't repeat that. She goes out with Joe Palmisano. But look, do you think you could just see if there are any accident reports or anything filed away somewhere in your office? Safety reports, maybe? Just take a look."

"Gee, I don't know, Chris," she said. "I could get in some real trouble, I think. What would you do if I found out that there are safety reports or whatever?"

"Well, you could maybe see if there's anything in there about Mr. Gorlukovich. Or even just about problems in the resin room, with the kettle."

"Wow, I don't know."

"Hey, if people are getting hurt, and that asshole Harrison doesn't care and isn't making that plant as safe as possible, don't you want to hold him accountable?"

I could tell I was pushing her a bit too much, but I could also see that she was thinking about my question. "OK, well, at least think about it," I said.

34

COMING OFF TWO GOOD WINS, THE TEAM WAS IN HIGH SPIRITS. But we knew the Ironton game was going to be a different story. They were always tough, and you couldn't take anything for granted. I was hoping that our new offensive approach would help us by throwing some surprises into the mix. Last year's game had been close, but we'd won it, playing our traditional take-it-to-'em, run-over-'em game. It would be great to open it up this year and win big.

At film night, Helwig was giving his usual pep talk to start off the meeting, and he said something like, "Boys, we've got two good wins under our belt. That's good, very good. But we've got a big test coming up on Friday night. Elmhurst is going to be tough; they're a big team, with lots of talent, blah, blah."

The other coaches looked at each other; we all looked at each other. Elmhurst? Who the hell was Elmhurst? This sounded like "win this one for Sarkovits!" Nobody said anything. Helwig kept going with his pep talk, and when he finished, he turned it over to Rudnik. Helwig looked like he was headed out into the corridor, maybe to have a nip, when Carpenter went up to him and said something. Helwig stopped and looked a little flustered, then turned to look at us and said, "Boys, I misspoke. Of course I meant to say Ironton, not Elmhurst. OK, coach—take over." And he went out into the hallway.

People in town seemed to be divided on Helwig. Maybe our first two games, with some razzle dazzle thrown in, had some people revising their opinions. Maybe he wasn't over the hill, after all. But then you still heard people saying it was time for him to go. We were behind him, like we had discussed at the boathouse. I really believe the whole team was behind him. But it was hard not to have doubts and worry when he said things like that.

On Fridays, Scourge and I had a study hall together. I actually made good use of study halls and tried to get as much homework done as possible. Friday nights were games, Saturdays I worked at Stenzel Agency, and Sundays I was usually hung over from Saturday night at the boat-house, or even if I wasn't drinking that much, I was proba-bly up late trying to get to third base with my new squeeze, Lilly Stewart. So I never felt like doing homework on Sunday, although sometimes I had no choice.

In addition to being the group's legal counsel and com-poser of writs, Scourge was our poet-in-residence. He also liked to come up with tongue twisters, and he got us all doing it. It was harder than you might think to come up with things that were really hard to say. The classics like "She sells sea shells by the sea shore" and "I slit the sheet, the sheet I slit, the unbeslitted sheet I slit" were harder than most of the stuff we invented. The ones we came up with were always more vulgar than clever. But even ours got harder to say after a few beers.

The Friday of the Ironton game, we were in study hall, Scourge sitting at the desk in front of me, like he always did. I was working on a math assignment or a paper of some kind. I didn't know what he was doing but he seemed to be more focused on his work than usual. After quite a while, he turned and handed me a piece of paper, folded in half. I took it and opened it.

I was stunned. Scourge had done it again. Another brilliant literary gem to add to his already impressive corpus of work. This was a poem about a tongue twister. Such a creative combination. Genius. He was a cheap little shit, but a giant among the literati of our time. This could elevate him beyond his already lofty post as the group's poet-in-residence. He could become Ganaway's first poet laureate. "Scourge. Brilliant!" I whispered. "You have to read this at the boathouse."

He bowed humbly and said, "Thank you, thank you very much" in his best Elvis voice.

Poetry was important, but football was paramount. After school we went home and got something to eat, then had to get back and get suited up and on the bus to Ironton. Like I've said, Ironton was a lot like Ganaway and Bell Island. Factories with their smoke and fumes and smell. Older houses, some of them looking pretty rough and weathered. Lots of corner bars. One big difference was that there was a Black neighborhood.

There was a good crowd coming into the stands as our bus arrived. We got off the bus and gathered in a room under the visitors' side bleachers. Visiting teams didn't have locker rooms. They dressed at their home school, and after the game went back there to shower. Ganaway always had a lot of fans who traveled to away games. Football was one of the most important and treasured things, a real source of pride, and people went out of their way to support their team. It wasn't just casual entertainment. Winning was expected. Ganaway had fielded winning teams for a long time, and a lot of the credit for that belonged to Helwig. That's why people were so concerned about what had been happening in the last several years, and why they were talking about Helwig, and wondering if he was past his prime. They wanted Ganaway to get back on track, start dominating again. Ganaway was supposed to be a power, a force to be reckoned with, *every year.*

We really felt ready for this game. Practice had been tough all week and the coaches had pushed us hard. We needed this win. Ironton was not Eastport or Summit. It wasn't Elmhurst either, but we'd tried to forget about that and concentrate on the game, not on Helwig's weird slipup. We took the field and the Ganaway fans made their presence known. The home team grandstand was larger than the visitors' bleachers, and there was a big home crowd, but the Ganaway fans filled the visitors' side.

We got off to a good start, scoring first with G in there. Dudek kicked the point after. He had improved, but he still wasn't as reliable as everyone wished he would be. Every time he lined up to kick the extra point, head down, looking kind of small out there, you held your breath. If the snap was good, and G got the ball down fast and positioned it just right, and Dudek plowed straight ahead into the ball and made a solid, front-on kick, and the ball sailed through the uprights, you breathed a sigh of relief. But all those things didn't happen like that every time. Dudek's percentage had improved, but still left something to be desired. And the backup place kicker, a sophomore, needed a lot of work. In practice I worked on holding the ball for the kicker, too. We obviously needed someone to back up G in case something happened and he couldn't do it. I felt like I was pretty good at it, but Helwig wasn't likely to put me in unless he had to.

We scored again, and Dudek had another good kick. With the score 14-0, Helwig put me in. We got a couple of first downs, with a couple of completed passes, and I was feeling pretty good. They stopped us and we turned the ball over, but our defense held, and they had to punt. I went back in, and again we moved the ball. We ran an option that got us about thirty yards. We threw a screen pass that had them totally faked out, and we were threatening to score when the clock ran out on the first half. Things were looking good.

But that didn't last long. We kicked off in the second half—a short kick by Dudek—and, son of a bitch, Ironton ran it back for a touchdown. One of our guys had a clear shot at the receiver, but he botched the tackle, and the Ironton guy twisted loose and headed for the sideline. The guy was fast! He literally outran three of our guys and trotted into the endzone. I looked over at Helwig, and he looked like he was going to have a stroke.

We returned the kickoff and G went in on offense. We got a couple of first downs, but then had to punt. It went back and forth, until toward the end of the third quarter, Ironton scored again and tied it up. I was really wishing Helwig would put me in so we could shake things up a little, give them a new look, get them off balance. But that never happened. We stuck with the tried and true, but the tried and true wasn't getting the job done. Ironton's defensive line was big and tough, and we weren't blowing them out. We tried a reverse, but our blocking broke down and we were stopped for no gain. Time was running out and it looked like maybe we were going to have to settle for a tie. But then, Lewandowski bobbled a snap from Fumb on a punt, Ironton blocked his kick, and they recovered deep in our territory. Damn! Three plays later, they scored, and we lost 21-14.

35

I COULD SEE THE PATTERN. We would start with G out there running the single wing. If we managed to get a decent lead, say, two touchdowns, Helwig would put me in. Then, if we scored, or at least moved the ball, had to punt, and the defense kept the other team from scoring, I'd continue to see some action. But if things started to get close, we would revert to the old model. The Ironton game was a perfect example. This really didn't surprise me much. Coach Parker was the main advocate for change, and he was doing his best to help us develop an effective, new-look offense. But his main responsibility was the JV team. The fact that he somehow managed to work with us as much as he did was kind of amazing, but he didn't have the time or support he needed to transform us into a confident, polished machine. It wasn't just the backfield that needed to be transformed. The offensive line was hugely important—critical. And Parker just didn't have enough time to devote to the whole task. Plus, he was always battling Helwig's reluctance to deviate from the strategy that had made him a legend in high school football in our area. Coach Carpenter was frustrated with Helwig too, but his focus was the defensive backfield. And Rudnik wasn't going to make waves.

We talked about this at Angelo's after the game. G agreed with my observation. He didn't agree with Helwig's strategy, if that's what you wanted to call it.

"We should be mixing things up all the time," he said. "Keeping them off balance. Now, they always know what to expect. And I'm sorry, but the Helwig thing about 'it doesn't matter if they know what we're going to do because we're just going to run over them' ain't working." Other guys nodded.

Sal Rizzo came over to our table from behind the bar and said, "What happened, guys? I heard you got off to a good lead and then blew it. What do you want, six Gennys? I'll buy you a round."

What could we say? We didn't want to get into the stuff we'd just been talking about. J.D. just said, "We've got some work to do. Wait till next week." And that was it. We ordered a couple of Mama's pizzas. We weren't a very jovial group. We were all wiped out from the game and feeling lousy about losing.

When I got home, Donna was still up, washing a few dishes. Everybody else was in bed. I asked her how she was doing, how her day had gone.

"I did something today that I hope I'm not going to regret," she said, and handed me a large manila envelope.

"What's this?"

"Take a look," she said.

I opened the envelope and pulled out a pretty large

stack of papers. There were memos, notes, reports, things like that.

"I made those copies on the Xerox machine," she said, "and that was risky because we're not supposed to use that machine very much. I was alone in the office for a while and I started looking through file drawers. I was nervous as all get-out that someone was going to come back and ask me what I was doing. It's not that I never look in the file cabinets. I file stuff and look for stuff all the time as part of my job. But, I don't know, I was really on edge. And like I said, I was nervous about the Xerox machine. Anyway, that stuff there came from a file folder labeled 'Resin Room.' I flipped through it very fast and it looked like it might have some information that could be pertinent to Mr. Gorlukovich's accident."

"Wow, thank you, Donna!" I said.

"That's OK. The more I thought about what Mr. Harrison said about polacks and dagoes and all that stuff, the madder I got. He really is a jerk. So maybe this can help. But Chris, that's all I can do. I can't go snooping around anymore, OK?"

"Sure, right, yeah," I said. "I'll look through this and see if there's anything that could be helpful. And this is the last time this will ever be discussed, OK? Never mentioned again. Between you and me, or anybody else. You didn't tell anybody that you made the Xerox copies, did you?"

"No."

"Well, don't. Ever. From this moment on, nothing happened. Same for me."

"So, what are you going to do with that stuff?" she said.

"OK, that's what I mean," I said. "No more discussion. Nothing. Nothing happened, OK?"

"Oh, OK, I get it," she said.

I went over to her and gave her a hug. I was going to say thank you, but then I remembered my own admonition and said nothing.

I took the papers up to my room and sat down at the little desk I used for doing homework. As I went through them, I started getting excited. There were safety reports, memos between managers, some correspondence with manufacturers. Maybe this stuff would be helpful to the lawyers. Now I had to decide what to do next. I put the papers back in the envelope and put the envelope in my desk drawer under a bunch of other papers and went to bed.

I couldn't fall asleep because I was thinking about what to do with the documents Donna had given me. It was brave of her to stick her neck out like that. She really didn't know G, or his dad, but she was a good person, and fair-minded, and she didn't like it when people like Harrison acted like superior assholes and showed no respect for regular people who worked hard to make a living. I wanted to make sure her efforts made a difference, and that she wouldn't get in any trouble for doing the right thing.

After lying there awake for what seemed like most of the night, I finally decided what I was going to do. I would send the documents, anonymously, to Lyle Stewart, Lilly's father, who was handling G's dad's case. Then, I could say something very vague to G, like, "Hey, this is all I can say, but Bullshit Law Firm may have some useful information." But then I thought, no, don't even say that. The Cone of Silence must descend upon me, and I must say nothing.

Nothing. That would be the smartest thing to do. The less said, by anyone, to anyone, the better. That was the way to go. As Sgt. Schultz on that new TV show, *Hogan's Heroes*, would say, "I know nothing!" Omerta all the way.

Once I had decided what I was going to do, I finally fell asleep. The next day I sealed up the envelope with the papers in it, addressed it to Lyle Stewart, Esq. at the Bullshit Law Firm, and took it with me to work. I used the postage scale at the Stenzel Agency to find out how much it would cost to mail it, then put stamps on it to approximate the amount. I was being so silent and secure that I didn't even want to give it to a person at the post office to weigh it and put postage on it. They might remember who brought that envelope in. Stupid, I know, but I was going to make sure that nobody ever knew where this stuff came from. At lunch I took it to a mailbox and dropped it in.

That night we got together at Striebig's for roast beef sandwiches and schuppers. The usual euchre players were there, and Mr. Striebig was surveying his domain, peering out over the barroom with his Scotch-taped eyes. Mrs. Striebig was kind of bitchy. Maybe she was sick of slicing roast beef.

I really wanted Scourge to recite his brilliant tongue twister poem, and I had figured out a way to bring it up.

"Brothers of the Backfield," I said, "I am pleased and delighted to inform you that our esteemed poet-in-residence has created another masterpiece. Being a man of great modesty and humility, he would not be inclined to bring this up on his own. Therefore, I have taken the liberty of bringing this to your attention, and I would like to ask him to recite his latest work." I pulled out Scourge's original manuscript and handed it to him. "Professor, would you please do us the honor?"

Scrooge—we often called him that at Striebig's because of his infamous attempt to weasel out of paying his share of the tab many months ago—looked surprised. But he rose to the occasion like a true celebrity. "My goodness," he said, "this is indeed a surprise. I am honored and flattered to be asked to share my work with you, dear friends." He took the manuscript, cleared his throat, and began reading "A Tongue Twister Surprise."

> *I slit the sheet, the sheet I slit,*
> *And the slitted sheet revealed a tit.*
> *How it got there, who could tell?*
> *But over me it cast a spell.*
> *I didn't know whose tit it was,*
> *And didn't really care because*
> *A tit is always nice to see,*
> *And since I saw this one for free,*
> *I thought, "That's good enough for me."*

The whole table erupted with applause. "Bravo! Bravo, Scrooge!" resounded within the back room of Striebig's. Mrs. Striebig peered out of the kitchen to see what was going on, looking even more annoyed than usual. The old guys at one of the euchre tables that was visible from ours looked up and stared at us. The Scrooge was truly a gifted poet. He took a bow and gave an Elvis thank you.

Mrs. Striebig called over to us and said our roast beef sandwiches were ready. We went up to the kitchen window and picked them up and took them back to our table. We got our third round of schuppers and toasted our poet-in-residence. We also toasted Coach Helwig. "May he lead us on to win one for Sarkovits!" When we finished our beers, we decided to go to Hollowell Circle and see if we could set a new record. We left the bar, piled into Fumb's car, and headed out. When we got to the circle, it was deserted; nobody in front of the hotel, no cop cars around. So we started driving laps around the circle, and kept it up until a drunk came staggering into the street. Fumb swerved and just missed hitting the old guy. Kind of surprising to see a drunk on the circle, because that was a pretty classy part of the City. The poor guy was still weaving around in the middle of the street and having avoided nailing him once, we decided not to press our luck. So we quit at thirty-seven laps, which was a new record.

36

THE WEEK OF THE ST. IGGIE GAME, a disturbing thing happened. The old man was always the first one up and off to work, and most of the time he was gone before we ever came down to breakfast. Lots of nights he was down in the basement until after everybody went to bed, including Mom. They had separate beds and she was used to being asleep when he came up to bed. One day Mom woke up and he wasn't in the bedroom or the bathroom. She came downstairs and saw that his car was still in the driveway. He wasn't in the kitchen, and she looked outside but didn't see him anywhere. She found him down in the basement, sound asleep and snoring on the old couch down there. When she went over to wake him up, she could smell the booze on him from six feet away. Apparently he had passed out. We knew he was drinking when he went down there every night, but I guess we didn't know how much. Maybe Mom knew and just didn't say anything or didn't think it would do any good. But this was kind of a warning sign. Anyway, Mom roused him, and he dealt with his hangover, got dressed, and went off to work. He might have been a little late.

I didn't give it much more thought. My focus was on the St. Iggie game. The coaches said they had a good team this year, but what would you expect them to say? Can't take anything for granted.

In the locker room one day at practice, J.D. told me that the cops had been to the market, talking to his dad. They wanted to know if he knew anything about the brick through the window at Amato's. Why would he know anything about that? he asked them. The cops brought up the thing about Amato's making a deal to sell their bread at The Union, all their locations. No idea what you're talking about, Mr. Palmisano told them. Anyway, Amato's could sell their bread anywhere they wanted to. Yeah, it was nice to be able to advertise that you could buy Amato's bread at Palmisano's, but not that big of a deal. But anyway, nope, don't know nothing about any deal between Amato's and The Union. News to me. That was the way to handle it. J.D. and I said we hoped that our guys would be able to do it that well.

———

WE WERE PUMPED FOR THE ST. IGGIE GAME. A must win to keep a winning record going at this point in the season. The St. Iggie cheering section was out in full force, and even before the kickoff, they cut loose with their famous Rat shit! Bat shit! cheer. But, unfortunately for them, the Saints did not give 'em—give us—hell that day. We kicked off and Dudek had his best kick of the year. He pounded it deep into St. Iggie territory. And Freckles Kramden was with us. Our kickoff team ran down the field with Freckles Kramden and slammed into the receiver, who didn't know what hit him. He fumbled the ball, we recovered, and two plays later we drove into the end zone on a 30 Power right up the middle. Our line blocked like they were supposed to, ShiThead smashed through with head down and knees pumping high and broke into the end zone standing up. And that kind of set the tone for the rest of the game. It wasn't a complete rout, but Parker must have been working on Helwig because I got to play most of the game. Of course it was never really close, but that did say a lot for our ability to move the ball from the T. We even pulled off another razzle dazzle, and the hometown fans loved it!

We were planning a rendezvous at the boathouse Saturday night. Now with the St. Iggie win, we upgraded to a horrendezvous and invited all the girls. It was Lilly Stewart and me; ShiThead and Sally Summers; G and Nancy Gregg; Scourge and Jill Long, the toothsome lass; J.D. and Peggy Harrison; and Fumb and Amy Strickland. We had the bar fully stocked with beer for the guys and 7 and 7s—well, Guck and 7s—for the girls, plus gourmet hors d'oeuvres, that being Schuler's potato chips and the best chip dip in the world, which you can only find in our area. Fumb had found a new cheapest-yet beer at one of the liquor stores. It was called Iron City. I guess they were trying to expand their market and bring it into our area. This stuff had quite a reputation. People would say, "That's not beer, that's Iron City." Didn't bother us Guck fans. We never had a repeat of the Drambuie and McDonald's orange drink cocktail. We survived it once, and I guess we thought we'd better not press our luck. Plus, no way Lilly could steal another whole bottle of the stuff from her father's liquor cabinet.

We had records on the record player: Dylan, I'm sure, probably the Beatles, the Beach Boys, the Byrds, lots of Bs. Definitely not the Monkees. What a phony, totally commercial, contrived joke they were. We loved "Flowers on the Wall" by the Statler Brothers, but you could only play that so many times before the girls threw a fit. We made sure everybody had a drink or a beer and just sat around, enjoying the good feeling of having won the game and having a girl on your lap.

I guess Scourge couldn't resist trying some of his famous clever humor. Fumb and Amy were sitting in the front corner by the windows, and he said, "Hey, how do you like the view from the coffin corner?" Fumb did not think this was funny. He glared at Scourge, looked really angry.

"What did you say, asshole?"

"Uh, just making a little joke."

"Well, your joke is not funny. I got news for you. You think you're a lot funnier than everybody else does."

"OK, hey I'm sorry. Amy, I'm really sorry. He's right, sometimes I think I'm a little too cute for my own good."

"Oh, don't worry about it," said Amy. "I'm not touchy, doesn't bother me a bit. You can't grow up being an undertaker's daughter without developing a bit of a thick skin. Actually, is there really such a thing as a coffin corner, or did you just make that up?"

"No, it's a real thing," said ShiThead. "In football sometimes you try to punt the ball out of bounds way down in your opponent's end of the field, down by the goal line. That's called a coffin corner kick, I guess because the ball is dead and your opponent can't run it back and they have to start way back in their own territory."

"Oh," Amy said, "OK, I'll take your word for it. Sounds kind of complicated. I don't know that much about football."

"Neither does Scourge, the smart-ass little shit wing-back," said Fumb.

"OK, well, like I said, no offense taken. So Pete, how is your dad doing?"

"I guess as well as can be expected. He's doing physical therapy, learning to get around better. Seems to be making progress. Thanks for asking."

"He got hurt at Cooper Chemical, didn't he?" Lilly wanted to know.

"Yeah, that's right."

"Well, the reason I ask is that I overheard my dad say something to my mom about getting an envelope in the mail, something about Cooper Chemical, he said, but there was no return address so he couldn't tell who sent it to him."

I looked over at Scourge. He was keeping a great stone face. God, I hope nobody else keeps talking about this, I thought.

"Well, this has nothing to do with an envelope," said Peggy, "but my dad was really upset the other night when he came out of work late and found all his tires slashed. Oh, in case some of you girls don't know, my dad works at Cooper Chemical. He's the manager."

At first nobody said anything, but then G said, "Oh man, that's too bad."

Oh god, G. Please don't say anything more. I was holding my breath. It must have been G who did that.

"Yeah, that is too bad," said Lilly.

"Not as bad as getting your foot cut off." Oh God, G. Stop! Shut up!

"Now why would anybody do a thing like that?" Oh shit. Now Nancy Gregg was keeping it going.

At least it appeared that G hadn't said anything to her about it. I decided to try to derail the discussion, so I said, "Well, that's not a great neighborhood over there. I wouldn't leave my car on the street overnight there."

"Why do you say that?" said ShiThead. "I wouldn't consider that a particularly bad neighborhood."

Oh please, just shut up!

"Well, whatever," I said. "These things happen." Please, drop it everybody.

"So, has anybody heard anything about the fire at The Union?" This was Nancy again. "My sister works there and she said nobody has said a peep."

I looked over at J.D. He had given all of us specific instructions to say nothing about this to anyone. Now we'd see if everybody had been able to keep their mouths shut. Silence. Good. But it was actually getting a little awkward, so I said, "Guess not. Hey, everybody, get a refill. It's time for *Get Smart*."

The girls groaned. "Do we have to? That show is so stupid."

"Now, now," said Scourge, "please show a little respect for an ancient tradition of ours. We always watch *Get Smart*. It is part of our heritage."

"How can it be a tradition?" said Lilly. "The show's only been on for like, a month, hasn't it?"

"You must remember," said Scourge, "that we live in a time warp, a parallel universe of our own creation."

More groans.

"OK," I said, "we're going to miss the beginning. Here, Fumb, have a beer." And of course he said, "That's not beer, that's Iron City." Then he threw his empty can at the waste basket, and it bounced off the wall and rolled across the floor. "Missed it by *that much*," he said.

37

I REALLY LIKED LILLY STEWART. She was smart, and funny, and she was giving me a lot more action than Karen Reinhardt ever did, although not the ultimate. Usually, we didn't get together with the guys or with girls during the week. We had practice, homework, and a couple of the guys had jobs that they would sometimes have to work, so socializing was pretty much confined to the weekends. But it was kind of hard to get to know Lilly better when we were in a big group, or hanging out at Gino's or Angelo's, so I invited her to go to a movie one night during the week before the Roosevelt game.

We went to the Tate, and G was working so we got in free. I don't remember what movie was playing because we spent the whole time making out in the balcony. There was hardly anybody in the theater. After the movie we went to Santori's, which was in Bell Island, for a slice of pizza and a Coke, and we had a chance to talk. She was nowhere near as uptight as Karen Reinhardt, not just about sex, but about the religion thing too. I found out that her family was Episcopalian but that they really didn't go to church much, if at all. Her dad was a Mason, which of course was strictly verboten for the Missouri Lutherans in Wittenberg. I didn't know much about the Masons, only that they were on the Lutherans' shit list.

She told me that she was a member of some organization for girls that was somehow part of the Masons—Triangle or something—but that she didn't really do much of anything with it. When she was telling me about all the secrecy, and the sacred rites, and the crazy bullshit stuff that Masons had to do, and the different degrees, and secret initiations, and handshakes, all that stuff, I was intrigued. I was really fascinated by the apron that she told me about. An apron? Why would they wear an apron? What was that all about? How had I missed out on all this? Did the other guys know about this shit, I wondered? Lilly told me that she would show me a picture of George Washington wearing his Mason's apron. George Washington? This whole thing was crazy. I decided I was asking her too many questions about Masons, and I didn't want to annoy her.

She started asking me about the IOOF, which she had heard one of us mention sometime or other. I couldn't tell her what the letters actually meant, because the guys had decided that would forever remain a closely guarded secret. Omerta. I did tell her that we sort of got the idea from the Odd Fellows, but that we put our own twist on it. She really wanted me to let her in on the secret, tell her what the initials meant. But I told her no, sorry, we're like the Masons. Mysteries and secrets. I guess we did sometimes use the term Od Farts now to refer to our group. That seemed to be gaining traction with us and replacing the Backfield. But the official name would not be revealed.

As we sat there talking and eating our pizza, the conversation turned to our recent horrendezvous at the boathouse. She thought the ren-dez-vouse thing was pretty funny. I told her how that got started with ShiThead pronouncing epitome as ep-i-toam way back in sophomore year. She said she had talked to Peggy Harrison since the boathouse meeting, and that Peggy was suspicious that maybe it was G—she called him Pete—who had slashed her dad's tires.

"Why did she think that?" I said. I was afraid of something like this.

"Well, I think it was because Pete's dad got hurt, and because Pete said something like getting your tires slashed isn't as bad as getting your foot amputated. I think that's what he said, didn't he?"

"Uh, did he? Maybe. I don't know." I was caught off guard. I had to be careful not to slip up. "What else did she say?"

"Oh, she didn't act mad or anything. I don't really know her that well. But I don't think she likes her dad very much. Remember what she said about him trying to get her to go to private school? And sending her brother off to prep school?"

"Yeah, that was pretty funny."

"She also asked me about that envelope that my dad got in the mail."

Oh shit, I thought.

"What did she want to know?"

"Just if I knew what was in it. If it maybe was about Pete's dad's accident."

"I wonder why she would think that."

"I have no idea. Oh, she also asked me if your sister works at Cooper. I told her I didn't know. Does she?"

"Uh, yeah. Just some kind of a low-level clerical-type job. I really don't know what she does."

"She also said Joe's brother Tony works there, too."

"Just a part-time job. He's going to college." I was thinking, fucking-A, Peggy's smarter than I thought. We're going to need another Omerta lecture from J.D. If she keeps going around talking about this stuff, the other girls are going to get curious and nosy and they'll start asking questions. Just like Lilly was doing.

"Well, anyway," said Lilly, "I've got something I want to show you." And she reached into her purse and pulled out a small hardcover book. It was kind of tan-yellow and the picture on the cover was pretty faded. She handed it to me.

"What's this?" I asked her.

"Just a goofy little book that I thought you'd get a kick out of. You know I have a part-time job at the public library."

"Oh, yeah," I said. I really didn't know that.

"Well, mostly I reshelve books when they're returned, or new books that we've purchased. I found this one on the shelf while I was reshelving. I don't think it's been checked out in a very long time. Like I said, I thought you'd like it."

I took a closer look at the cover and opened the book to the title page. *Famous Fimmales, witt Odder Ewents from Heestory,* by Milt Gross. I looked at the table of contents and saw chapters with titles like "De Insite Sturry from de Woild," and "How it Got Bomped Huff Julius Sizzer," and "How It Got Inwanted Tenksgeeving Day." What the hell is this, I thought. I went to one of the chapters and started to read. I could hardly figure out what it was saying. It was trying to sound like some kind of dialect or something. I read a few lines out loud and Lilly said, "You do a very good

Yiddish accent." Aha! So that's what it is, I thought. Yeah, it really is pretty clever. And really funny, once you get into it.

"God, Lilly, this is great!" I said. "Thank you for thinking of me, of us. Yeah, this is perfect for our weird group. This can become our sacred book, our ancient scripture. The guys will love it. You're amazing! How can we get a copy of it? Maybe you could return it, and then just steal it. No, I know you can't do that. How about you return it, then I check it out, and I say I lost it, and then I just pay for it? You said it hasn't been checked out in forever. The library won't even miss it."

"Well, you could do that, but you really shouldn't. The library works on trust, and depends on people being responsible, and doing the right thing. I can ask the librarians how to get a copy. It's possible to buy books that are out of print. They know all that stuff."

"Yeah, yeah, definitely do that, OK? We need to have our own copy of this masterpiece of literature."

I was loving this discussion with Lilly. I was learning a lot and got some great ideas for the group. I loved the apron thing. We would have to get aprons to wear at our boathouse meetings. We could get them at the hardware store, the kind carpenters and workers wore, and yeah, come to think of it, masons wore them. I'd seen them laying bricks and they had on aprons. Holy shit. And we would have readings from our new sacred text, *Famous Fimmales.*

I didn't want to stay out too late. Had to be in good shape for practice with the Roosevelt game coming up. It was going to be a tough one. They had a lot of starters returning from last year's team and they were 4-0 coming into the game. All of their wins had been lopsided. We paid our tab, actually I paid it, and we headed out to the car. I thanked Lilly again for the book and told her how much I'd enjoyed our date. We talked some more on the way to her house, which was in the Forest Hill section.

When I got home, I decided to give J.D. a call, even though it was kind of late. One of his sisters answered the phone and went to get him. He was still up.

"What's up, man?" he said.

I told him about stuff that Lilly was talking about and how that was making me nervous. "If these broads start talking among themselves and then start asking us all kinds of questions, I just have this fear that somebody's going to slip up and say too much. Maybe in the heat of the moment, if you know what I mean. That could snowball into some real problems."

"Yeah," he said, "all it takes is for somebody to let on that they know something about something, and all of a sudden up goes the Cone of Silence."

"Right. I was thinking that maybe you could give another little lecture on Omerta. Just to the guys, obviously. Just to reemphasize how critical it is to be Sgt. Schultz at all times."

"Yeah, I agree. I can do that. Probably won't have a chance to do that until this weekend, though, right?"

"Probably. But maybe we can find opportunities to casually mention it to the guys when we have the chance. Remind them to be discreet and tell them we have to talk about some stuff at a meeting."

"OK, sounds good," he said. "See you tomorrow."

38

THE ROOSEVELT GAME WAS ONE I'D REALLY LIKE TO FORGET. Of course, we had to hear all about the suntanned boys again. I'm ashamed to say that, back then, that kind of talk didn't really bother me much at all. Unfortunately, that's just the way it was. Well, the suntanned boys of Roosevelt that year, like most years, were some pretty damn tough and talented football players. They were big, and fast, and eager to kick the shit out of the white boys, whose bus rumbled into their town along the lake, a town that looked a lot like Ganaway, with its huge steel mill belching smoke and stench and God knows what else into the atmosphere.

No point going into the gory details. We played our usual game. Since we were never in the lead, I didn't play at all. I don't know if I could have done any good if Helwig had put me in. Probably not. Their defense was big, and fast, and not to be pushed around. But I still had to believe that if we'd worked more at adding some variety to our game, and being less predictable, then in general that would have helped.

It was a lot like the year before. I guess we shouldn't have expected it to be much different. We lost 28-6. Not a total humiliation, but certainly a big disappointment and tough on morale. Last year coming into the Roosevelt game, we had been 4-0. This year we were 3-1 coming in, so now we were 3-2. This was our senior year. We had hoped—I guess hoped against hope, you would say—that we might have an undefeated season to wrap up our high school career. Now we were going to have to scramble like hell just to make sure we had a winning season. Parsons should be—*should be*—a sure win. Norfolk, not so sure. And then Bell Island. God, you could never predict that game. There had been years, if you looked back at the record books, when one of the teams came in with a 7-0 record, and the other had maybe a 2-5 record, and the 2-5 team won. The BI-G game was just different. I don't know how or why that could be, but I guess there was just so much pride, and tradition, and crazy energy involved there, that you just never knew what could happen.

When we got back to school and into the locker room and showered, nobody was in much of a mood to go anywhere. So we just all headed home, and agreed we'd do something on Saturday night.

I worked until noon on Saturday and then stopped in at Palmisano's. J.D. was sweeping the floor. He was the only one working as far as I could see. When he saw me come in, he waved me over and said, "Hey, man, come on over and sit. Want some lunch?"

"Nah, I don't want to bother you, man," I said.

"No bother at all. Sub? Assorted? Oil?"

"Well, if you're sure. That sounds great."

"Yeah, I'll make two." He put away the broom, washed his hands, and started building our subs. He sliced everything fresh, but it didn't take him long. He'd made a lot of subs. He brought our sandwiches over and sat down.

"So, how's business on a Saturday?" I asked him.

"Usually pretty slow. Actually, it's been slow in general lately. It's the big supermarkets—The Union, Zollner's. We just can't compete with those guys. They're too big, they buy in huge quantities, they can afford to sell everything cheaper."

"Yeah, I can see that," I said. "So what can you do? Sounds like a really tough situation."

"Not really much of anything we can do. We do deliveries and they don't. That gives us something of an edge there. But it also cuts into profits, which are already paper thin. Mostly we deliver to little old ladies or old couples, like Mrs. Mancuso and her husband. We've even started making some deliveries in the Third Ward. We don't sell pierogi, but some people just like the convenience. Or they don't have a car, or they're just too old and shaky, and it's hard for them to get out."

"Doesn't sound like a bright future," I said. "All kinds of small businesses are struggling, I think, trying to compete with the big chains. My old man knows a guy who owns a hardware store, not in town here. The guy says people will come in and explain a project they're working on and ask all kinds of questions about what parts and stuff they need, then go and buy everything at K Mart or Sears or someplace like that."

"Yeah, aren't people wonderful? I can tell it's really wearing on my dad. I hear him and Rocco going at it sometimes and I can tell Rocco is frustrated, looks ahead and doesn't see much of a future. He's almost thirty, wants to get married and probably have kids, the whole bit, but he thinks the market's a dead end. And he's probably right. The old man probably knows it too, but he can't admit it. So, they argue about having a plan, needing a plan, making a plan for the future. But it just seems that they go around and around, and so far I haven't heard of any kind of plan."

"That really sucks," I said. "My old man's not happy either, that's for sure. He got shit-faced down in the basement one night and passed out down there, and my mom had to roust him out and get him to work."

"I bet she was thrilled about that. My old man's always got a glass of dago red going, so I'm sure he's shit-faced most of the time, but he doesn't really show it. I hope he's not drinking during the day. I don't think he is."

"So, what about this Omerta lecture?" I said. "Like I told you, Lilly was talking about stuff that Peggy had told her, and stuff that came up at the boathouse. I obviously did a Sgt. Schultz. You and I can talk about some stuff, and we have, like the brick through our window, but even then, I know we've agreed that it's best just to never mention any of this shit. And the more people that say something, and somebody then comments on it or asks about it, that just is not good. And how about Peggy? Is she asking questions? About her dad's tires, and my sister and your brother working at Cooper?" I was going to mention the anonymous envelope mailed to Lyle Stewart, but then I caught myself. Even though I could really talk about anything with J.D., still it would be best not to even bring it up.

"I'm doing the Sgt. Schultz with her, just like everybody

else," he said. "Of course, I can't deny that I know my brother works at Cooper. Obviously. But I just say as little as possible and try to change the subject."

"Well, you are the master of Omerta. Our role model. So, what are we doing tonight? Boathouse? Striebig's? Angelo's? If we can get everybody together, we can talk about it. You can deliver your lecture."

"Yeah, OK," he said.

We finished our subs and J.D. had to wait on a customer, the only person who'd come into the market the whole time we were talking. I left and when I got home nobody was there except Sam, so I asked him if he wanted to go out and play catch. He was happy to be asked and we went outside and I had him running patterns, firing the ball at him hard. He didn't flinch and made some really good catches. He was planning to go out for football in high school.

We had a bunch of oak trees at the back end of our yard and there were squirrels all over the place. One of them ran right in front of Sam when he caught the ball, and Sam quickly gripped the ball and threw a nice spiral right at the little devil, just missing him by about a foot. "Almost nailed the little bastard!" he yelled.

"Nice throw," I told him. "Is this a new form of squirrel hunting you've developed?"

"Yeah, come on, let's see if we can nail one of the little fuckers." Little brother was showing off his cool guy vocabulary, I thought.

So we started looking for another target, and we saw one coming down the trunk of one of the trees near where I was. "Here," Sam threw me the ball. "Get him! Grandma Lindke can cook us some yummy squirrelbraten." Gee, little brother was getting quite clever. I guess I hadn't noticed how fast he was growing up and developing a nice warped sense of humor.

I threw a wicked spiral right at the poor little critter and I swear I missed him by about two inches. Missed him by *that much.* Not sure what I would have done if I'd actually killed it. Squirrelbraten, maybe? The Lindkes were from solid farmer stock, but I don't think eating rodents was a part of the Prussian culinary tradition. We decided to cut the hunt short before we actually bagged a squirrel and had to deal with a dead animal. But Sam's invention of football squirrel hunting really caught on with the group, and we made any number of hunting expeditions to Forest Park, where the squirrel population was very dense. Little brother had done good, and we even awarded him a Certificate of Achievement for his impressive creativity.

It wasn't easy to get free from the girls on a Saturday night, but somehow we all managed to come up with one excuse or another, and we met at Striebig's. We didn't have to worry about getting discovered because the girls really didn't know much about our fondness for Striebig's, and wouldn't have been caught dead there anyway. We got our schuppers and ordered roast beefs and sat at "our" table in the back room. Once we got settled in, J.D. got into the main topic.

"Guys," he said, "we need to update on a few things. And this might be kind of an odd conversation, because we need to talk about some stuff without talking about it."

"What the hell are you talking about?" said ShiThead. "Or not talking about? How many beers did you have before you got here?"

"OK, bear with me." J.D. took a big slurp. "Now, think back to our last gathering with the girls at the boathouse. Do you remember Peggy saying certain things about certain things? And then G said a couple of things related to what Peggy said." You could see wheels turning in guys' heads.

"And then Lilly said some things." A couple of blank looks.

"Something about mail." You could see the lights coming on.

"Think a minute, now. Are you with me?"

Looking around, I could tell that everybody knew what he was talking about now.

"OK, well now here's the thing. We need to make every effort, go to extraordinary lengths, to Know Nothing! Know Nothing! Just like Sgt. Schultz. For the good of the Order, and for all individuals who might have information that we don't want anybody else to have. Get what I'm saying?"

Everybody nodded yes.

"So, I will leave you with one word, a word I'm sure you're familiar with. Omerta. OK? OK, so that's my lecture for tonight. Should we go see what's up at Nick's?"

That sounded like a good idea. We hadn't been to Nick's in quite a while. We had another schupper, paid the bill, and went out into the chilly fall night and walked over there. Nick's parking lot was pretty crowded. When we got inside there weren't any tables open, so we went up to the bar, the guys who were eighteen ordered beers, and we just hung around the bar, stepping aside and making room when somebody came up to get a drink. We stood there, listening to the band, a local group trying to sound like the Beatles and not succeeding very well. ShiThead gave me a poke and looked over toward the entrance, and said, "Look who's here."

There was a small group, three or four people, just coming in the door. I didn't recognize any of them and I gave ShiThead a look that said, "Yeah, who?"

"That's Sally's brother, Dale, with the BI letter jacket on. I don't know the other guys."

"Oh, yeah, now I recognize him. I guess he's having a pretty good season." BI's record at that point was 5-0. Didn't really want to think about that. They started heading over toward the bar. Dale came over to ShiThead and said, "How ya doin', man?"

"Good, good." He gestured toward me and said, "You know your fellow QB, here, right?"

"Yeah," Summers said, "the only QB who's never thrown a pass. Ha ha, just kidding. How ya doin', man?"

"Hey, how are ya?" I said.

ShiThead made a little small talk with him, and then he and his buddies, who I guess were on the BI team, wandered off and started talking to other people. Man, it would be sweet to beat those bastards. Only three weeks away. I'd have to ask Pastor Reinhardt to beseech the Lord to help us kick their asses.

We hung around for quite a while. The band took a break, or so we thought, but it turned out that they were done and a different band came on. They were pretty good. A table opened up, so we sat down and had a few beers and listened to the music. The guys who had proof were able to go up to the bar and get beers for the ones who weren't eighteen. It was too busy for the bartender to notice. It was too loud to talk, and it was nice just to be there and relax. The smoke was pretty thick, a blue haze over the whole space, but we were used to that, and it didn't really bother us much. When the second band wrapped up, we decided to take off. We thought about going over to Angelo's, but it was pretty late, so we just figured we might as well go home. Can't remember how many cars we had driven over to Striebig's, but as we walked back across the street, I said to ShiThead, "Do you think Sally knows that her brother is a complete flaming asshole?"

"I don't know," he said, "probably. You want me to ask her?"

"I guess that won't be necessary," I said. "I'm sure it's painfully obvious to her. Just like it is to everybody else."

39

AFTER GETTING OUR ASSES KICKED BY ROOSEVELT, we were really hoping that we could come back and kick the shit out of Parsons. Luckily for us, the Pussies didn't let us down. We got off to a quick lead and never looked back. This was an especially good game for me, since Helwig apparently felt comfortable using it as an opportunity to appease Parker and the fans who wanted to see us updating our game. I got a lot of playing time in, and Helwig had me running mostly from the T. We probably passed more in that game than we had for the entire season up to that point. But he also sent in some of the standard single wing stuff, so he could see how I would do with that. I felt that my blocking was good, and that made me feel good, although I should have realized that a lot of my performance was directly related to the fact that Parsons had a pretty shitty team. I'm sure this was not lost on Helwig, but he came up to me after the game and told me, "Good job, Simpson, good job."

After the game we went to Angelo's and soaked up the kudos. Johnny V bought us all beers, and the old flower lady who came around most nights gave each of us a flower of some kind. I didn't mind taking the beer from Johnny V, but I felt kind of guilty about the flower lady. We never knew who she was, or where she lived, or how many flowers she actually sold. Everybody just took her for granted and she kind of blended into the woodwork. She would go out and start walking up Samuels Street and hit the other bars and, I suppose, every once in a while somebody would buy some flowers from her. I hope so.

Before we all left, we talked about what we would do the next night, Saturday. The girls were not happy being left out of the activities on the previous Saturday night, so we knew that we'd have to include them this week. The boathouse was always good for that. We could drink, make out, watch *Get Smart*, and act like the assholes we were, and it was cheap. In preparation for the gathering, I bought aprons for all the guys at the local hardware store. I was tempted to see if I could get them cheaper at a discount store or something, but then I thought about what J.D. and I had talked about at the market, and just bought them. They weren't very expensive anyway, just made out of some kind of cloth, canvas maybe, with a few loops and compartments to hold nails, or screws, or hammers, or whatever.

When everybody was there and had their drinks, I stood up and banged on the Guck-filled Seagram's bottle to get everybody's attention. "Ladies and gentlemen," I said, "and I use those terms loosely, give me your undivided attention, please." It took a while for everybody to shut up, but when they did, I continued. "As we all know, one of the ancient and honorable traditions of the Backfield, also known at times throughout history as FOCC, FOCCU, FOCCNA, and

IOOF, is the wearing of ceremonial aprons by the members. Recently, as you recall, a tragic fire at our organization's headquarters resulted in the loss of all members' aprons, which were kept, from time immemorial, in the ceremonial storage chamber."

"What are you talking about?" said ShiThead.

G added, "How much have you had to drink?"

"Hear me out, please," I continued. "Thanks to our dear friend, Lilly Stewart, we have been able to acquire replacement aprons from the Masonic Lodge. The Masons, many years ago, adopted our apron tradition for their members, and as an expression of their gratitude and friendship, they have very generously donated these aprons to us. Gentlemen, please come forward and receive your apron, which has been pre-stocked with several cans of Iron City, plus an engraved can opener."

Everybody thought I was nuts, and said so, but once they realized that the aprons were actually stocked with beer, they were more than happy to take them. This was how things worked with us. Somebody would come up with a ridiculous idea, and if it was stupid enough, it would be adopted and added to the history and lore of the brotherhood. And to my credit, I'm proud to say that everybody started wearing their aprons at boathouse rendezvouses from that time forward. I was going to introduce *Famous Fimmales* next, but thought I'd probably tried the patience of the group enough for now, so I took a modest bow, donned my apron, popped a beer, and sat down.

Somebody asked Scourge if he'd written any new poems. I don't know if this was a prearranged setup; I think it was, because he just happened to have a folded-up copy of a poem with him.

"Oh, is Tyler a poet?" Lilly sounded surprised.

"He thinks he is," said Jill.

"Hey, now show a little respect for the poet-in-residence," said Fumb. "Have you heard his classic 'A Tongue Twister Surprise'? Brilliant, simply brilliant."

"Oh no, no, no," said Jill. "Do not read that disgusting poem. If you can even call it a poem. I mean it, Ty. We don't want to hear that."

"Why, is it really that bad?" said Lilly.

"Yes, it's that bad. It's very bad."

"Oh, come on," said Fumb, "where's your sense of humor? I thought it was really funny."

"Well, now you've got me really curious," said Lilly. "I want to hear his poem."

"How about we let him read his new one," said Peggy. "Have you heard the new one, Jill?"

"No, and I'm not sure I want to."

"Oh, come on, Jill, let him read it." This was G weighing in.

"Hmmm," was all she said.

"OK, thank you so much," said Scourge. "I give you my latest modest attempt at poesy."

"Wait a minute," said ShiThead, "what do you mean 'poesy'? I thought it was poetry."

"He's just being literary," said Fumb. "I'll explain it to you sometime." I was always surprised and impressed by how much Fumb knew about stuff like this. For a car guy he was quite cultured.

"OK," said G, "go ahead and read it. Whatever it is."

"Ahem," Scourge cleared his throat ceremonially. "Here you are. 'I Wandered Lonely Through the Crowd.' With apologies to William Wordsworth."

> *I wandered lonely through the crowd*
> *Of fans who came to watch us play;*
> *And some of them were well-endowed,*
> *Which caused my wayward eyes to stray.*
> *Would some sweet lass come up and say*
> *She wanted me to touch her breast?*
> *Perhaps then I could have my way,*
> *And let my throbbing member rest.*

"Ewww," said Jill. "Really, Ty, you're so disgusting. Do you really think that's funny?"

"That's it?" said ShiThead. "All that bullshit buildup for that? But wait a minute, who is William Wadsworth? And why do you have to apologize to him?"

"It's Wordsworth, dickhead, not Wadsworth," said Scourge. "Famous English poet. He wrote a poem called 'I Wandered Lonely As a Cloud.' So my poem is a takeoff on that. So I say, 'With apologies to William Wordsworth.' Get it?"

"Seems like you're overthinking it," said ShiThead.

I couldn't stay out of it any longer. "No, ShiThead, that is a standard literary convention. But I know you're not into literature. Girls, did you know that the reason we pronounce rendezvous as ren-dez-vouse is because ShiThead once read a passage in class and pronounced epitome as ep-i-toam."

"Oh, blow it out your ass. How many times are you going to tell that story?"

I thought this might be a good time for a passage from

our sacred text. "People, people," I said, "it is time for a reading from our sacred text, the book that instructs and enlightens us, and binds us in mutual respect for, and devotion to, one another. Please, refresh your refreshments, and give heed to our worshipful scripture."

"Now what the fuck is he talking about?" demanded ShiThead. "This 'ron-day-voo' is turning into some kind of weird shit show!"

"Patience, patience," I implored. "Listen and learn." And I started reading from *Famous Fimmales,* the chapter titled "De Insite Sturry from de Woild." Once they got the hang of the Yiddish accent, everybody had to admit that it was pretty clever. And funny. Even the girls. Then I gave Lilly credit and thanks for finding this gem and bringing it to us.

All in all, I thought that my introduction of the aprons and of our sacred text went pretty well. With our group, you could never be quite sure if a new absurdity would catch on and have staying power. At one point we decided to invent some cool new slang words and expressions. One example I can think of is the adjective "scenic," which we were supposed to use instead of "cool." We tried to incorporate that into our twisted culture, but it never really caught on. But that didn't matter. We would use the term every once in a while just to remind ourselves of how creative and different we were. We never cared much if we succeeded or failed at something. As we often said, "Mediocrity can pay off," and "The key to success is to lower your expectations."

Anyway, my scripture reading was saved by the clock, when somebody said, "OK, it's time for *Get Smart*. Enough of this other bullshit. Let's get down to the real bullshit!"

"Yi yi yi!" said Fumb. He had picked that up from the *Famous Fimmales* reading, and it would become one of his favorite expressions.

And so we all got another drink and totally ignored the groans and rolling eyes of the girls, and settled back to enjoy our favorite show.

40

I HADN'T TALKED WITH MY MOTHER ABOUT THE BRICK through the window, or the old man's debt trouble, or even about the thing where he passed out in the basement. She didn't seem to want to talk about any of this, at all. In a way, I kind of would have liked to discuss some of this with her, but I could definitely see a lot of good reasons for keeping the Cone of Silence down on it. I did notice that a couple of times Dad went walking down the street in the evening instead of going straight down to the basement. I guess she didn't have a problem with him going out to a bar once in a while, but just in the neighborhood, no driving a car. And not staying out late. Hmmm, I thought, I wonder how that's going to work out. One night I heard him say that he had been at Hoffmann's, not Volcker's, his old haunt, and that there were other vets there. Some people he could talk to, I guess. I thought it was probably good for him to have some kind of social life, as long as he didn't start getting plastered and getting back into his old ways, doing things that got him in trouble. He really was not a happy guy, I could tell that for sure. And he still raved on sometimes about Reinhardt and the peace that passes all understanding, and what would a draft dodger like Reinhardt know about peace?

More and more he was skipping church, which did not please Mom, but she wasn't making too big a deal about it. I think him skipping was preferable to him going off on something that Reinhardt said. One Sunday we were supposed to go over to Grandpa Lindke's for lunch after church, but Dad was so pissed that Mom called up and said he wasn't feeling well and wouldn't be able to make it. He was upset about what was said when somebody died. On the day that someone died, the church bells would ring, and there would be one gong for every year the person had lived. So everyone in Wittenberg would count the bells and try to figure out who had kicked the bucket. Then in church the next Sunday, the minister would say, "It hath pleased Almighty God to summon out of this vale of tears to Himself in heaven the soul of [name of person who died]." Well, this always irritated the old man, and on this particular Sunday, when we got home from church, he cut loose. "I'm sorry George Dietrich died. He was a good guy. But what is this crap about the vale of tears? 'It hath pleased Almighty God to summon out of this vale of tears the soul of George Dietrich.' Doesn't make any sense. Why the hell did Almighty God put poor George Dietrich into a vale of tears anyway? More to the point, why the hell did Almighty God create this vale of tears in the first place? So he could put his creatures there and torture them? And then when it pleases him, summon them out of it? What a crock of horse shit! What kind of a god would do that?" That's when Mom called Grandma and said Dad had a headache.

When I was going out with Karen Reinhardt, we had some discussions about things like this. I probably wasn't as emotional about it as the old man. It wasn't the only reason I never got to second base with her, but it didn't help. As for the old man, I felt bad for him, felt sorry that he was so unhappy and sad all the time, but I had to focus on football, on the rest of the season. We couldn't let the Parsons win go to our heads or give us a false sense of our competitive ability. The rich pricks from Norfolk were always contenders, even though that was annoying as hell. But we had to face facts. Last year's loss to them had been a bitch. We had played the Helwig game, and I felt because of that we'd missed some opportunities, but why should we expect things to be any different this year?

I was kind of disappointed that the old man showed virtually no interest in football and hardly ever attended one of our games. But I wasn't going to say anything about it. Growing up he hadn't been involved in sports and now he had enough problems and if he wasn't interested then that was fine. We had plenty of enthusiastic fans in town to cheer us on, and they were out in force for the Norfolk game, which was a home game for us this year.

The weather was getting cold at the end of October, and we'd been having a lot of rain. The field at the stadium was always well maintained but still, if it was soaking wet, it could get pretty muddy. I didn't think that would be a factor in this game, but when we got to the stadium and went down into the locker room, it started to rain again. Helwig's pep talk was pretty standard, but he seemed to be slurring his words. He didn't come up with anything like "let's win this one for Sarkovits," but he just sounded a bit off. I figured I wouldn't be playing much, since Norfolk had a good team with a good record, and it would probably be a tight game. I looked over at G and he was listening intently to what Helwig was saying. He'd be the guy leading the team tonight.

My predictions turned out to be accurate. We ran our standard offense. We scored first, and Dudek made the point after. The crowd went nuts. Our defense was doing a good job, but so was theirs, and there was a lot of back and forth. At halftime we were ahead 7-0 but not feeling terribly confident. The second half started out pretty much the same way. They'd stop us and we'd punt, we'd stop them and they'd punt. Then in the fourth quarter, on one of our punts, their receiver dropped the ball and we recovered deep in their territory. We got a first down, then J.D. scored on a good old 46 Power. Dudek kicked another extra point, and we were starting to feel like maybe we had it in the bag, 14-0. Maybe I'd even get some playing time.

But that was not to be. Dudek's kickoff was not great, and they ran it back to about our forty-yard line. It only took them a few plays to get down inside our ten. Our defense seemed to be falling apart. Maybe we were getting tired. They scored on a pitch-out. But they missed the extra point. Whew! That was good. 14-6. But things quickly took a turn for the worse. They kicked off, a really good kick. Our guy, I can't remember who it was, caught it on about our fifteen-yard line. He got a couple of good blocks and headed for the sideline and it looked like he might have a shot at going all the way. But he had two guys to get past. One of them came at him and slammed into him with a jarring tackle that snapped his head back to the point where it looked like it might come off. The ball flew out of his hands and he hit the ground with a sickening audible thud. The ball rolled backward toward our end zone and it looked like it might roll out of bounds. But the other defender ran after it and scooped it up just before it went out. He tried to stay in bounds but he couldn't, which was very lucky for us. Now they had the ball back, deep in our territory. Shit! Everything was falling apart.

Helwig called time out and the defense gathered around him on the sideline.

I could barely hear his voice over the noise of the crowd, but I could see his hands waving over his head and it was obvious that he was really worked up. Whatever he told the defense got them fired up, and they gave a loud "Go Ganaway!" and headed back out onto the field. We held them and it was something like fourth and five from our fifteen. If we could make them turn it over, we'd have a good chance, as the clock was running down. They ran an option. It looked like their quarterback was going to hand off to the fullback, and our defensive line converged on him, and would have stopped him, except the QB didn't give him the ball. He faked the handoff, kept the ball, and when one of our linebackers moved up on him, he flipped the ball to the halfback who had a clear path to the end zone. Touchdown. A perfectly executed option play. We were totally sucked in. I thought Helwig was going to expire. He was jumping and screaming and it looked like his head was going to explode. Parker and Carpenter, and even Rudnik, looked concerned and came over to him and tried to calm him down.

Meanwhile, out on the field, Norfolk was setting up for the extra point. Obviously, they would go for two. The ref put the ball down, blew his whistle, and started the clock. Less than three minutes to go. No time to think and talk about what to do. They lined up, the QB took the snap, and it looked like another play just like the one before. But this time, instead of keeping the ball or pitching it out, the QB faked a handoff to the fullback, then dropped back to pass. Their left end was all alone way back in the corner of the end zone, not a single one of our guys anywhere near him. The QB had plenty of time and threw a perfect spiral that seemed to sail in slow motion over the heads of the battling linemen, right into the waiting arms of the receiver. Shit! Faked us out of our jocks. Again. I was almost afraid to look at Helwig. I thought he might have expired. Norfolk kicked off and it was a good kick, so we started deep in our own territory with less than three minutes to go. We didn't make a first down, punted, and were lucky that the clock ran out before they scored again. 14-14 tie.

We went to the locker room as the disappointed hometown fans filed out of the stadium. Our senior year and we were 4-2-1 with the BI-G game coming up. I don't even remember what Helwig said in the locker room. We were all feeling terrible and depressed, and just wanted to get the hell out of there. We didn't want to see anybody or talk about the game, so we didn't want to go to Angelo's. But we didn't want to just go home either. So we decided to go to Spivak's, a fairly rundown, anonymous gin mill on Samuels Street at the corner of Oneida Street. We had been there before on our occasional attempts to conquer Samuels Street, and we knew it wouldn't be very busy and there wouldn't be any high school kids there. We got a table off in a corner and all six of us sat there and drank a lot of beer and didn't talk much about the game or anything else. What was there to say?

We were all getting pretty shit-faced, especially G, who always tended to really get into it. And when he reached a certain point, you couldn't reason with him when you saw that he was getting too blitzed. He would get belligerent and then we would have a hard time cutting him off and getting him into somebody's car and delivering him home. I think Fumb was driving, and when we headed out to the car to go home, G started weaving his way across Samuels and started going down Oneida towards the river. That part of town had a lot of warehouses and storage buildings, as well as a lumberyard and not many streetlights, so it was pretty dark. Somebody yelled at him to come back and get in the car but he ignored us and kept walking down Oneida. We all went over there and followed him, hoping he wouldn't be too big of an asshole and would come with us.

He had gone around the side of one of the buildings, three or four stories high, with a fire escape that looked like it was hanging down kind of low. He was jumping up and trying to grab onto it, and after a few tries he managed to get hold of it and he pulled it down and started to climb onto it. ShiThead got to him and tried to drag him down off of the ladder, but G kicked him away and kept climbing. It had been raining on and off all evening, all through the game, and the temperature had dropped so now the rain was freezing on the streets and sidewalks.

"What are you doing?" ShiThead yelled at him. "Get down off of there, you crazy asshole!"

"Blow it out your ass, man," G said. "It's nice up here. Come on up. Or are you too scared, you fucking pussy?" As he said this, he climbed up the ladder to the next landing of the fire escape, up to the third floor.

This was getting to be quite a problem. When G got like this, it was impossible to reason with him. Scourge gave it a try.

"C'mon, G. We're freezing our asses off and we need to get the hell out of here. Just come down off that fucking thing."

"Come and get me."

"Tell him you'll buy him another beer," J.D. said.

"Come down and I'll buy you a beer at Fran's," Scourge said. Fran's was across the street from Spivak's, and for some reason G seemed to like it there. Maybe because Fran's daughter, who worked there, was pretty hot.

Well, it took a lot of back and forth, and coaxing, and bribing, but finally I think the cold was getting to him, and he started slowly coming down. When he got to the first landing, he stepped off onto the ladder and jumped up and down a little to make the ladder go down to the ground. He probably should have come down backward, holding on to the ladder, but he didn't. He just started walking down like he was descending a regular staircase, and when he got to about the fourth or fifth step, his foot slipped on the icy metal and he came crashing down onto the sidewalk. God, that was a sickening sight. When he hit the pavement, his right foot went sliding under him and he hit the ground hard. His right hip and right shoulder slammed into the concrete and he let out a terrible yell. Oh man, this was not good.

Scourge ran up, bent over him, and said, "Shit, G! Are you all right?"

G was obviously in a lot of pain, his face all screwed up. "Ahhh! Shit! My ankle is really fucked!"

"How about your shoulder?" Scourge asked. "Can you stand up?"

"I don't know. Shit! Goddamn it!" He sounded really pissed, like someone had done something to him. But it was his own damn fault. Still, we all felt bad for him and were worried about him.

"Here," Scourge reached out his hand to him. "See if you can get up."

G managed to get upright, but he couldn't put any weight on his right foot. It obviously hurt like hell.

"Do we need to take him to the hospital?" said Fumb.

"No, no! I don't need to go to the fucking hospital. Give me a minute and maybe I'll be able to move on it a little."

We all stood around, wanting to help but not having any idea what to do. After a while it became obvious that G's ankle was really messed up and it wasn't just going to start feeling better. But he absolutely refused to be taken to the emergency room, so finally we managed to help him hop to the car on his left leg, and we had to be really careful because the freezing rain was still making everything slippery as hell. We got him in the car and drove him home, and when we got there, we went through the same thing helping him get into the house. We were trying to be quiet and not wake up his mom and dad, but they heard us and came out into the kitchen. His dad was using one crutch. I'm sure the situation hit all of us right then. Jesus Christ, just what Mr. and Mrs. Gorlukovich needed, another member of the family with a fucked up foot.

"What in the world happened to you, Peter?" His mother had a horrified look on her face.

"It's nothing, Mom. I just slipped on the ice. I'll be fine. I just want to go to bed."

Mr. Gorlukovich didn't say anything. He just looked at G and then looked down at his foot and shook his head. Then he said, "Peter, are you sure you're OK? Do you need to go to the emergency room?"

"No, Dad, I just need to put my foot up and go to bed and get some sleep. I'll take a couple of aspirins and I'm sure I'll be fine in the morning."

This sounded highly unlikely and we just glanced at each other and didn't say anything. After a kind of awkward moment, Fumb said, "Well, if you don't need a ride anywhere, I guess we'd better get going."

"Thank you, boys," said G's mom. "Thank you for bringing him home and taking care of him."

We all mumbled something and left the three of them standing there in the kitchen. I guess somehow G got up the stairs to his bedroom. Their house was a small Cape Cod, with one bedroom downstairs and two small bedrooms upstairs with the slanted ceiling of the roof. What a day. And night. What a fucking mess.

41

WHEN I WOKE UP THE NEXT DAY, the first thing that flashed through my mind was the image of G, standing there on one leg in his kitchen, with his mom in her bathrobe and his dad on his crutch looking on with scared, worried expressions on their faces. The next thing that hit me was, holy shit, I might be starting in the BI-G game. Oh my God! I certainly hadn't anticipated this development. Of course, maybe G's ankle wasn't that bad and he'd be fine to play in the game on Friday. Much as I had always wanted to be a starter, at that moment I desperately hoped that G would be OK. I wanted to call him, but it was too early. I'd have to wait till later.

I went downstairs and got some cereal. I was scheduled to work a half day at the Stenzel Agency, as usual, and I left to get there by eight thirty. I couldn't stop thinking about the possibility of me playing QB against BI. Helwig would probably want to run single wing. I knew, and he knew, that I was not as good a blocker as G. I would certainly give it everything I had, but G was bigger and stronger than me, and he'd been playing the position since the start of our junior year. He knew what he was doing, and the offensive line, and the whole backfield—everybody—was familiar and comfortable with his style and his leadership. My playing time had been pretty limited. I hadn't done too bad when I'd had the chance to play, but we virtually never ran from the T when we were in a tight game. So my confidence level was quite low. Especially since BI was having a hell of a year, and they were 7-0 going into the game.

Around ten o'clock I called G. I couldn't wait any longer to find out how he was. His dad answered and said that Mrs. Gorlukovich had taken him to the emergency room. I asked him how bad he thought the ankle was, and he said it was really swollen and very sore and that G couldn't put any weight on it, so he had given him a spare set of crutches to use. Luckily, he didn't ask me any questions about the night before or details about how G had messed up his ankle. I didn't know what G had told him and I didn't want to contradict anything that he'd said. I asked him if he could have G call me when he had a chance and he said sure. Then I called J.D. and asked him if it would be OK if I came over to the market after I got off work. I told him I had talked to G's dad, and that it sounded like G was going to be out for the game. He said fine, come on over, so right at noon I headed over there.

J.D. made a sub for us to split. I wasn't very hungry, probably because I was so nervous thinking about the BI-G game and how the hell I was going to manage as starting QB. J.D. tried to reassure me, and he gave me a little pep talk about of course I could do it, and I had a great arm, and we'd have a chance to throw some new shit at 'em, and they wouldn't know what to expect, and we'd have the element of surprise, and on like that. It was nice of him to try to build me up, but I had a lot of doubts.

I said, "Thanks, J.D. I really appreciate you saying that. But I have to admit I'm basically scared shitless. For one thing, there's no guarantee that Helwig is even going to let us run from the T. You know how he is. When things are tight, he reverts to the old tried and true. Except with me as blocking back, it's going to be a different story. The single wing is G's thing, and everybody knows it, including BI. They'll be licking their chops. I'd much rather run from the T, but you know as well as I do that we're not super effective with that because we don't practice it much. We only use it in games when we've got a pretty good lead, and usually that's against a fairly weak team. BI has a hell of a team this year. It ain't gonna be easy."

"Well, I'm sure Parker will work with us in practice this week, and we'll have a good game plan lined up," said J.D. "Don't worry about it. We'll just work hard and we'll be ready for 'em."

"I hope so," I said.

We talked some more and then a customer came in. I said I'd better get going, and I headed home. When I came in the house my mom was in the kitchen. She didn't work at Stenzel on Saturdays, and she asked me if I wanted some lunch. I told her thanks, but I'd eaten a sub at Palmisano's.

"How is Joe?" she said. "Are you guys ready for your big game? Your BI-G game?"

I figured this was as good a time as any to tell her about G's sprained ankle, and that I was going to be starting QB on Friday night. She looked surprised, or concerned, or I don't know exactly what.

"Oh my goodness! Well, that's quite a development. Are you excited?"

I couldn't say that I was shitting my pants, so I just said, "Yeah, sure."

"We'll have to tell your father. I'm sure he'll want to go to the game and see you play."

"Yeah, well, he hasn't been to any of our games so far this year, so I don't know if he'll necessarily want to come to this one."

"Oh, I'm sure he will," she said. "This will be a big night for you. I know he'll want to come watch. I'm going to tell him I want to go too. We'll be there. This will be very exciting."

Actually, I didn't particularly care whether my father and mother came to the game or not. They had never been into sports, and they didn't know anything about football or understand why it was so important to me. Their interest or lack of interest was the last thing on my mind then. I needed to talk to the guys, just needed to talk to them about the game. I didn't know exactly what I needed to talk about, or what that would accomplish, but I just needed the feeling of teamwork, that we were in this together, that we knew we could win.

Sometime during the afternoon, I got a call from G. He was home and resting with his foot up. He said his ankle was pretty fucked up. Not broken, but the doc had said that a sprain can be worse than a break and can take longer to get completely better. G should have put ice on it right away when it happened, but he didn't know that and didn't do it. Now he had the ankle wrapped in an ace bandage and was supposed to stay off of it and keep it elevated and put a heating pad on it periodically. Obviously, he was out of commission. I didn't even want to ask if he could maybe meet at the boathouse that night. It sounded like he should take it easy and not be driving around and climbing rickety stairs and taking any chances. But damn! I really wanted to get together, and he needed to be there. "I'd like to see you, man," I said.

"Why don't we all get together here at my house, tonight?" he said. "For old time's sake. I can get down to the basement, and my mom will be working, and my dad would be fine with it."

"Really?" I said. "No kidding, man, that would be great! I'll call everybody. What time?"

"How about nine or so. We've got a crappy little TV down there now so we can watch *Get Smart* and shoot the shit about the BI-G game and talk strategy. I'm so pissed that I was so damn stupid and now I'm in this mess. But you're a great QB, Croc, and you've shown you can lead the team, and you're gonna do great."

"Well, thanks for the vote of confidence," I said. "I wish I was as confident as you are. Or at least as confident as you sound."

"Hey, c'mon, man. You can do it. Think of the great backfield you've got. And the whole team. You know we're going to be pumped up and ready for those BI bastards."

"Yeah, you're right," I said. Not sure I actually believed it, but I had to get past the self-doubt and step up and be a leader. No time or place for hesitation. I remembered my Little League baseball coach's favorite expression: "He who hesitates is lost."

So G called everybody and we met in his basement that

night. Just like old times, when we first started hanging out together. Fumb brought a bottle of Guck, and we had some traditional refreshments while we shot the shit and listened to our old favorite records. We talked about football, of course, but it didn't seem like there was all that much to say. We were going into the biggest game of our lives without our starting QB, and we would have to step up. I would have to step up. We speculated about whether Helwig would have us playing old school, or if Parker would influence him to try some other stuff. We guessed it would be old school. I would bust my ass to try and fill G's shoes. We'd have to see how things looked in practice on Monday.

We listened to the Statler Brothers, Dylan, and Mitch Miller. Then it was time for *Get Smart*. We freshened up our drinks, settled back, and in spite of everything we were happy.

42

THE WEEK OF THE GAME, THE WEATHER WAS TERRIBLE. Typical for late fall in our area. From one day to the next you didn't know what you might get. This particular week started off with rain and temperatures in the high thirties. We were used to it, but still, you always felt chilled to the bone and everything was damp and cold. The practice fields were a mess, as you can imagine. They had been trampled on daily for ten weeks and even the varsity practice fields were mostly mud by this point. It didn't make much difference which field we used, they were both in bad shape. But that was probably a good thing, because it prepared us for what the game might be like. BI had a nice stadium and they took good care of it. But the condition of the field was going to be a factor if the weather didn't improve.

In the locker room before practice on Monday, Helwig got everybody together. The truth about G's accident had been effectively suppressed by our group. The official story was that he had slipped on an icy sidewalk uptown while walking to Fumb's car from Gino's. This lie had gone over surprisingly easily. Nobody, including G's parents, had asked for a lot of details. Slipped on the ice while walking to the car seemed to satisfy everybody. Lucky for us.

"Boys," said Helwig, "you've probably heard by now that Gorlukovich had an accident and seriously sprained his ankle. He'll be fine, but he will definitely be on the sidelines for the game. Simpson will be starting at QB/blocking back. Simpson, are you ready to lead the team?" He pointed at me. Took me completely by surprise. I hesitated for just a split second, then said in what I hoped was a very confident tone, "Yes, sir! Absolutely!" I hoped my lie would get me through this awkward moment. Helwig continued.

"Boys, four days from now, you will play the most important GAME of your life. It may well be one of the most important DAYS of your life. I cannot state that too strongly. This one game, this one day, you will remember for the rest of your life. We've been thrown a curveball here, with Gorlukovich's accident. But luckily for us, we have Simpson to step in. He is a talented, experienced player, who is as committed to Ganaway football as any player I have ever seen."

Geez, thanks, Coach, I thought.

"We have just a few days to prepare for Bell Island. They are good. Their record is 7-0. But we have a mission, and we will not fail to achieve it. We WILL prevent them from having a perfect season. We WILL defeat them on their own field on Friday night. We WILL make our hometown and our fans proud. We WILL bring a victory back to Ganaway! Now, we've got a lot of work to do, so let's get out there and work like we've never worked before. Let's focus on our fundamentals. Let's be Ganaway tough. Let's be Ganaway smart. A-gile! MO-bile! HOS-tile! Let's take it to 'em!"

We yelled and hooted and hollered and clattered up the stairs and headed across the street to the practice fields. That day, and every day that week, we concentrated on running the offense without G. We worked on adapting to me as QB, with my strengths and my deficiencies, and we tried to develop a strategy that would keep us in the game. Coach Parker was leading this effort, but it wasn't at all clear how much actual authority he would have to call the shots during the game. My guess was, not much.

The week went by very fast. I couldn't think about much of anything other than the BI-G game. I was distracted in my classes and it was a struggle to keep up with my homework. Crazy how a game can have such a grip on your life. Mom told me that she and Dad would definitely be at the game. I'm not sure if that made me happy or annoyed. Maybe some of each. Nice that they were interested in seeing me play—this one time—but now just one more thing to add to the pressure I was already under. I didn't dwell on it. I had bigger things to deal with.

———

THE WEATHER ON FRIDAY WAS THE SAME AS IT HAD BEEN ALL WEEK. Constant rain and cold, truly miserable. We suited up in our locker room and boarded the bus to Bell Island High. Everybody was nervous as hell and just wanted so badly to win this goddamn game. Helwig gave a rousing pep talk, as usual, and even though we'd heard him do it so many times, he never failed to strike some nerve in our high school heads that got us fired up and itching to do battle.

By the time the game started, the temperature had dropped and there were some snowflakes floating around in the air, kind of a mix of rain and snow. We kicked off and Dudek had a good kick, maybe to their ten-yard line. The field was soaked and muddy and very slippery, and it was hard to get any footing. We stopped their receiver inside the twenty. Their offense took the field and tried a couple of running plays, which got them nowhere. I was thinking that the shitty weather was going to be an advantage for us, because they were known to be fast and nimble on offense, and the sloppy field was going to slow them down. Going into the game, hardly anybody in town, even our most loyal fans, gave us much of a chance of winning this one. For us, especially seniors on the team, winning this game was unbelievably important. We just couldn't go through four years of high school football and never beat BI. With third and long, Summers tried a pass, but the ball slipped from his hand, and it wasn't clear if it would be considered a fumble or an incomplete pass. He fell on it and the ref placed the ball at that point, so it was a fumble. Watching this, I couldn't help but thinking, Yikes, if Summers is having trouble out there, what's going to happen to me? It didn't take long to find out.

BI punted, and it wasn't a good punt, so we had good field position, starting from about our forty. As I took the field with our offense, all kinds of thoughts were flashing through my head, all of them bad and scary. Helwig was going to be sending in the plays; I didn't know if I'd get to call any plays myself. In some ways, that was kind of reassuring, like, well, if we fuck up, that's his fault, not mine. On the other hand, I was the one out there, and I'd be the one people were watching, and expecting to perform.

Our first series of downs, no surprise, we ran from the single wing. J.D. was probably the best guy you could have out there. Even though the field conditions were terrible, he had great balance and power and speed. If anybody could run on that field, he could. ShiThead was similar. Raw power, very stable. Scourge, at wingback, was small but very agile—and mobile and hostile, I thought, ha ha. If there was any way we could get the ball to him, either by a pass or a reverse, maybe he could navigate the slush and get into the open. As things turned out, neither team was able to do much of anything. I did complete a couple of passes from the T. Parker had probably talked Helwig into it. When the first half ended, the score was 0-0. In the locker room, the guys who had been playing were covered in mud, and their shoes and socks were totally soaked. We listened attentively to the halftime Helwig pep talk, and got repumped-up, gave a rousing "GO GANAWAY!" and headed back out onto the field for the second half.

We were the receiving team, and we got a break. It was a short kick, and our receiver, I think it was Gary Dempsey, took it on about our thirty, broke one tackle, got a couple of good blocks, and headed down the sideline, where the field wasn't quite as soggy and slippery, and ran it down to the BI thirty-five. I couldn't believe it when Parker grabbed me by my jersey, pulled me over to him on the sideline, and told me to run a pass play. On first down. He shoved me out onto the field and yelled, "Let's see you do it, Simpson!"

When I called the play in the huddle, ShiThead said, "Are you sure?"

"Yes, I'm sure! You think I'm making this shit up?"

"Seems like it."

"OK, no discussion!" And I repeated the call.

We broke the huddle and set up on the line of scrimmage. Fumb snapped me the ball, I turned to my left and faked a handoff to J.D., who was heading to the right, to the strong side. Then, hiding the ball as well as I could, I drifted back and checked my receivers. Jimmy Kowalczyk, the tight end, had started across the center, then pivoted toward the left sideline. The guy covering him tried to change direction too, but slipped in the mud, and Kowalczyk was open. It was a tough throw to make, because I had a lot of territory to cover with the pass, turning and throwing back to my left and hoping I didn't lose my footing. Or drop the damn ball. It was bitter cold and the snow had turned to freezing rain. As soon as the ball left my hand, I knew it was going to be good. My grip was solid and the ball went sailing—a hell of a spiral under those conditions, if I do say so myself. Kowalczyk caught it on about the twenty, and there was nobody anywhere near him. He sprinted toward the goal line and sailed into the end zone. Touchdown, Ganaway! Eat shit, Summers! I guess the QB who never threw a pass just threw a pass. So, blow it out your ass!

We lined up for the extra point. I had held for Dudek many times in practice, never in a game. It shouldn't be any different, I told myself. And it really wasn't. Fumb sent me a perfect snap, the ball didn't slip out of my hands, I got it down quickly, and Dudek came toward the ball. Everything looked good. But then Dudek's left foot slipped a little, just enough to throw off his kicking motion. His right foot grazed the muddy ground and it hit the ball right in the middle, sending it forward, but not up. The ball hit Fumb in the back of his head as he blocked the defensive line. Damn! Damn! Damn! At least we were ahead, but 6-0 with a whole half to go? Shit!

Our quick score did not set any kind of trend, for us or them. Possession went back and forth, back and forth. Considering the terrible playing conditions, this wasn't surprising. As the clock continued to tick away and we moved into the fourth quarter, it started to seem like maybe we could win this thing, 6-0. But that hope was short-lived. BI returned one of our punts all the way down to our thirty-yard line. For a second, it looked like they might go all the way, but our deep safety made a great tackle and prevented a disaster. We held them and it was something like fourth and five. They weren't going to punt from there, so this was a make-or-break play. We had to keep them from getting a first down. Unfortunately, that's not what happened. Instead, Summers made one of the best plays of the game. Rolling out to his right, and finding his wide receiver open over the middle, he drilled a perfect pass—on the run—and the guy caught it, turned upfield, and sprinted into the end zone. The extra point was good. 7-6.

At this point it seemed as if BI was getting some kind of second wind, and we were losing steam. I didn't want to think that way, but the feeling was there. And when we didn't get a first down on our next possession after the kick-off, the feeling only got worse. We punted, a good punt that had them pretty deep in their own territory. But on their first play, Summers threw another nice pass, again straight over

the middle, and they picked up a first down. This was starting to look really scary. They ran for about five yards, then
Summers completed another pass for another first down.
Damn, the son of a bitch was good. Couldn't deny that. And
they seemed to be fired up, not letting the weather or the
cold mess with their heads or with their game.

They lined up quickly and our defense seemed to be
slow to respond, struggling to get in position, getting out-
hustled. Again, Summers went back to pass, but this time his
foot slipped on the soggy turf. He stumbled, then regained
his balance, but we had a blitz on, and one of our linebackers had a clear shot at him. Summers set up to throw, but as
soon as he did, our guy, Phil Bassetti, hit him with a hel-
met-to-helmet blow that made a crack you could hear all
over the field and on the sidelines. Summers's head snapped
back and he went down and his head hit the ground hard.
You could actually hear a collective groan coming out of
the stands, it was such a brutal hit. He dropped the ball, and
Bassetti fell on it, and our fans in the visitors' stands went
wild. But then suddenly things got quiet when Summers
didn't get up. Didn't even move. He just lay there sprawled
out on his back in the mud. The refs called time out, and the
BI coach and team doctor came out onto the field and knelt
down over him. He wasn't moving. People were starting to
get worried. I hated the guy's guts and even I was getting
worried. Finally, after what seemed like a really long time,
two of the coaches who were hovering over him helped him
sit up. And then after a few seconds they got him to his
feet, but he was definitely shaken up. With help, he walked
off the field and they took him to the locker room. The

announcer said something, the crowd clapped, and then he was forgotten, and we got back to the game.

This was our big chance. Good field position, clock running out but still time. If it had been up to me, I probably would have tried something daring. But Helwig had us playing old school. We made a couple of yards, then another couple of yards, and before you knew it, we were fourth and five from maybe the twenty. And we were down to less than two minutes on the clock. I was ready for another run, but when our tight end came in with the play, it was a pass from the T. My big chance. I took the snap and started to run back into the pocket when I saw the blitz coming. I didn't even have a chance to set up, or look for my receivers. I was smothered by two of their linebackers, who had broken through almost untouched, and they flattened me. So we turned the ball over.

With Summers out of the game, BI had to revert to their backup QB, who was just a sophomore who hadn't played much all season. But maybe that wouldn't matter if they could just run out the clock. We really needed to get the damn ball back, and fast. We had a couple of time-outs left, so that was good, but we didn't have much time, not much time at all. They played it smart and were eating up the clock with running plays and we had to use one of our time-outs to stay in the game. Now we had one time-out left, and they were fourth and eight or something, and they lined up to punt. This was it. It looked like we were going to lose, lose our fourth BI-G game, and maybe be the only class in living memory that had never beaten BI. Dave Messing, our defensive captain, had the defense in a huddle and was yelling and jumping, trying to pump our guys up. BI lined up, their center snapped the ball, the clock started. The snap was wobbly, the punter bobbled it briefly, then set up and kicked, but the kick was blocked! Blocked! Holy shit! We blocked the kick and recovered on the seven-yard line with seven seconds left in the game. Seven and seven. Guck and seven. Why would I have a thought like that at a time like this? Time out!

Helwig was waving at me furiously, waving me to the sideline. Parker and Carpenter were standing right there with him, and he looked pale. And he smelled like booze. Parker was very agitated, talking passionately, almost yelling. "Coach, coach, we've got to try something different! The field is too wet and sloppy. We can't run the standard stuff at 'em, our blockers can't get traction, they're slipping and sliding all over the place. We need to run a screen, give a receiver some running room. Or a reverse, spread things out. Or an option, keep 'em guessing."

Helwig looked overwhelmed, confused, uncomprehending. Carpenter said, "Coach, you have to decide. We only have a few seconds and they're going to blow the whistle, and we've got to get back out there." Helwig took off his hat and was rubbing his head. Carpenter and Parker were both desperate for a decision.

"46 Power!" he said.

"No, coach," Parker groaned.

"46 Power. We've gotta take it to 'em. Now go!" And that was it. I headed back out onto the field and we huddled up.

"OK, here we go," I said. "This is for all the marbles. We gotta do this. Take it to 'em. 46 Power."

"What?" yelled ShiThead. "Are you shitting me? Seriously? 46 Power?"

"That's what coach said. Parker tried to talk him into something else, but that's what he said."

"No," said ShiThead. "Just fucking no! This is our senior year. We're not going to lose to fucking BI." This was not good. Time was running out; the ref was going to make us line up any second.

"Well, what do YOU wanna do?" I asked him, as belligerently as I could.

"Field goal."

"What? Are you shitting me? Dudek can only kick an extra point about half the time. He already missed an extra point. Even under the best of conditions, we're too far out for a field goal. And Helwig won't send him in. We have to do what Helwig says."

"Fuck Dudek! Fuck Helwig!" said ShiThead. "I'm gonna kick a field goal. Now enough talk. Croc, you hold the ball for me, and I'm gonna kick a goddamn field goal."

I couldn't believe what I was hearing. This was truly crazy. I had to make a decision. I did some of the fastest analysis of my life. Would we score a TD on a 46 Power? Given the condition of the field and the experience so far in this game? Almost zero chance. But a field goal? Could I go against Helwig and do something like that? Something as crazy as that? And ShiThead? ShiThead kick a field goal? He'd never kicked a field goal in his life. Think! Think!

"OK, fuck it! What have we got to lose? We're going to kick a field goal. Everybody—block like your life depends on it. Let's go. Ready, break!" and we broke the huddle and lined up. This was crazy. This was crazy.

I took my position behind Fumb, got down on one knee, ready to take the snap. ShiThead backed up and started lining up for the kick. Then he took about three steps to his left. Where was he going? What was he doing? My God, he's going to kick it soccer style!

I called for the snap. Fumb sent it back to me in a perfect spiral, right into my hands. I set the ball down and ShiThead started his approach. I got the ball on the ground and a split second later ShiThead's leg whipped through the air and his foot hit the ball with a powerful smack and the ball sailed up and over the linemen battling with each other and kept on going right through the absolute center of the goal post. Field goal! Three points! The clock runs out. We win 9-7!

The fans poured out onto the field, and we were quickly surrounded. It was a total mob scene. We were getting hugs, and slaps on the back, and bangs on the helmet from our ecstatic fans. We wanted to get to the sideline to join the rest of the team and the coaches, but it was hard to make any headway through the crowd. I wanted to see Helwig's face. Or maybe I didn't. I didn't really know what to think. And then I saw that the team had hoisted Helwig up onto their shoulders and were bouncing him up and down and chanting something. What were they saying? Something with three syllables, but it wasn't Gan-a-way. No, oh my God, they were screaming Sar-ko-vits! Sar-ko-vits! Who had started that? It was perfect! We would analyze that forever. The cops who were there didn't even try to clear people off the field. As long as everyone was just celebrating peacefully, they let things play out. After a while, we were able to make our way to join the rest of the team, and to head to the bus. You can imagine how crazy the bus ride was back to the school and the locker room.

I won't even try to describe the locker room scene. I can say that we were experiencing what for many of us was the happiest time of our lives. Before we showered, when things had settled down a bit, Helwig came out and we all gathered around him. I had no idea what to expect. We had directly contradicted his orders. We had pulled a stunt that was truly unprecedented in the history of Ganaway football. We had taken a crazy risk—although under the circumstances it was probably no riskier than Helwig's approach. But that risk had paid off. Had paid off big time. What would he say? What could he say?

"Boys," he began, "I'm at a loss for words. And as you know, I am seldom at a loss for words." Everybody chuckled nervously. "So, here's what I will say, and I'll keep it short." You could hear a pin drop in that room. "We won!" Silence. Everybody waited for the rest. But there was no more. That's all he said. "We won!" After a couple of seconds, the locker room erupted with shouts and cheers and insane banging on lockers and slamming of locker doors. Yes, dammit, we had won. Sure as shit, we had won!

43

THE SPORTS REPORTER FOR THE *COURIER-TRIBUNE* WAS WAITING outside when we came out of the locker room. We hadn't been thinking about that at all, that the paper would want to know all about the soccer-style kick. He identified ShiThead, and came up to him and said, "That was quite a surprise, Hanuszewicz, and quite a kick. Where did that come from? And what were the players saying on the sideline? They were chanting something."

Man, this could be dangerous. What if he said the wrong thing? None of us had ever talked to a reporter before. Thankfully, ShiThead kept a cool head, and all he said was, "Gee, I can't really comment on anything. You'll have to ask Coach Helwig any questions you have about the game."

"OK," he said, "is the coach still down there?"

"Oh yeah," said ShiThead, "I imagine he'll be out in a minute."

"Well, great game," the reporter said. "Amazing kick. I'd like to talk to you about that sometime if it's OK with the coach."

"Yeah, OK," said ShiThead, "see what he says. Well, we gotta go celebrate. See ya." And we headed for the parking lot.

We had told the girls to meet us at Angelo's after the game, but the guys needed to have a little talk before we met them, and the public, and started getting all kinds of questions about the field goal. So we all piled into Fumb's car, and we sat there for a minute trying to get our heads around what had happened.

Then I said, "I'm trying to figure out what we're going to say about what we did out there. And I know we all have a lot of questions for you, ShiThead, you secret, sneaky, weird-ass soccer guy."

"Yeah, what you did was amazing, but what the hell! Where did that come from?" said G, who hadn't suited up, and had watched the game from the sidelines, leaning on his crutches.

"Yeah, so like Croc said, what are we going to say when everybody starts asking us about ShiThead's soccer kick? This is going to be very weird. And tricky."

"I think, if there's any way, we should try to avoid getting into it until we see what Helwig says to the reporter," said Scourge. "There's definitely going to be a story in the paper tomorrow morning. I have no idea how Helwig is going to explain it, but it would be good if we didn't contradict what he's going to say."

"Well, yeah, I agree," said Fumb, "but think about all the other guys who were out there. They're probably going to be blabbing all over the place."

"That's true," said J.D. "but that doesn't mean we have to be blabbing too. We can play it cool, say as little as possible. Say something like, 'Yeah, we always have some surprises up our sleeve.' That would be a version of Omerta, maybe. See what Helwig says. He's the one who's really on the spot. I think we should try to stay behind him, support him. Like we always have, even when other people are giving him shit."

"Yeah, that makes sense," said Scourge. "But here's another thing; who started yelling, 'Sarkovits, Sarkovits'?"

"Uh, that was me." G looked very sheepish. "I don't know, I just was going nuts that we won, and Helwig's 'Let's win this one for Sarkovits' just popped into my head. And then everybody started yelling it too. We were just all so damn happy!"

"I have to admit, it was perfect," I chimed in. "I think if anybody asks about that, we just say it's an inside joke, just for the team. If somebody else wants to tell the story about what Helwig said, well, we can't stop them. But again, us guys, we can stay out of it."

"So, is that what we're gonna do? Does everybody agree? Are we together on this?" said Scourge. "Everybody good with the company line?" He looked around, turned to look into the back seat. We had agreement.

"Yup."

"Got it."

"We're good."

"So, let's get our asses over to Angelo's," said ShiThead. "The broads will be waiting for us and getting pissed. And we don't want that, right?"

A couple of other guys had cars, so we broke up and went to our cars, and headed for Angelo's. It was a short drive but when we got there, the place was already a mob scene. Really, I don't think I had ever seen or heard Ganaway as happy and joyful as that night. The whole town. I know we couldn't be everywhere in the town, but you just had the feeling that this night was magical. Our unbelievably crazy win against Bell Island made everything good. Didn't matter that the union at the foundry was probably going on strike. Didn't matter that the Ford plant was going to lay off a hundred workers. Didn't matter that you had to go into work at Cooper the next morning and breathe that filthy air for another shift. All that mattered was that we had won the BI-G game. And won it in a way that nobody would ever, ever forget.

Everybody wanted to buy us beers. Johnny V even bought us shots of Crown Royal. I had never tasted Crown Royal before. It lived up to its reputation. The flower lady gave us flowers again and we chipped in and bought her a drink. And yes, the questions were coming at us, about the kick, and the Sarkovits thing. But we were able to execute the Omerta-ish plan and deflect them pretty easily. There was so much commotion, and people buying rounds for each other, and just celebration, that nobody really pressed us. Some of our girls had never had a sloe gin and Squirt, so we bought them some of those, and they liked them. What had we done? Now we'd have to stock up the bar at the boathouse. Guck and Seven might not be good enough anymore. We thought about going somewhere else, maybe even to the boathouse, but decided against it. We were too smashed, and we certainly didn't want to take any chances, with G hobbling around on crutches. So somehow we managed to get the girls home, and get ourselves home, in one piece.

It was late when I got home, and everybody was in bed. The next morning I was hung over and really felt like shit, but I had to get up and go to work at Stenzel. My mom was up and offered to make me some breakfast, but I was running late and had to get going.

"That was quite a game last night," she said. "Really exciting, even though I don't know much about football. You did a great job! There's a nice story in the paper. It's over there." She pointed to the table where the paper was spread out. Even though I was late, I grabbed the paper and turned to the sports page. The headline said, "Ganaway Wins BI-G Game with a Big Shocker." And the subtitle was: "Helwig Drops Another Shocker."

I read through it as quickly as I could. Regarding the soccer-style punt, Helwig was playing it kind of like we were. He didn't go into any details about how Hanuszewicz learned to kick a football soccer style, or why he had never done it in a game before. The reporter asked those questions, but Helwig just said something like J.D. had said, that "we always like to have some surprises up our sleeve." So he was going to stonewall it too. And probably manage to take credit, or try to take credit, for making the crazy, surprising call that won us the game. Well, there were six guys besides J.D., ShiThead, Scourge, Fumb, and me who had been in that huddle and had heard the exchange between me and ShiThead. They knew that Helwig had sent in the call for the 46 Power. They knew that ShiThead had said, "Fuck the 46 Power, I'm kicking a field goal." They knew that I had gone along with him and disobeyed Helwig. It wasn't likely that they'd keep their mouths shut. But, like Scourge had said in the car the night before, the six of us would play it cool. At least for now.

The other shocker referred to in the subtitle was almost as big as the field goal. Helwig had announced that he was retiring! In the story he made it sound like he had been planning, or at least contemplating, this for quite some time. The BI-G win had been the final deciding factor. This year marked his fortieth year as head football coach at Ganaway High. He couldn't ask for a better finale than the BI-G win. It was time for new leadership to take over. It had been a great run, and he was incredibly grateful for the loyal support of the Ganaway fans and the whole Ganaway community over all those years. He said all the standard things that you say at a time like this, and he sounded good, and sincere. Who would replace him? the reporter wanted to know. That would be up to the Ganaway athletic director and the school board, Helwig said. I folded up the paper and tossed it back onto the table. I was really late now. I rushed out the door and headed for the Stenzel Agency.

44

WITHOUT A DOUBT, WE NEEDED TO GATHER AT THE BOATHOUSE THAT NIGHT.
We figured the girls wouldn't mind too much being left out
of this one, since we'd all been together after the game and
had partied pretty hard. Fumb surprised us all by bringing a
bottle of Guck—a virgin bottle, unopened.

"So, ShiThead," I said, "we're dying to know. Where
the hell did that come from?"

"Well," he said, "I told you when you were making your
ignorant comments about soccer, when we were at the Eagle
that time, that I played a lot of soccer when I was younger."

"Yeah, but I asked you if maybe some good soccer
player could be a placekicker in football, and you said no,
that kicking a soccer ball is totally different from kicking a
football. And, I might add, you acted like I was some kind
of an idiot for even asking that question."

"OK, well, much as I hate to admit it, or give you any
credit for anything at any time, your question actually did
get me thinking. So, whenever I had a chance, before or
after work at the Eagle, I would go out on the field and work

on kicking the football around. The kid who lives in one of the houses behind the field—he's in the band, I think—saw me doing that a few times. I waved at him once and he yelled over and asked me what I was doing. I told him I was just trying a little experiment. He offered to retrieve the ball and throw it back to me so I could spend more time kicking and less time chasing the ball. After a while, I got pretty good at it."

"Did you ever think of bringing this up to Helwig? Especially considering that Dudek, well, you know." I figured I knew the answer to my question.

"Yeah, right. Sure, Helwig would just jump at the idea. So, no. Maybe I considered mentioning it to him for a split second, but then common sense took over."

"Since when did you ever have any common sense?" said J.D. ShiThead flipped him the bird.

"So, what made you do what you did in the game?" G wanted to know.

"Something just snapped. We just couldn't lose to BI. Go through four years of high school and never have a win over BI? No. So I probably wasn't actually thinking those exact thoughts, but that's the emotion that I was feeling. I don't know. I just blurted it out."

"Well, I'm sure glad you experienced that emotion, or whatever. What a fucking incredible end to that game," I said.

"Well, give yourself some credit, Croc. Oh God, here I go again, giving you credit. What's happening to me? I'm becoming a weak pussy. But seriously, you made the call. You made the decision to go along with my batshit idea. If you would have said, no, gotta do what Helwig says, gotta run the 46 Power, then that's what would have happened. I couldn't have done a thing about it."

The other guys started clapping. Fumb raised his glass and said, "Here's to Croc, our beloved backup QB, who had the balls to make a really stupid decision that won us the game of the century."

"Hear! Hear!" everybody yelled. Then Scourge added, "Here's to the smartest dumb Crock of Shit who ever lived."

Again, everybody yelled, "Hear! Hear!"

Then I raised my glass, "And here's to ShiThead, the Polish Placekicker Par Excellence! Pass the pierogi!"

"Hear! Hear!"

"All well-deserved kudos," said J.D. "Now, what I want to know is, how do we handle the questions that aren't going to go away? I don't have to tell you that I'm a big fan of Omerta, but with something this public, this high-profile, the old 'I know nothing' Sgt. Schultz approach is going to be hard to pull off."

"I think we need to come up with a party-line story," said Scourge. "It would be something like, 'ShiThead played soccer as a kid, and just for the heck of it he started kicking a football around soccer-style at the Eagle, and he mentioned this to some people'—do we say Helwig?—I don't know. But it was such a goofy idea that we never really got serious about it, but in the BI-G game, the way it was going, the field conditions, and the final seconds, and blah blah. That kind of thing."

"Sounds like you've got a good start on a party-line story right there," said Fumb, "and it's actually sort of true, partly true, anyway."

"OK, I'll work on that," said Scourge.

"So, let me get this straight," said G. We're not going to do the Cone of Silence thing on the field goal, is that right?"

"Right," said Scourge, "there's already too many people who have information about it, and there's going to be all kinds of talk, and everybody knows that all of us were right in the middle of it, so we're not going to be able to stonewall it completely. It just wouldn't work in this case. So we'll all stick to the party-line story. Once I draft it and we all approve it."

"OK, so how about the other shit that we're not talking about? Like my dad's injury and the lawsuit, for example. Or the fire at The Union. Oops, excuse me, not supposed to say the words."

"OK, here's my opinion," said J.D. "We know we can trust each other. So it does seem a little weird to never utter a word about any of the shit that we're aware of. But it's still safer, in my opinion, to not talk about any of it. What do you guys think?"

"I agree," said Scourge. "There will no doubt come a time when we can look back and hash over all this shit. But for now, why not just avoid it? In fact, since the topic has come up, this might be a good time to share with you a little poem that I wrote in study hall the other day."

ShiThead groaned, "Oh no, here we go again with the 'poesy.'"

"No," said Fumb, "let's hear it. Give it to us, Scourge."

Scourge set down his drink and pulled out a sheet of paper with the handwritten poem. "Gentlemen, I give you 'Ode to Silence.'" He stood up, cleared his throat dramatically, and delivered his latest masterpiece.

If you're thinkin' of tellin' some tales outta school,
Always remember dis one simple rule:
You keep your mouth shut and you keep your head
    down,
And you never let on if you shit your pants brown.
If da boys or da cops come and ask what you know,
You don't know nuttin' and you tell 'em so.
Omerta is what dis here principle's called,
And you better observe it, or your ass will be
    hauled
In front of da boys, and your balls will be mauled.
So like I just told ya, have nuttin' to say,
And you might be around for at least one more day.

"Hooray!" Fumb raised his glass. "Another brilliant achievement by the poet laureate. To Scourge!"

"To Scourge!" we all joined in.

"OK, now I've got something to propose," I said. "I'm going to propose the formation of a new organization. An organization to commemorate and preserve forever in our memories our incredible win over BI, and our beloved coach, and our deep love of stupid shit. I think the Sarkovits cheer was brilliant. Great job, G. Very creative. Very impromptu. That cheer just said so much about our crazy group, our crazy year, our crazy coach who is obviously losing it, but who is loved by all of us in spite of his failings. We won it for Sarkovits, and we have no idea who the hell Sarkovits is. And we don't care. We don't want to know. But we won it for him. He is worthy of our love and respect. So, I have here a Declaration of Formation, which I hereby move that we adopt, to wit:

Know all men by these presents, that on this
Sixth Day of November, in the Year of our Lord Nineteen
Hundred and Sixty-five,
we do hereby declare and approve the formation of the
Society for the Encouragement of Sarkovits Adulation,
to be known henceforth to us and to all men as
SESA.

"Do I hear a second?" said Scourge.

"Who made you presiding officer?" said ShiThead. "But yeah, I second the motion."

"All in favor, please say 'Cleah is not a cullah,'" said the presiding officer.

The motion passed unanimously.

"Yi! Yi! Yi!" Fumb exclaimed. "Anudder horganazashun to kipp trek huff." Fumb was really into Milt Gross speak. We were starting to worry about him.

The rest of the evening went like that. It's hard to imagine a more blissful time. There were lots of things ahead of us. Would the Bullshit Law Firm succeed in sticking it to Cooper and that dickhead Harrison? Would the old man find his way out of the depression he was obviously in? Would Palmisano's survive the betrayal of Amato's and the competition of The Union? Would some of us, or all of us, wind up in Vietnam? Or maybe Canada? There was a lot of shit that we didn't know. We didn't know what we didn't know.

We watched *Get Smart*, and drank some more Guck, and then we turned off the TV and put on a Dylan album, the one that had "Bob Dylan's Dream" on it. I will never forget that song, and that night, all together in our boathouse refuge, reveling in our big win and not knowing what we didn't know, and not caring one bit that we didn't know. Many times since that night I've thought about that song, and our friendship, and thought that, yeah, no matter what the price, I'd give it all gladly if our lives could be like that.

ACKNOWLEDGEMENTS

I want to thank my wife, Alice, who encouraged me to write this novel, served as my astute sounding board and editor, and cheered me on along the way. I also want to thank her, from the bottom of my heart, for putting up with me for more than a half century.

A big thank you, also, to Tanya Muzumdar and Sarah Meiers at Mission Point Press. Their editorial and design expertise, and their outstanding responsiveness to all my questions, made the publication process smooth and even enjoyable.

ABOUT THE AUTHOR

J.R. Krull played football in high school and college during the 1960s. He had a long career as a librarian and library administrator. Now he spends his time volunteering for several nonprofits, reading, writing, and walking on the beach in Florida. This is his first book.